James Grant

The King's Own Borderers

A Military Romance

James Grant

The King's Own Borderers
A Military Romance

ISBN/EAN: 9783337053703

Printed in Europe, USA, Canada, Australia, Japan

Cover: Foto ©Andreas Hilbeck / pixelio.de

More available books at **www.hansebooks.com**

THE

KING'S OWN BORDERERS.

A Military Romance.

BY

J A M E S   G R A N T,

AUTHOR OF

" SECOND TO NONE," "THE ROMANCE OF WAR," "THE YELLOW FRIGATE,"

ETC. ETC.

" Memories fast are thronging o'er me,
  Of the grand old fields of Spain;
How he faced the charge of Junot,
  And the fight where Moore was slain.
Oh the years of weary waiting
  For the glorious chance he sought,
For the slowly ripened harvest
  That life's latest autumn brought."

IN THREE VOLUMES.

VOL. II.

LONDON:

GEORGE ROUTLEDGE AND SONS,

BROADWAY, LUDGATE HILL.

1865.

LONDON :
SAVILL AND EDWARDS, PRINTERS, CHANDOS STREET,
COVENT GARDEN.

CONTENTS

OF

THE SECOND VOLUME.

KING'S OWN BORDERERS.

CHAPTER I.

A LAST REJECTION.

> " Ae fond kiss and then we sever!
> Ae farewell, alas for ever!
> Deep in heart-wrung tears I'll pledge thee,
> Warring sighs and groans I'll wage thee;
> Who shall say that Fortune grieves him
> While the star of hope she leaves him?"
>
> BURNS.

IGNORING the source or cause of the excitement among the household, Cosmo lounged into the breakfast-parlour, where the silver urns were hissing amid a very chaste equipage, and where the September sun was shining in through clusters of sweet briar and monthly roses, and as he seated himself he handed to his father a long official-like document, at the sight of which his mother changed colour, and even Flora, who looked charming in her smiling radiance, lace frills, and morning dress of spotted white muslin, lifted her dark eyelashes with interest.

"What's the matter, Cosmo?—your leave cancelled?" asked Rohallion.

"Oh no, my lord—nothing so bad as that."

"A summons from headquarters, I see."

"Something very like it," drawled Cosmo; "read it to the ladies. Spillsby, some coffee—no cream."

The letter ran briefly thus :—

"Horse Guards, &c., &c.

"Sir,—I have the honour to acquaint you, by direction of His Royal Highness the Field-Marshal Commanding-in-Chief, that it is now in his power to appoint you to one of the second battalions lately raised for the line and for immediate foreign service, provided that within a fortnight you are prepared to assume the command, in which case your name shall appear in the next Gazette.

"I have the honour to be, &c., &c.

"Major the Hon. C. Crawford,
&c., &c."

"A fortnight!—are we to have you only for a fortnight, my dear, dear Cosmo?" exclaimed Lady Rohallion, all her maternal tenderness welling up at once.

"You will not, I fear, have me so long, my dear mother," said he; "and you, Flora, he added in a low voice, as he purposely held his plate across her for a wing of grouse; "and you——"

" Give you full leave to go, with my dearest wishes, and your heart unbroken. Come, Cosmo," she added in the same low voice, and with a soft smile ; " let us part friends, at least."

Cosmo's eyes seemed to shrink and dilate, while a cold and haughty smile spread over his otherwise handsome features, as he turned quietly to discuss his grouse, and said to the butler,—

" Spillsby, tell the groom to have a horse saddled for my man—take Minden, the bay mare—as I must despatch a letter to Maybole within an hour."

Breakfast was hurried over in silence and constraint, then Cosmo, kissing the brow of his mother, who was already in tears,—for the only real emotion that lingered in the Master's heart was a regard for his mother—played with the silk tassels of his luxurious dressing-gown, and lounged into the library to write his answer to the military secretary, and profess himself to be completely, as in duty bound, at the disposal of His Royal Highness, and proud to accept the command offered him.

He soon penned the letter, and sealed it with the coronet, the shield *gules* and fess *ermine* of Rohallion, muttering as he did so,—

" The line—the line after all ; a horrid bore indeed, to come down to that !"

He threw open his dressing-gown, as if it stifled him, almost tearing the tasselled girdle as he did so, and planting his foot on the buhl writing-table, lounged back in an easy-chair, where he strove to read up Sir David Dundas's "Eighteen Manœuvres," and fancied how he would handle his battalion without clubbing the companies or bringing the rear rank in front; by taking them into action with snappers instead of flints, as old Whitelock did at Buenos Ayres, or committing other little blunders, which might prove very awkward if a brigade of French twelve-pounders were throwing in grape and canister at half-musket range.

Soothed by pipe, and by the silence of the place, and by the subdued sunlight that stole through the deep windows of that old library, so quaint with its oak shelves of calf-bound and red-labelled folios and quartos, its buhl cabinets, and square-backed chairs of the Covenanting days, its half-curtained oriel window, through which were seen the ripe corn or stubble fields that stretched in distance far away to the brown hills of Carrick. Soothed, we say, by all this, Cosmo dawdled over the pages and the diagrams of the famous review at Potsdam for some time before he became conscious that Flora was seated near him, busy with a book of engravings.

Then begging pardon for his pipe and his free-and-easy position, a bachelor habit, as he said, he arose and joined her. Leaning over the back of his chair, as if to overlook the prints, while in reality his admiring eyes wandered alternately and admiringly over her fine glossy hair, the contour of her head, and little white ears (at each of which a rose diamond dangled), and her delicate neck, which rose so nobly from her back and beautifully curved shoulders, he said in a low voice, and with considerable softness of manner, for him at least,—

"'Pon my honour, friend Flora, I believe you really begin to love me, after all."

"How do you think so, or why?" she asked, looking half round, with her bewitching eyes full of wonder and amusement.

"Because we always quarrel when we meet, and that is called a Scots mode of wooing, isn't it?"

"So our nurses used to say, long ago."

"And were they right?"

"Now, dear Cosmo, let us talk of something else, if you please," she urged pleadingly.

"Why so?"

"A dangerous topic has a strange fascination for you."

"Dangerous?"

"Unpleasant, at least," said Flora, pettishly.

Cosmo flung the "Eighteen Manœuvres" of Lieutenant-General Dundas very angrily and ignominiously to the extreme end of the library, and folding his arms stood haughtily erect before Flora, whose bright eyes were fixed on his, with a smiling expression of fear and perplexity combined.

"Can it be possible," he began, "I ask you, can it be possible, Miss Warrender——"

"Oh, you are about to address me officially—well, sir ?"

"Can it be possible, Flora, that you still love this unknown protégé of my foolish mother—this nameless rascal, who has run away, heaven knows where ?   By-the-bye, I wonder if Spillsby has overhauled the plate chest since he went !"

Flora was silent, but his *brusquerie* and categorical manner offended her, and filled her eyes with tears.

"This weeping is enough," continued the exasperated Cosmo, who, though he had no great regard for Flora, felt his self-esteem—which was not small—most fearfully wounded ; "you *do* love him."

"And what if I do ?" she asked, very quietly, but withal rather defiantly.

"Very fine, Miss Warrender—very fine, 'pon my soul !   That old jade, Anne Radcliffe, with her ' Romance of the Forest,' her ' Castles of Athlin and Dunbayne,' and this new Edinburgh fellow, Scott, with his ' Marmion,' and so forth, have perfected your education.   Your teaching has been most creditable !"

"This taunting manner is not so to you," replied Flora, resuming her inspection of the book of prints.

"Oho ! we are in a passion again it seems ?"

" Far from it, sir—I never was more cool in my life," said she, looking up with a wicked but glorious smile.

" And where has this runaway gone ? His friends in the servants' hall heard something of him last night or this morning, if I may judge from the pot-house row they made."

" He has gone into the army," replied Flora, with a perceptible modulation of voice.

" The army !" replied Cosmo, really surprised ; " enlisted—for what ?—a fifer or triangle boy ?"

" No," replied Flora, curling her pretty nostril, while her eyes gleamed dangerously under their long thick lashes.

" For what, on earth, has he gone then ?"

" A gentleman volunteer."

" A valuable acquisition to His Majesty's service !" said Cosmo, laughing, and, greatly to Flora's annoyance, seeming to be really amused ; " do you know, friend Flora, what a volunteer is ?"

" Not exactly, sir," said Flora, again looking down on her book of prints with a sigh of anger.

" Shall I tell you ?"

" If you please."

" We never had any in the Household Brigade —such fellows are usually to be found only with the line corps."

" Ah—with corps that go abroad and really see service—I understand."

" Miss Warrender, the Guards——"

"Well, *what* is a volunteer?" asked Flora, beating the carpet with a very pretty foot.

"A volunteer is a poor devil who is too proud . to enlist, and is too friendless to procure a commission; who has all a private's duty to do, and has to carry a musket, pack, and havresack, wherein are his ration-beef, biscuits, and often his blackball and shoebrushes; who mounts guard and salutes *me* when I pass him, and whom I may handcuff and send to the cells or guard-house when I please; who is not a regular member of the mess and may never be; who gets a shilling per diem with the chance of Chelsea, a wooden leg, or an arm with an iron hook if his limbs are smashed by a round shot; who is neither officer, non-commissioned officer, nor private—neither fish, flesh, nor good red-herring (to use a camp phrase). Oh, Flora, Flora Warrender, can you be such a romantic little goose as to feel an interest in such a fellow as I have described?"

Mingling emotions, indignation at the Master's insulting bitterness, pity for Quentin, and pure anger at the annoyance to which she was subjected, made Flora's white bosom heave as she quietly turned her eyes, with a flashing expression however, upon the cat-like regards of the sneering questioner, and said,—

"Who are you, sir, that would thus question or dictate to me?"

"Who am I?" he asked, while surveying her through his glass with amusement, perplexity, and something of sorrow in his tone.

"Yes, sir—who are you?"

"I am, I believe, Cosmo, Master of Rohallion, and Colonel to be, of a very fine regiment; so I can afford to smile at the pride and petulance of a moon-struck girl."

"Oh, how unseemly this is! Whatever happens, let us part friends," said she politely, perhaps a little imploringly.

"So be it," said he, kissing her hand as she retired.

"Now, the sooner I am off from this dreary paternal den the better. Away to London at once. Andrews!—Jack Andrews," he shouted, in a tone almost of ferocity; "show me the last newspapers." They were soon brought, and Cosmo's sharp eyes ran rapidly over the advertisements. "Let me see," he pondered, "travelling by mail is intolerable; one never knows who the devil one may be boxed up with for a week, a fever patient or a lunatic, perhaps! The smacks are crowded with all manner of rubbish, travelling bagmen, linesmen going home on leave, sick mothers and squalling babies. What is this? The good ship *Edinburgh*, pinck-built, near the new quay at Leith, sails for England without convoy—carries six 12-pounders—master to be spoke with daily at the Cross—to be *spoke*

with. Faugh! what says the next advertisement?
'A widow lady, who is to set out for London
next week in a post-chaise, would be glad to hear
of a companion. Enquire at the *Courant* office,
opposite the Old Fishmarket-close, Edinburgh.'
Egad! the very thing—widow lady—hope she's
young and good-looking. I'll answer *this!*"

Such advertisements in the London and Edinburgh papers were quite common in those days,
when travelling expenses were enormous.

He replied to it, and departed from Rohallion
in a great hurry soon after. Whether with a fair
companion or not, we are unable to say.

We hope so, and that on the journey of about
four hundred miles to London, the amenity of the
fair widow consoled him for the final rebuff he
met with from Flora Warrender.

CHAPTER II.

THE MESS.

" He is more fortunate! Yea, he hath finished;
For him there is no longer any future.
His life is bright; bright without spot it was,
And cannot cease to be.

      O 'tis well with him,
But who knows what the coming hour,
Veiled in thick darkness, brings for us!
                   Wallenstein.

THE mess-room of the 2nd battalion of the 25th Foot, in old Colchester Barracks, was a long room, and for its size rather low in the ceiling, which was crossed by a massive dormant beam of oak. Good mahogany tables occupied the entire length of the room, with a row of haircloth chairs on each side thereof. It was destitute of all ornament save a few framed prints of the popular generals of the time, such as the Duke of York, so justly known as " the soldier's friend;" Sir Ralph Abercrombie, who fell in Egypt; Sir David Dundas, the hero of Tournay; Sir David Baird, flushed with triumph and revenge, leading on his stormers at Seringapatam; the sad and gentle Sir John Moore, and others.

The room was uncarpeted, but the number of tall wax candles, in silver branches, on the long table, and in girandoles, on them antelpiece and sideboard, together with the quantity of rich plate that was displayed, and the brilliance of the assembled company, about thirty officers in full uniform, their scarlet coats all faced and lapelled to the waist with blue barred with gold, and all their bullion epaulettes glittering, had a very gay appearance; thus the general meagreness of the furniture passed unobserved.

At mess the coats were then worn open, with the crimson silk sash inside and over a white waistcoat. Nearly all the seniors still indulged in powdered heads, while the juniors wore their hair in that curly profusion introduced by George IV., then Prince of Wales. A few who were on duty were distinguished by the pipe-clayed shoulder-belt and gilt gorget, which was slung round the neck by a ribbon which varied in every corps according to the colour of its facings.

Amid much good-humour and a little banter, they seated themselves, and the president and vice-president—posts taken by every officer in rotation—proceeded to their tasks of dispensing the viands.

Quentin was seated next his host, Major Middleton, about the centre of the table, and he surveyed the gay scene with surprise and pleasure, though looking somewhat anxiously for the face of his kind friend Warriston, who was to be a guest that evening, but was still detained on duty.

To him much of the conversation was a perfect mystery, being half jocular and half technical, or that which is stigmatized as " shop." It chiefly ran on drills, duties, and mistakes—how badly those 94th fellows marched past yesterday, and so forth; while the standing jokes about Buckle's nag-tailed charger, Monkton's old epaulettes, Pimple's last love-affair, and the old commandant's state of mind on discovering that Colville had a fair visitor in his guard-room, seemed to excite as much laughter as if they had all been quite new, and had not been heard there every day for the last six months.

Some rapid changes would seem to have taken place at the headquarters of the 2nd battalion. The old colonel of whom Quentin heard on the march from Ayr, had sold out, and a Major Sir John Glendinning come in by purchase. One gazette contained a notice of this, and a second announced the death of Sir John in a duel with an officer of the Guards. The lieutenant-colonelcy was thus again vacant, and all present, even Monkton, hoped the step would be given in the regiment, that old Major Middleton would get the command; thus all would have a move upward, and who could say but Quentin Kennedy might obtain the ensigncy which would thus be rendered vacant? But poor Middleton had served so long, and had seen so many promoted over his head, that he ceased to be hopeful of anything.

Some of the youngsters drank wine again and again with our young volunteer, a spirit of mischief being combined with their hospitality. To " screw a Johnny Raw" was one of the chief practical jokes at a mess-table then, as it is at some few still; but Middleton's influence soon repressed them.

The cloth removed, the regimental mull, a gigantic ram's head, the horns of which were tipped with cairngorms and massive silver settings, was placed before the president, and was passed down the table from left to right, according to the custom of all Scottish messes. The mull was the farewell gift of Lord Rohallion, and the gallant ram was the flower of all that he could procure in Carrick.

The proposed expeditions to Spain and Holland soon formed the staple topics for discourse and surmise; but none present had the slightest idea on which of these the regiment might be despatched.

When Quentin looked round that long and glittering mess-table, and saw so many handsome, pleasant, and jovial fellows, all heedless and full of high spirits, who welcomed him among them, spoke cheeringly of his prospects and drank to his success, he felt a pang on reflecting that he must owe it to the death in battle of *one* at least among them !

There was plenty of laughter, fun, and joking. Many of those present were more or less dandies ; but the military Dundreary, the—to use a vulgar phrase—" heavy swell," who affects the style of Charles Mathews in " Used Up," was unknown in the days of the long, long war with France, for men joined the army to become soldiers indeed. Their predecessors were usually killed in action, and they had the immediate prospect of finding themselves before the bravest enemy in the world.

The solemn regimental snob, or yawning ya-hoo, whose private affairs became so " urgent" in the Crimea ; the parvenu Lancer or lisping Hussar, cold, sarcastic, and unimpressionable, are entirely the growth of the piping times of peace, and to them the stern advice of the old officer of other times, " Be ever ready with your pistol," is meaningless now.

" I joined the service as a volunteer," said Rowland Askerne, the burly captain of the Grena-diers—as his massive gold rings announced him—turning to Quentin.

" Were you long one ?"

" Longer than I quite relished," replied As-kerne, laughing.

" Indeed !" said Quentin, anxiously.

" Yes—four years; and long years they seemed to me."

" On foreign service ?"

" Of course; and pretty sharp service, too, sometimes. I carried a musket with Middleton's company at the capture of Corsica, in '95, and again with the Gordon Highlanders on the recent expedition against Porto Ferrajo, in Elba, where I had the ill-luck to be the only man hit. A French tirailleur put a ball through my left leg, but he was shot the next moment by my covering file, Norman Calder, now a sergeant. Some of the Irish in '98 proved better marksmen than the French; they knocked a number of ours on the head, so I won my epaulettes fighting against the poor fellows under General Lake, at Vinegar Hill. I had many a heart-burning before they promoted me; (by *they* I mean the Horse Guards) and I swore that when the day came that they did so, I would tread on my sash and turn cobbler; but I had not the heart to quit, so I wear my harness still—a captain only—when I should be lieutenant-colonel by brevet, at least; but Middleton's case is a harder one than mine, for he has been longer in the service."

" We are most likely bound for North Holland," said the adjutant; " and there many an evil will be ended."

" The French are in great strength there, and

hard knocks will be going," added Monkton. "Many among us are fated perhaps to find a last abode among the swamps of Beveland; so, if you escape, Kennedy, you must certainly gain your pair of colours, with five shillings and threepence per diem—less the income-tax—to spend on the luxuries of life—damme !"

"Glad to hear we are to be off so soon, Monkton," said a smart, but somewhat blasé-looking young lieutenant, "for we have a most weary time of it here in Colchester. The course of drill—drill, always drill—with club, sword, or musket, and the whole routine of barrack duty, with inspections and guards, are decidedly a bore !"

"What the deuce would you have, Colville ?" asked the adjutant, bluntly. "What did you come here for ?"

"I came to be a soldier," replied the "used up" sub, with a suave smile.

"To be a soldier ?"

"Yes—not to doze life away by marching to and fro at the goose-step, in that gravelled yard, or by lolling over the window in shirt-sleeves, to save my shell-jacket. Where are all the castles I built——"

"To storm, eh ?" asked Buckle, glancing uneasily at the commanding officer, who was forming his walnut-shells in grand-division squares, for the edification of the second major.

"Yes—I had hoped to have achieved something decidedly brilliant ere this."

"Console yourself, Colville, and pass the port. Ah, you consider yourself sharp—up to every sort of thing—a common delusion with young fellows of your age; but ten years' more soldiering, and the rubs of life between your twenties and thirties, to say nothing of those afterwards, will cure you of thinking so. Believe me, Colville, wherever we go, we shall find plenty of desperate work cut out for us all. Well, Monkton, in recruiting, you could not pick up an heiress—eh?"

"No. Heiresses are not to be found under every hedge."

"In Scotland, especially."

"I have considered the matter maturely, my dear friend," said Monkton, in his bantering tone, "and have come to the sage conclusion that, if a man marries, with his pay only, he had better hang; if otherwise, and his wife have a long purse, and expectations, to enhance the charms of her blushes and orange-buds, let him send in his papers, and quit; so the service loses your Benedict any way."

"Purse, or no purse," said Colville, "as Paragon says in the comedy we acted at York, 'when you see *my* wife, you shall see perfection, though I never met the woman I could conscientiously throw myself away upon.'"

" Pimple, we hear, has been romantically tender on a flax-spinner's daughter; and that the route came only in time to save him from the arms of Venus for those of Bellona, and he is burning now to forget his loved and lost one amid the smoke of battle," said Colville, with a tragic air. "Ah, there were great men even before old Agamemnon."

" But Pimple shall show us by his glorious example, that we have at least one greater since."

" Let me alone, Colville, and you also, Monkton," said Boyle, becoming seriously angry; " I hope to do my duty with the best among you."

Attention was speedily drawn from the irritation of the little ensign by the entrance of Warriston, who apologized briefly for being late, having been detained on duty at the quarters of his own regiment; then drawing a chair near his friend Middleton, he handed to him the last number of the *London Gazette*, pointing to a paragraph therein, and leisurely filling his glass with claret, passed the decanters.

When Middleton read the passage referred to, a crimson flush passed over his features, and he crushed up the paper as if an emotion of rage and pain thrilled through him.

" What is the matter, major ?" asked half-a-dozen voices; " nothing unpleasant, I hope ?"

" The lieutenant-colonelcy has been given *out* of the regiment," replied Middleton, with his

c 2

brows knit, while his hand still crushed up the paper; then, as if remembering himself, he smiled, but very disdainfully.

"He must have seen much service to be appointed over *your* head," said Monkton.

"Service—yes, the Guards fight many bloody battles about Hounslow, Hyde Park, and the Fifteen Acres," replied the justly exasperated field-officer. "Here is my advancement stopped by the promotion of a fellow who has some petticoat interest about Carlton House, whose cousin is groom of the backstairs, and who has been compelled to 'eschew sack and loose company;' so he comes from the Household Brigade to the Line, and may go from the 25th to the devil, perhaps."

"Be wary, my good friend—be wary," said Warriston, glancing round the table hastily.

"And *who* is he?" asked several, full of curiosity.

"The son of a general officer—the Master of Rohallion."

On hearing this name, Quentin felt as if petrified! Here, even here, his evil spirit seemed to be following him!

"It is an old name in the regiment," said Monkton.

"Yes," replied the major; "his father was a gallant officer; I was his subaltern in America; but here it is;" and he read, "'25th Foot; to be Lieutenant-Colonel, Major the Honourable Cosmo Crawford, from the 1st Guards, *vice* Sir John Glendinning, deceased;' so he comes over us, in virtue of that court rank which is one of the worst abuses of our service."

" Promotion is always slow among the Household troops, so they indemnify themselves at the expense of the line," said Warriston, in answer to a question of Quentin's; "every rank among them having a grade above us; but take courage, my good old friend, this kind of thing is not likely to happen again."

With a smile that grew scornful in spite of himself, the worthy old major strove to conceal the bitterness of his heart, though all present condoled with him on his disappointment and hard usage by the powers that be ; and for reasons known to himself alone, none shared his chagrin more than Quentin Kennedy.

He had been formally enrolled as a member of the regiment, and had ordered his equipments for it; his name, as a volunteer, had been sent by Middleton to Sir Harry Calvert, the Adjutant General, at the Horse Guards, that he might obtain the first vacant ensigncy (*subject to the approval of the commanding officer*), and that he might have his passage abroad provided, either by the commissariat department, or by the commandant at Hillsea, near Portsmouth. His own honour, and all the cir-

cumstances under which he stood prevented him
from quitting; but *now,* what hope had he of
comfort or prosperity in remaining? His very
chances of advancement depended on the veto,
whim, and caprice of this Master of Rohallion,
his bitterest enemy! Of what avail would now
be the endurance of campaigning, the hardship
of serving as a volunteer, and risking all the
perils of war?

Perhaps Flora Warrender may come with him
as his bride was the next idea; and it added
greatly to the bitterness of the others.

That night Quentin slept but little, and he
seemed barely to have closed his eyes when he
heard the drum beating the assembly.

Then he sprang from bed just as the grey
dawn was breaking, and proceeded hastily to
dress, remembering to have heard last evening
that, at daybreak, the regiment was to have a
" punishment parade," which, to his uninitiated
ears, had a very unpleasant sound.

CHAPTER III.

THE PUNISHMENT PARADE.

" Most worthy sergeant, I have seen thee lead,
 Where men among us would be slow to follow ;
 Udsdaggers, yes !   By trench and culverine,
 Where men and horses too, lay foully heap'd
 On other ; and hath it come to this, good sergeant,
 Beshrew my heart—a prisoner and afeared."
Old Play.

PLAIN though it was, being destitute of lace
or epaulettes, poor Quentin was very proud of
his volunteer uniform, and being eminently a
handsome young man, he looked very well in it.
The coarse buff crossbelts, the pouch, and bayonet, and, more especially, the Brown Bess he had
to carry, did not suit his taste quite so well. He
had imagined that he would have to shoulder a
kind of Joe Manton, or something like a smart
Enfield rifle of the present day, with a "draw"
of ten pounds or less on the trigger, instead of a
long blunderbuss like the regulation musket of
those days, weighing fourteen pounds, with its
enormous butt-plate of brass and so forth.

Thanks to the teaching of the old quartermaster, he proved himself so apt a pupil under the

sergeant-major and old Norman Calder, that within a week he was reported as "fit for duty," as Monkton said, "doing as much credit to his preceptors as to the cabbage-stalk," for so he designated the army tailor.

But we are anticipating.

His first parade was an inauspicious one, in so far as it was for *punishment*.

A sergeant of the regiment had been recently tried by a regimental court-martial for permitting spirits to be brought by a woman to the main guard-house at night, while he was in command, and by these means certain prisoners became intoxicated and riotous. He alleged that he was asleep on that luxurious couch, the guard bed, after posting his sentinels, and that the fault lay with his corporal and others; but the plea was urged in vain—the corps was under orders for foreign service—an example was necessary; so he was now to receive the award of his dereliction of duty, and as the drum-major had received some special instructions over night, all knew that it involved the application of the now (happily) almost obsolete instrument—the cat!

The degradation of a non-commissioned officer is always a painful duty; but when flogging is added thereto, it is doubly painful to the witnesses, and maddening to the culprit.

"I told you old Middleton was a Tartar," said Monkton, as he and Quentin hurried downstairs from their quarters; "he'd certainly flog ensigns if he could; and the *Gazette* of last night wont have improved his variable temper. But here he comes, mounted, with holsters and blue saddle-cloth, but looking for all the world like an old woman trotting to market with her butter and eggs. Such a seat—such a queer length, or rather want of length, in the stirrup-leathers! Good morning, Buckle—so we are to have a flogging—ugh? that isn't lively."

Quentin being a young hand, felt somewhat awed, as he knew not what was about to ensue. The sun had not yet risen, and the September morning was chilly and misty; the men of the regiment were falling in by companies under arms in light marching order—the tall grenadiers on the right with their black bearskin caps; the smart light company on the left with green plumes in their shakos, and Saxon horns on all their appointments; the sergeants were calling the various rolls; the officers were gathered in a somewhat silent group, and the face of every man wore a sullen, or rather dejected expression, for a punishment parade is the kind of parade least liked by soldiers of all ranks. It acts as a damper on the spirits of all; on this morning the atmosphere was dense; the sombre sun seemed to linger behind the uplands of Suffolk, and the shadows to lie deeper in the silent barrack square.

Impressed by the taciturnity and gloomy expression of the men, whose faces wore the pallor
incident to all who come from bed in haste at an
unusual hour, Quentin remained silent and full
of expectation and anxiety as he fell into the rear
rank of Captain Askerne's company, to which he
was to be permanently attached. He was sen-
sible, however, that the soldiers viewed him with
interest, as a volunteer is always popular. It
was to rescue Thomas Grahame, when lying
severely wounded, and then serving as a simple
volunteer in the red coat of the Caledonian Hunt,
that our troops in Holland made one of their
most desperate rallies, and gained to the service
the future Lord Lynedoch, the hero of Barossa.

The inspection of the companies and the drum
for coverers rapidly followed the calling of the
muster-rolls; a bugle sounded; the officers fell in;
the bayonets were fixed, and the regiment, without
music, was marched silently by sections to a secluded part of the barracks, where, surrounded by
high stores and magazines, no stranger's eye could
oversee the proceedings, and then it was formed in
a hollow square, in the centre of which Quentin
perceived three sergeants' pikes (weapons not dis-
used till 1830) strapped together by the heads,
an equilateral triangle being formed by the shafts,
which were stuck in the earth. Near these were
the drummers and drum-major, who carried in his
hand a canvas bag, which, as Quentin was in-

formed in a whisper by the next file on his right, contained " the cats."

" The officer with the cocked hat, and without a sash, close by, is the doctor," he added.

" The doctor—for what is he required ?"

" You'll too soon see that, sir," was the ominous response.

" Steady, rear rank—silence," growled old Sergeant Calder.

At that moment one of the drummers drew forth a cat, and Quentin could perceive that it consisted of nine tails of whipcord, each having nine knots thereon, and these were firmly lashed to a handle about the length of a drum-stick. A slight shudder with an emotion of sickness came over him ; and he looked anxiously at the face of Major Middleton, but it seemed immovable as he said to the sergeant-major with studied sternness of tone,

" March in the prisoner."

A section in the face of the square wheeled backward and permitted the unfortunate, with his escort, consisting of a corporal and two men of the barrack-guard, to march in and halt before the major, on which the culprit took off his forage-cap and stood bareheaded, the centre of all observation.

He cast a haggard glance at the triangles ; another half furtively and restlessly at the stolid faces round him, and then he seemed to become

immovable. There was little need for Mr.
Buckle, the adjutant, to read over the proceedings of the Court, for the hopeless sergeant knew
at once his double degradation and his doom!

He was to be reduced to the rank and pay of
a private, and to receive *three hundred and fifty
lashes*, the utmost number a regimental court could
then award; with the option, if he would avoid
this extreme punishment, of volunteering to serve
for life (*i.e.* till disabled by wounds or age) in
the York Chasseurs, or any other condemned
corps, in Africa or the West Indies.

His name was Allan Grange, the colour-ser-
geant of the Grenadiers, who always considered
themselves the *corps d'élite* of a regiment.
Altogether he was a model of a man, erect and
strong in figure, his hair was a little grizzled
about the temples, and his face was somewhat
careworn, as if he had known or suffered much
anxiety and trouble in his time. His eye was clear
and keen, and save a little nervous twitching
about the muscles of the mouth, he seemed unmoved and unflinching—unflinching as when on
the glorious field of Egmont-op-Zee, he commanded the Grenadiers of the 25th, after all their
officers had fallen, and with his pike broken in
his hand by a musket shot, led them to that
bloody hand-to-hand conflict on the road that
leads to Haarlem.

Perhaps the poor fellow was thinking of that

signal and bloody day—perhaps of his boyhood
and his home ; it might be of the future, that
was all a *blank ;* for he seemed as in a dream
while the adjutant read over the formula of the
trial, the list of charges and the sentence, till he
was roused by the drum-major proceeding to
rip off with a penknife the three hard-won
chevrons from his right arm. It was done
gently, but " the iron seemed to enter his soul"
at the moment, and a heavy sigh escaped him
as his chin sank on his breast.

" Allan Grange," said Major Middleton, raising his voice clearly and distinctly, that the
whole of the hollow square and even its super-
numerary ranks might hear, " you are the last
man in the whole Borderers whom I could have
expected to see standing before us as you do
to-day. In cutting off your stripes I feel extreme
reluctance and sorrow, and I think you have
known me long enough to be aware of that."

" I am, major—I am aware of it," said the
reduced man in a hollow voice.

" Allan Grange, you have come of a respectable
old Scottish stock in Lothian ; you were born in
my native place, and are one of the many fine
lads who came with me to the line from the
Buccleugh Fencibles. I know well how, in your
native village, the Stenhouse, your name and progress have been watched by early friends and old
schoolfellows ; by none more than your father,

who now lies in Liberton kirkyard, by the good
old mother who nursed you; by the old dominie
who taught you; by the grey-haired minister
who will ere long see your name affixed, as that
of a degraded man, on the kirk-door. I know
how, at the village inn on the braehead, in the
smithy at the loan-end, at the mill beside the
burn, it would be known that Allan Grange had
been made a corporal—that he had gained his
third stripe—that he had been made a colour-
sergeant; and I can imagine how the listeners
would drink to your health and to mine, in the
hope that we should one day see you an officer;
and now—*now*—by one act of folly you are
again at the foot of the ladder!"

A heavy sigh escaped the sergeant; the drum-
major's knife gave a final rip, and he stood once
more a private on parade!

"The worst part of your sentence yet remains
—unless—unless you volunteer into the York
Chasseurs."

"Major Middleton," said Grange, firmly, and
standing erect, like a fine man as he was, "I'll
not leave the regiment!"

The man was fearfully pale, and it was evident
to all that Middleton, though a strict and sometimes severe officer, was greatly moved.

"You will rather take three hundred and
fifty lashes than volunteer?" he asked.

"I'd volunteer for a forlorn hope; I've done

so before now, sir, as you know well, but I'll not
quit the old 25th for a condemned corps. I'll
take my punishment—I've earned it like a fool,
and with God's help, I hope to bear it like a
man."

"Then strip, sir," said Middleton, playing
nervously with the blue ribbons of his gorget.

All emotion seemed to pass away as the culprit
proceeded deliberately to unclasp his leather
stock and unbutton his coat; but before it was
off the major exclaimed in a loud voice, as he
drew a letter from his pocket—

"*Stop !*"

Grange paused, and looked up with a haggard
and bloodshot eye.

"I remit the rest of the sentence, for the
sake of one who intercedes for you."

"Sir?"

"I have had a petition from your wife, and
willingly grant it. Take away the triangles.
Conduct yourself as you did till this misfortune
came upon you, and ere long, Grange, you may
regain the stripes you have to-day been deprived
of. Rejoin your company."

"I thank you, sir, for the sake of my poor
wife and her bairnie. I have proved that I would
rather take my punishment than leave the regiment and you ; and—sir—sir——"

Here Grange fairly broke down and sobbed
aloud ; and no man among the nine hundred

there thought the less of him, because his stout heart, which even the terror of the lash could not appal, now became full of penitence and gratitude. At that moment many an eye glistened in the ranks, and many a heart was swelling.

"There, there—don't make a fuss," said Middleton, testily; " I hate scenes! Prepare to form quarter-distance column right in front—stand fast the Light Company."

And so ended an episode, that, like the warm rising sun now shining cheerfully into the barrack-square, shed a brightness over every face, and lent a lightness—a sense of pleasure and relief to every heart, as the regiment marched back to quarters, and to what was of some importance after being two hours under arms in the morning air—breakfast.

CHAPTER IV.

THE OLD REGIMENT OF EDINBURGH.

"Such is our love of liberty, our country and our laws,
That like our ancestors of old, we'll stand in freedom's
    cause;
We'll bravely fight like heroes for honour and applause,
And defy the French, with all their art, to alter our laws."
                                        The Garb of Old Gaul.

FROM Major Middleton, who took somewhat of a fatherly interest in him, Quentin learned much of the past history and achievements of the regiment he had joined.

It was one with which the stories of his old military friends at Rohallion had made him familiar from boyhood; thus, he was in possession of so many old regimental names, so many stock stories and anecdotes, which Middleton deemed unknown beyond the circle of their mess-table and barrack-rooms, that he considered the lad an enigma, and was puzzled how, or where, he had gained all this information about the corps; for Quentin, though looking forward to the arrival of Cosmo with a disgust that almost amounted to terror, kept his own counsel

with wonderful prudence, and never permitted
the name of Rohallion to escape him.

As there is no offiical record of the Borderers'
achievements prior to 1808, the account given by
the major is perhaps the only one extant.

Under David Leslie, Earl of Leven, the 25th
Foot were formed on the 10th of March, 1689,
from a body of six thousand Covenanters, who,
on the news of William of Orange landing at
Torbay, marched from the West Country and
laid siege to the castle of Edinburgh. On their
banners were an open Bible, with the motto,
" For Reformation according to the Word of
God."

Marching north against the loyal Highlanders,
they left their compatriots, all of whom served
without pay or remuneration till the conclusion
of the siege, when the fortress was surrendered
by the Duke of Gordon after a noble defence,
and after being warned by a spectre—pale as he
" who drew Priam's curtain at the dead of night "
—in fact, by the wraith of the terrible Claver-
house in his buff coat, cuirass, and cavalier wig,
all stained with gouts of blood, that he had been
shot by a silver bullet on the field of Killycrankie. In one of the rooms of the old fortress this vision is alleged to have appeared to
Colin, Earl of Balcarris, then the duke's prisoner,
and the truth of the episode is admitted by a
delirious biographer of the viscount, who affirms

that he is frequently in communion with the ghost in question, and with others.

The Earl of Leven, though colonel of infantry under Frederick Wilhelm, Elector of Brandenburg, and of a regiment which came over with the Prince of Orange, who made him Governor of Edinburgh Castle and Master of the Scottish ordnance, was a Whig noble, chiefly famous for the rapidity of his flight from Killycrankie, and the vigour with which he horsewhipped the Lady Morton Hall. It is said that he rode six miles from the Pass without drawing his bridle, though his regiment, the future 25th, and Hastings, the future 13th, were the only troops that made any stand against the victorious Highlanders.

Leven's regiment having been raised in the capital while Sir John Hall, Knight, was Lord Provost, was designated of Edinburgh, and bore the insignia yet borne on its colours, the triple castle of the city, with its crest and motto, *Nisi Dominus Frustra.*

As Leven's regiment—the same in which "my uncle Toby" fought at Landen, and with which he went to "mount guard in the trenches before the gate of St. Nicholas in his roquelaure" —it served in all King William's useless wars for the well-being of his darling Dutch, and all the great barrier towns of Europe have heard the drums of the 25th. It was the *first* British regiment which used the socket in lieu of the

screw bayonet, which its lieutenant-colonel, Max-
well, adopted in imitation of the bayonets of the
French Fusiliers. Prior to this, our bayonets
were screwed into the muzzles of the muskets,
and to fire with them fixed, was, of course, an
impossibility. After fighting at Sheriffmuir, as
Viscount Shannon's Foot, it served with distinction in the wars of the Spanish and Austrian
succession, and shared in the disasters of Fon-
tenoy, ere its soldiers had again to imbrue their
hands in the blood of their own countrymen at
Falkirk, at Culloden, and in defending the
Comyn's Tower in the old Castle of Blair against
Lord George Murray, till we find them again
among the troops defeated at Val through the
cowardice and incapacity of the Duke of Cum-
berland.

During the seven years' war it suffered severely
at the siege of a small German castle, by the
heroism of a sergeant of the enemy. Under
Lord Rohallion a party of the Edinburgh Regiment had made themselves masters of an outwork, in which they established themselves at the
point of the bayonet. *Under* this work was a
secret mine, which (as the "Ecole Historique et
Morale du Soldat" relates) was entrusted to a sergeant and a few soldiers of the Royal Piedmontese
Guards. The mine was ready, the *saucisson* led
through the gallery, the train was laid, and a single
spark would blow all below and above to atoms!

With admirable coolness the sergeant desired his comrades to retire, and request the king to take charge of his wife and children. He then, inspired by a spirit of self-devotion, set fire to the train and perished, as the mine exploded. The outwork rose into the air and fell thundering into the fosse, Lord Rohallion, a corporal, and two men alone escaping, covered with bruises and cuts. The name of the sergeant was said to be Amadeus di Savillano, son of the Castellan of the fortress of that name in Piedmont.

The Edinburgh regiment served at the battle of Minden. The Earl of Home was then its colonel, and it was in the second line, and on the left of Kingsley's famous brigade. Landing in England, on the homeward march, near the Borders, the old colours borne in the seven years' war were buried by its soldiers, with all honour, and three volleys were fired over them.

In those days, when any regiment approached London, the colours were furled and cased, and no drum was beaten or fife blown during the march through its limits. The 3rd, or Old East Kentish Buffs, were alone excepted, and had the exclusive privilege of marching through the City of London with all the honours of war, in memory of having, at some period, been recruited from the City Trained Bands.

Likewise no regiment could beat a drum within the walls, or through the portes of the

Scottish capital, with the exception of the 25th, or old Edinburgh Regiment. But not long after the battle of Minden, it chanced that a certain thick-pated lord-provost objected to their drums beating up for recruits, on the plea that none should beat there but those of the City Guard. On this, the colonel, Lord George Henry Lennox (M.P. for the county of Sussex, who died in 1805), was so incensed, that on his special application the title of the corps was changed, and its facings were altered from the royal yellow of Scotland to the royal blue of Britain, and after a time it was styled the " King's Own Borderers."

Egmont-op-zee, Martinque, and Egypt added fresh honours to those of other times ; but still on drum and standard are borne unchanged the castle, triple-towered, with the anchor and motto, *Nisi Dominus Frustra,* usually the first little bit of latinity learned by the Edinburgh schoolboy.

Such is a rapid outline of the past history of this famous old corps, in the ranks of which Quentin Kennedy hoped to achieve for himself a position and a name—perhaps, rank and glory too ! What boy does not look forward to some such vague but brilliant future,—

" In life's morning march when the bosom is young."

The evening subsequent to the punishment parade was the *last* on which the battalion mess would assemble, and Quentin was Monkton's guest. He was again seated near the worthy major, and from him he learned much of what we have just narrated, many a quaint regimental story being woven up with what was actual military history.

"You should tell him of that startling adventure, or rather, I should say, of those series of adventures, which happened to you when commanding an out-picquet in America," said Colville, with a significant but hasty glance at Monkton, for the frequent repetition of this story formed a kind of covert joke against the worthy major.

"What—which out-picquet—at the siege of Fort St. John?"

"Exactly, Major," said Monkton.

"St. John, on the Richelieu River?" asked Quentin.

"Yes," said Middleton, with an air of gratification; "you are a very intelligent young man, and have no doubt read of the defence of that place."

Quentin hastened to say that he *had* heard of it; in fact, the defence with all its details—the bravery of Majors Preston and André of the Cameronians, and so forth—formed one of the stock stories of his old friends, the quartermaster and Jack Andrews; and so frequently had he heard it, that he was somewhat uncertain at times that he had not served there too.

"But the episode of yours, with that devilish

Indian fellow, may scare Kennedy when on sentry," said the adjutant, " a duty he must do as a volunteer."

" Scare—not at all !" said Middleton, testily ; " it is the very thing to sharpen his wits and to keep him wide awake. There are others here who never heard the story, and it is worth listening to ; but before I begin we must send away the marines and replenish the decanters."

" Right !" cried Askerne, who was president ; " this is the last night of one of the jolliest messes in His Majesty's service. To-morrow the plate, which has glittered before us so long— the crystal from which we have imbibed the full bodied port, the creamy claret, and the choice Madeira, the sparkling champagne, the old hock, in fact, ' the entire plant,' to use a commercial phrase, will be packed up and stored away among dust and cobwebs, while the Borderers march in quest of ' fresh fields and pastures new.'   A long farewell to our glorious mess !" exclaimed the handsome grenadier, as he poured a glass of port down his capacious throat.   " Mr. Vice-President, order the last cooper of port before the major begins his story."

" Ah, the mess !" sighed Buckle, the adjutant ; " when we come to be frying our ration beef in a camp-kettle lid, under a shower of rain, perhaps, there will be an exchange with a devil of a difference !"

With the aforesaid " cooper" there came in hot whisky-toddy for the major and a few select seniors, for it was *then* the custom at the messes of Scots and Irish national corps to introduce the Farintosh and potheen ; though I fear our dandies of the Victorian age (especially such as are horrified at the sight of a black bottle) might consider such a proceeding a deplorable solecism in good taste.

" And now, major, for your story," said Askerne, while Colville, perhaps the only affected man in the regiment, gave his shoulders a shrug, perceptible only by the glittering of his epaulettes, and Monkton responded by a sly wink behind his glass of wine, while he pretended to be looking for the beeswing.

CHAPTER V.

THE ADVANCED PICQUET.

" All quiet along the Potomac, they say,
    Except now and then a stray picquet,
Is shot as he walks on his beat to and fro,
    By a rifleman hid in the thicket.
'Tis nothing. A private or two now and then,
    Will not count in the tale of the battle;
Not an officer lost—only one of the men,
    Breathing out all alone the death-rattle."

" In the spring of the year '75, a party of ours,
under Lord Rohallion, then a captain, was sent
to the Fort of St. John, on the Richelieu River,
to strengthen the garrison, which was composed
of some companies of the 7th Fusiliers and the
26th, or Cameronians, under Major Preston, of
Valleyfield, in Fifeshire, as gallant a fellow as
ever bore the King's commission.

" We were in daily expectation of the advance
of the rebel General Montgomery, with a great
force, so the duties of guards and sentinels were
performed with great vigilance, as the whole
country for miles around, if not actually in
possession of the armed colonists, was full of
people who were favourable to their cause,

and were consequently inimical to the king and to us.

" Montgomery was expected to approach through Vermont county (now one of the states) by the eastern shore of Lake Champlain, a long and narrow sheet of deep water, which forms the boundary between it and the State of New York; thus, on an eminence which commanded a considerable view of the country southward, and at the distance of two miles from Fort St. John, Major Preston, of the 26th, had an outpost or picquet, consisting of one officer and twenty men, stationed in a log-hut, from whence they were relieved every week. The officer in command of this advanced party had to throw forward a line of sentinels, extending across the road by which the Americans were expected to approach. At the hut was also a small piece of cannon, taken from a gunboat recently destroyed on the Lake, a 6-pounder, which was to be fired as a signal for the troops in Fort St. John to get under arms, and the picquet was well supplied with rockets to give the alarm by night.

" Our sentinels there had frequently been found dead and scalped, without a shot being fired. Sometimes they disappeared altogether, without leaving a trace, save a few spots of blood on the prairie grass. Their desertion was never suspected by those in authority ; but that savages and assassins lurked in woods along the eastern and western shores of Lake Champlain we had not a doubt; thus the solitary outpost before the Fort of St. John was a duty disliked by all, and always undertaken with sensations of doubt and anxiety.

"It was on a beautiful afternoon in the month of September, that with a sergeant and twenty men of the Borderers, I took possession of this log hut, relieving a Lieutenant Despard, of the Fusiliers, from whom I received over my orders, and posted my line of six sentinels at intervals across the highway and a kind of open prairie which it traversed. These orders were written and delivered with the parole and counsign, by Major André, of the Cameronians (afterwards named 'the unfortunate'), and they were simply, that during the night the sentinels were to face all persons approaching their posts, to stand firm in a state of preparation at half-cock with ported arms, and to fire instantly on all who could not give the countersign.

"Despard informed me that excessive vigilance was necessary, as he had lost five sentinels in one week, information which made my fellows look somewhat blankly in each other's faces; 'and these assassinations have occurred,' he added, 'though we have an Indian scout, Le Vipre Noir, an invaluable fellow, however unpleasant his name may sound, attached to the picquet-house. I would advise you to keep off that bit of prairie in front, Middleton. Zounds! one is always over the ankles in mud there, and mid-leg deep occasionally; so it's more like snipe-shooting in an Irish bog, than knocking over Yankees and Iroquois.'

" I now found that there was another scout, a Cornishman, named old Abe Treherne, attached to the post, as well as the native mentioned by Despard.

" Abe Treherne was a white-haired squatter and pioneer, who, for more than forty years, had been in the district, living by the use of his rifle and hatchet. He wore an Indian hunting-shirt and deer-skin mocassins, and had so completely forgotten the civilization of his native England, that he had almost become an Indian by habit, if not by speech. He was brave, however, and a most faithful fellow to us. Active and hardy, brown and weatherbeaten by constant exposure; privation could not impair, nor toil weary his strength, which was wonderful, for, by the wild life of nature he had led, every muscle had been developed, till it became like a band of iron.

" The savage scout, Le Vipre Noir, as he was named, was one of the Lenni-Lenappe—or un-mixed race as they boast themselves—who once occupied all the vast tract of country which lies between Penobscot and the shores of the Potomac; but we styled the most of them Delawares, and by that name they became known.

" Well, this devil of a Delaware—I think I can
see the fellow now !—was a model of muscular
strength and manly beauty, so far as form and
sinew go. He was like a colossal statue of
polished copper. His usual expression was fierce
and sullen ; his eyes were keen, black, and glittering, and his red and yellow streaks of war-paint
lent a fiendish aspect to his dusky visage, the
features of which were otherwise clean cut and
regular. He was somewhat of a dandy in his
own way, as his fur mocassins and hunting-shirt
were gaily ornamented with scarlet cloth, wampum, and beads, by the Delaware girls.

" His head had been denuded of hair entirely,
save the scalp-lock, in which two feathers were
stuck. At his girdle hung his pipe and hunting-
pouch, a large musk-rat skin, in the tail of which
his keen-edged scalping-knife was sheathed ; he
had also a pouch for ammunition, a long rifle, and
a tomahawk, which were never from his side by
night or day.

" This Delaware was from one of the native
villages about the upper end of the Penobscot
river, where the chiefs had signed a treaty of
alliance, offensive and defensive, with our government, and had sworn to have no communication
with the Americans or others, the king's enemies,
without the knowledge of the officer commanding
the British forces in North America.

" One of our men, named Jack Andrews, had

quarrelled with the Delaware, about a wild goose
they had shot. Blows were exchanged; the
savage drew his scalping-knife; but the Borderer
clubbed his musket, and laid the red-skin
sprawling among the reeds. Peace was enforced
between them; but the savage was more than ever
sullen and reserved, doubtless brooding on the
vengeance he meant to take.

"Such was Le Vipre Noir, who will bear
rather a conspicuous part in my little story.

"It was a lovely evening, I have said, when we
took possession of the sequestered picquet-house.
The rays of the setting sun, as he sank beyond
those grand and lofty mountain ranges, which rise
between the source of the Hudson and Lake
Champlain, shed a red glow across the water, and
bathed in warm light the foliage of the mighty
primeval forest, which for ages had clothed the
shores of that magnificent lake. In the immediate foreground the bayonets of my sentinels
seemed tipped with fire, as they trod slowly to
and fro upon their posts in that voiceless solitude.
Before the log-hut the arms were piled, and my
soldiers, with the Cornishman, were cooking their
supper, while the swarthy Indian scout was squatted
on his hams at a little distance, smoking listlessly
or half asleep, as the duty of searching in the
woods usually devolved upon him after nightfall.

"I, too, lit my pipe, and the pouch from

which I took my tobacco called back to mind
some half-forgotten thoughts and fancies.

"They were lovely hands that embroidered
that pouch for me, and it was associated with
many a promenade in Paul Street, when we were
quartered in Montreal, with balls at *her* father's
house, in the Rue de Notre Dame, flirtation and
ices in the Place d'Armes, where the French
troops used to parade of old—for, in short, that
tobacco-pouch had been made for me by Ella
Carleton, the belle of that old colonial city.

" She had a dash of the old French blood in her,
and hence her dark hair and eyes, which contrasted so wonderfully with her pure English
skin, and hence her continental form of eyelid and
drooping lash.   So I sighed as I thought of a
year ago—cursed the emergencies of the service
that banished me to Fort St. John, and passed
my fair Ella's present to the sergeant of the picquet, that he might supply himself, for active
service is a true leveller, and without impairing
discipline leads to a spirit of *camaraderie* not to
be found in such tented fields as Hyde Park or
the Phœnix at Dublin.

"After the sun set and twilight stole on, I
walked restlessly to and fro before the log-hut,
within which my men were now gathered with
their arms, as the dew was falling.   I had seen
all carefully loaded and had examined the flints
and priming.   I was resolved that due vigilance

on my part should not be wanting if the post were attacked or my sentinels surprised; and to prevent them from wandering unconsciously from their beat in the dark, I had six white stakes placed in the ground, and gave orders that they were to remain close by them during the night, until relieved, and every hour I went in person with the reliefs, a most harassing duty.

" Leaving my sergeant at the picquet-house, a few minutes before midnight, I went with six men to relieve my sentinels, who were all posted on the skirts of an open space, a large tract of waste ground which for some miles was covered with long prairie grass, and which stretched away towards the forest that was traversed by the main road leading to Fort Edward on the Hudson, about sixty miles distant.

" Save the gurgle of a runnel that stole under the prairie grass, there was no sound in the air— not even the whistle of the cat-bird; there was no moon, but the stars were clear and bright, and guided by their light we went straight from post to post, relieving the sentinels; but as we approached the place where the sixth should have been, on the extreme left of the highway, we advanced *unchallenged* to the stake that marked his beat: the place was solitary and the man— was gone.

" His musket, undischarged, was lying there, and a pool of blood beside it at once refuted any suspicion of desertion. But how came it that he had perished without resistance—without giving an alarm, and where was his body? All round the place we searched for it, but did so in vain.

"Posting another man, I gave him reiterated orders and injunctions to be on the alert, and wistfully the poor fellow looked after us as we returned to the picquet-house with the tidings of another mystery, which added to the conster-. nation that prevailed concerning this devilish outpost. Neither le Vipre Noir nor Treherne had yet returned; they were as usual scouting in front of our advanced sentinels, and when they came back, not together, but separately, they each reported the country all quiet for miles towards the mountains. Who then was this determined assassin, unless it were Satan himself?

"Next night the sentinel on the extreme right was missing, without leaving even a trace of blood, and without the grass being bruised or trodden near his beat; and on the night following, the sentinel on the roadway was found lying dead on his face; his musket was undischarged, his head cloven behind, and his scalp gone.

"The consternation of my picquet had now reached its height. Still our scouts asserted the country to be quiet around us, though, with a strange gleam in his eyes, the Indian said, that when he shouted in the woods he heard an echo.

"'From whence?' I asked, suspiciously.

"'From the great barrows by the lake—where the bones of my forefathers lie. The white man treads there now; but they were great warriors, and many were the scalps that dried before their tents.'

"I was but a young officer then, being fresh from our Scottish Fencibles, otherwise I would have doubled my sentinels; but the idea never occurred to me, and my sergeant failed to suggest it. The affair was becoming intolerable. This mysterious assassination of brave men roused my blood to fever heat, and I resolved that on the next night I should take the duty of sentinel with a firelock, and remain on my post as such, not for one hour merely, but for the entire night, in the hope of solving this terrible enigma.

"On the evening I came to this conclusion the post was visited by Charley Halket from the fort, the captain of our first company, who came cantering up on a fine bay horse. I was glad to see him, for Halket was one of the most lively and devil-may-care fellows in the corps, and he sang the best song and was the best stroke at billiards in our whole brigade. Charley would drink his two bottles at mess overnight and wing a fellow in the morning, without keeping his arm in a cold bath, and with an accuracy that showed he had a constitution of iron; he hunted fearlessly, shot fairly, rode like a mad-cap; gambled, but simply for excitement, and spent his money like a .

E 2

good-hearted fellow. He was always laughing and
jovial, and I was about to relate the disasters
that had befallen my party, when the pale and
anxious expression of his usually merry face
arrested me, and I feared that the fort had been
taken by surprise in rear of our post.

" ' What the devil is the matter, Halket ?' said
I: ' I have always predicted to Preston that we
should never have our legs under his mahogany
at Valleyfield again—never taste his Fifeshire
mutton, or test his fine old Burgundy. What
is up ? Has the fort fallen, Charley, that you
come here with your bay thoroughbred covered
with foam, even to its bang-up tail ?'

" ' No, my dear Middleton ; but I wish to pass
your post.'

" ' To the front ?' I asked, with astonishment.

" ' Yes.'

" ' It is impossible !'

" ' Even if out of uniform ?'

" ' In or out of uniform, none can pass or
repass save our scouts, whose lives are of
little value. Preston's orders are strict and
decisive.'

" ' But if in disguise ?' he urged, earnestly, and
lowering his tone, as he stooped from his saddle.

" ' Worse and worse !'

" ' How ? explain, pray,' he demanded, as his
earnestness became tinged with irritation.

" ' You might be deemed a deserter by General

Burgoyne if found more than two miles from camp or quarters.'

" ' A deserter!—I?—pooh, man, absurd!'

" ' A general officer has joined the rebels already. Then you might be hanged as a spy by Montgomery, whose troops are certainly closing up, if we may judge from the murderous outrages committed by his Indian allies upon the picquets stationed here.'

" ' It is for that very reason, Middleton, that I am most anxious to ride southward for about twelve miles into the country along the shore of the lake, towards Misiskoui.'

" ' You could not return; my sentinels have positive orders to fire instantly on all ——'

" ' Who have not the parole and countersign,' said he, smiling; ' they are *Quebec* and WOLFE. You see that I have both!'

" ' From whom?'

" ' My friend André, of the Cameronians—the fort-major.'

" ' He is very rash! I wish he had this infernal picquet to command; the duty might teach him caution.'

" ' But, my dear Middleton——'

" ' Say no more, Charley—come, don't be rash; duty is duty; and I must perform mine. Moreover, I value your life and my own honour too much to risk either to further some mad-cap ramble of yours.'

"'Zounds, sir!' he began, furiously.

"'Now don't call me out, Charley; I am on duty and can't go, and when I am relieved and you are cool, you wont ask me. But tell me, Charley, what affair is this that seems so urgent? The country in front is full of perils; already eight or nine sentinels have been assassinated, and yonder grave covers one of three fine fellows I have lost.'

"'Listen to me, Jack,' said he, dismounting, and throwing the reins of his horse over his arm, and leading me a little way apart from the soldiers who were smoking and lounging before the log-hut; 'you remember Ella Carleton?'

"'I should rather think I *do*,' said I, reddening, and giving him a very knowing wink, to which he made not the slightest response; 'Ella, whom we used to meet so much a year ago at Montreal.'

"'The same,' said he.

"'I remember her perfectly—a charming girl, with features that were pale but beautifully regular, and with eyes and hair so dark.'

"'Exactly,' said Halket, whose eyes sparkled with pleasure. Her father, you are aware, is a rich land-owner, in the American interest.'

"'Many a bottle of champagne I have drunk in his house in the Rue de Notre Dame!'

"'Yet he is an old curmudgeon who hates us red-coats, and for that reason, as well as for a few others that were more cogent, Ella and I were privately married about a year ago.'

"'Married?—whew! Here's news for the mess to discuss over their wine and walnuts!' I exclaimed, while laughing to conceal an irrepressible emotion of pique.

"'I depend on your honour,' said he, earnestly.

"'To the death, Charley; but you have quite taken my breath away. Married—you never looked a bit like it!'

"'We were married a year ago at the cathedral in the Place d'Armes unknown to all—even to yourself, Rohallion, and others my most intimate friends,' said Halket, speaking rapidly and with growing emotion; 'in a month she will be a mother—think of that, Jack! She is residing at one of her father's country clearings near the Missiskoui River, in an old hunting-lodge, built by Simon de Champlain, who first discovered the lake. She has written to me by a circuitous route, saying that Montgomery's advanced posts are within a few miles; that her father and all his men are with the rebels; that the Iroquois are ravaging the country, burning, killing, and scalping all before them; and thus, for the love I bear her, and for the sake of our child that is yet unborn, I must strive to save her, and have her conveyed to Fort St. John. This is all my story, Middleton. She is about twelve miles distant from this outpost; I think I know the

way, aud am certain I should be back before
the morning-gun is fired. If not, I must risk
all—commission, rank, reputation, everything—
but Ella must be saved! You understand me
now, don't you, my dear friend?' said he,
earnestly, as he grasped my hand, and I could
see that the poor fellow's eyes were filled with
tears.

" ' Perfectly, Charley; I would risk my life to
save or serve her or you; but I think we may
find those who will do both more effectually than
either you or I.'

" ' Who do you mean?'

" ' The Delaware scout, and old Abe Treherne,
the hunter, will get over the ground in half the
time, and knowing, as they do, every track and
trail in the forest, with ten degrees more safety
than you could ever hope for.'

" I at once proposed the affair to them, and
Treherne entered into it with great readiness.
His reward was to be a pair of handsome pistols
and ten guineas. He knew the old hunting-
lodge on Carleton's clearing quite well, and with
the assistance of the horse, undertook to bring
the lady to the picquet-house in safety, and long
before sunrise. The Delaware, however, shook
his head.

" ' Le Vipre Noir has some darned doubts, I
guess,' said the hunter; ' the woods about the
Missiskoui are full of the mocassin prints of the

Yankees and the Iroquois; the tracks, I reckon, are dangerous enough; and there will be an almighty trouble in bringing a fine lady a-horseback through the bush; for all that, Delaware, you'll venture to bring the White Chief his squaw safe from the hunting-place beyond the river?'

" ' From the Missiskoui, where once I had a wigwam, and where *my* squaw and her little papooses perished at the hands of the white men?' said the savage, in a husky and guttural voice, while his stealthy eyes filled with a malevolent gleam, as he sat sullenly smoking under a tree.

" ' You're a darned fool, Vipre,' said Treherne, angrily. ' Look ye har—what's the use o' thinking o' that now? What's past is past, ain't it?'

" ' She appealed to them, and they laughed at her. She appealed to Manitto, but his face was hidden behind a cloud, and he saw neither her nor what the pale-faces did to her. She is with Manitto now—but I yet am here.'

" ' We may have a scrimmage, Delaware—can you bite yet?' asked Treherne, testily.

" The savage pointed to his scalping-knife and grinned.

" ' Will you venture with me for twelve bottles of the raal Jamaiky fire-water?'

" ' Oui, ja, yes!' said the savage, eagerly, in

his mixed jargon; 'I neither fear the feathered arrows of the rebel Iroquois, or the lead bullets of the Yankees.   Go! Le Vipre Noir is a warrior!'

"'Delaware,' said I, patting his muscular shoulder, 'what are the greatest of human virtues?'

"'Courage and contempt of death,' he replied, loftily, while shaking the two heron's plumes in his scalp lock.

"'Good,' said Halkett, who had listened to all this preamble with irrepressible anxiety and impatience; 'here are ten guineas as an earnest of future reward, Delaware.   You will risk this for me?'

"'For *you*?' said the Indian, scornfully, putting the coins, however, in the musk-rat pouch, which dangled at his wampum girdle.

"'For her, then?' said Halket, persuasively.

"'For neither,' replied the Delaware, while a lurid gleam shone in his sombre eyes.

"'How, fellow?' asked Charley, with alarm.

"'I do so for the reward—for the fire-water and gold that will buy me powder and blankets; but neither for the squaw nor the papoose of the pale-face.'

"'Risk it for what you will, but only serve me'; and you, Treherne——'

"'Make your terms with this darned crittur of a Redskin, and you can settle with me after,

sir,' said Treherne, who had been regarding his
compatriot with a somewhat doubtful expression.
'Come, Vipre Noir, we must keep the hair on
our heads, if we can, certainly; so put fresh
priming into the pan of your rifle, my dark serpent, for the dew is falling heavily; if the rebel
Redskins come on us, it must be our scalps
agin theirs! I'm your brother—let us be off to
the bush ere the sun sets.'

"Charley Halkett hastily wrote a note to his
wife, telling her to place implicit confidence in
the two scouts as true and tried men, who would
convey her safely to the British outpost in front
of Fort St. John, where he, all eagerness and
impatience, awaited her; and on being furnished
with this, Treherne slung his long rifle across his
body, stuck a short black pipe in his moustachioed
mouth, mounted Halkett's horse, and, with the
swift-footed and agile Indian running by his
side, crossed the open bit of prairie before the
log-hut, and rapidly disappeared in the dense and
virgin forest that lay beyond.

"That forest soon grew dark; twilight stole
along the shores of the silent lake; the last red
rays of lingering light faded upward from the lone
mountain tops; one by one the bright stars came
twinkling out, and the old and clamorous anxiety
occurred to us all; and each poor fellow, as he
was left on his post, felt himself a doomed man,
who might die without seeing his destroyer, or

who might disappear as others had so mysteriously done, without leaving a trace behind.

"Slowly and wearily our autumn night wore on, and with our pistols cocked, Halkett and I visited the sentinels almost half-hourly. The sky was moonless, and the silence around our lonely post was oppressive; to the listening ear there came no sounds save those of insect life among the long and reedy prairie grass.

"All at once, afar in distance from the deep recesses of the vast pine forest, there rose the shrill war-whoop of the red man!

"Like the yell of an unchained fiend, it rung upon the still night air; but died away, and all became silent—more silent apparently than before, and I felt the hand of Halkett clutch my arm like a vice, while hot bead-drops rolled over his temples.

"I had terrible forebodings, but remained silent, and with reiterated advice to my sentinels to be 'on the alert,' returned to the picquet-house. Poor Charley Halkett's alarm excited all my compassion; the boldest, frankest, and jolliest fellow in the corps had become a nervous, crushed, and miserable wretch!

"I thought that lingering night would never pass away. It passed, however, as others do; the morning came in, bright and sunny, and without one of our sentinels being missed or molested; and it seemed, certainly, a very singular feature in those mysterious deaths, that the only night on which no fatality occurred, should be that on which we actually had an *alerte,* and when Treherne and the Delaware were away in the direction of Missiskoui, and *not* scouting in front of the post !

" Morning had come, but there was yet no appearance of our messengers or Ella Carleton, and old sympathies made me doubly anxious on her account.

" Halkett, who was pale with sleeplessness and intense anxiety, walked with me a little way beyond our advanced sentinels, who were now shouting to each other their happy congratulations that nothing had occurred during the night—in short, that they were *all* there.

" Lake Champlain, in its calm loveliness, shone brightly under the morning sun, its surface un-ruffled by the wind, and not a sail or boat was visible in all the blue extent of its far stretching vista. The gorgeous azalias were still in their bloom, so were the snowy blossoms of the sumach, and the glorious yellow light fell in flakes be-tween the towering pines of the ancient forest, while the dewy prairie grass glittered as it rip-pled beneath the pleasant breeze.

" The distant landscape and the dim blue hills that look down on the winding Hudson seemed calm and tranquil, the silence around us was intense, the hum of a little waterfall alone breaking the stillness of the autumn morning.

"Poor Charley was like a madman, and it was in vain that I suggested to him that Treherne and the Delaware might have been compelled to make a long detour; that Ella might be ill and unable to travel on horseback, that her father might have returned, that Montgomery's advanced guard might be now far beyond the Missiskoui, that our scouts might have lost their way in going or in returning, not that I believed either possible for a moment, but I was glad to say anything that would serve to account for their delay, or soothe his gnawing anxiety; so in exceeding misery he returned to Fort St. John. The moment that morning parade was over he hastened to me again, and slowly the terrible day passed over, without tidings of Ella Carleton or her guides, and as night drew near I had almost to use force to prevent Halkett from setting out on foot for the old hunting-lodge on the Missiskoui, a place he could never have reached alone.

"Suddenly we were roused, about sunset, by a shout from the picquet, and as we looked up, the Delaware stood before us—alone!

"His aspect was fierce but weary; his hunting shirt was torn and bore traces of blood. His story was brief. They had been attacked by Indians in a deep gulley some miles distant, in the grey dawn of the morning; Treherne had been killed and the lady carried off! The Indian showed his wounds, and then claimed his reward.

" Poor Halkett, on hearing of this catastrophe, fell, as if struck by a ball, and was laid on the hard bed of planks whereon the soldiers slept. He was in a delirium, yet passive and weak as a child.

" So the hostile Indians were in our neigh. bourhood! I thought with horror of what the poor girl—on the eve of becoming a mother— might suffer at their merciless hands; and all her delicate beauty, her merry laugh, the singular combination of elegance and *espiègleric* in her manner, came vividly back to memory, as I had seen her last, happy, radiant, and smiling, amid the glare and glitter of a garrison ball in the city of Montreal.

" I questioned the Delaware closely; but his story was simple and unvarying, so he received food, rum, and the reward which Halkett had promised.

" An irrepressible anxiety stole over me as night deepened, so taking my servant's musket and bayonet, I primed, loaded, and fixed a new flint with care ; and proceeding to the distance of fifty yards in front of my line of sentinels, on the open space where the prairie grass grew thick and rank, I resolved to pass some hours there as an advanced sentinel.

" The sky was dark and cloudy, the stars were

obscured by vapour, the silence was intense, and
it smote upon my heart with a sense that was in
some degree appalling, though I knew that my
sentinels and the rest of the picquet were all with-
ni hail. The tall prairie grass waved solemnly
and noiselessly to and fro ; the sombre forest
beyond, with the myriad cones of its black pines
stretched far away to the distant mountains, but
not a sound came from thence, nor from the lone
shores of the vast lake of Champlain, whose vista
receded away for miles upon my right. Even if
the night-herons were wading among its waters
I could not hear them, and the whistle of the
cat-bird was silent.

"Through the dark, I could see where the wild
sumach, with its white blossoms and scarlet
berries, waved over the graves of those who had
perished on this fatal out-post. Their aspect was
solemnizing in such a dark and silent hour, and
the familiar faces of the dead men seemed to
hover before me. But there was something
mysterious and unaccountable in the total dis-
appearance of those whose blood we had only
traced upon the grass of the prairie.

"Around where I stood this grass was more
than a yard in height and thick as ripened corn.
It was waving steadily to and fro as the breath
of the night wind agitated it.

"I had been in that solitary place about two
hours, and midnight was at hand, when an

emotion like a thrill—a tremor, not of fear, but of *warning*—a ' gruc,' as we Scots call it, came over me. I felt the approach of some unseen thing, and cast a hurried glance around me. Something unusual about the appearance of the prairie-grass caught my eye.

" Where, when hitherto I had looked in a direct line to the front, the surface, while swaying to and fro, seemed a flat and unbroken mass, there was now visible a dark line, a hollow furrow, as if some animal was crawling slowly and stealthily through it.

" With every nerve braced, with all the powers of vision concentrated, I watched this new appearance, and the hollow track seemed to draw nearer and nearer *to me,* slowly, silently, and almost imperceptibly, as if a snake or some such reptile were crawling towards my post ; and, ere long, it was not more than fifteen yards distant.

" I placed a handkerchief over the lock of my musket to muffle the click of the lock in cocking, then I took a steady aim and fired !

" On this, ' piercing the night's dull ear,' there rang a wild, shrill, and savage cry—a cry like that we had heard on the preceding night—and a dark figure, bounding from among the grass, came rushing towards me, but I stood, with bayonet charged, ready to receive him on its point.

" He was an Indian, brandishing a tomahawk ; but, within a few feet of where I stood, he fell prone on his face, wallowing in blood. The report of my musket, and his cry, brought all the picquet to the front. We dragged him into the log-hut, and discovered that I had shot our missing scout, the Delaware, Le Vipre Noir, the ball having entered his left shoulder, and traversed nearly the entire length of his body. He was mortally wounded, but the powers of life were strong within him. I was greatly concerned by this misfortune, which might procure us the enmity of his entire tribe; but why was he stealing upon our post in the manner he had done?

" Before this could be resolved, and while we were staunching the welling blood, and doing all in our humble power to soothe suffering and prolong existence, a pale and bloody figure, who had given our sentries the pass-word, staggered into the hut, and sunk, half fainting, against the guard-bed. He was old Abe Treherne, the scout, cut, gashed, and apparently dying.

" He was almost as speechless as the Delaware; but, on seeing each other, though weak and deplorable their condition, the eyes of these men glared with rage and hate, and they made such incredible efforts to reach each other, knife in hand, that the soldiers of my picquet had to hold them asunder by force.

" ' Search the hunting-pouch of the darned thief—the accursed red-skin !' said Treherne, in a hollow voice. ' May I never hew hickory again if I don't have his scalp and his heart tew!'

"I was about to make the search, when Charley Halket anticipated me, and shudderingly drew forth its cold and clammy contents.

"There were four human scalps; three were recognised as belonging to our own men, the murdered sentinels, and the fourth had attached to it the long, black, silky hair of a woman—the soft and ripply tresses of Ella Carleton!

"'The red-skin fell on us suddenly in the bush, with knife and tomahawk,' said Treherne, speaking with difficulty, and at intervals; ' he took me unawares from behind, and well nigh clove my head—darned if I don't think the tommy's stickin' there yet! I fought hard for my precious life—harder for the poor lady, I guess; but I swowned, after a time, and then he dragged her into the bush.'

"'Ella—Ella!' exclaimed Halket, wringing his hands.

"'The last I saw, 'tween the leaves and the blood that poured into my eyes, was the glitter of his scalping-knife; and the last I heard was her death-cry. Shoot the varmint, captain! I searched the bush for her till I was weary. Shoot the critter dead, soldiers! Ah! he was well named Le Vipre Noir, by that son of a Delaware dog, his father.'

"The savage scarcely heard the end of this,

F 2

for Halket, maddened by the contents of the hunting-pouch, and brief story of Treherne, placed a foot upon the prostrate body of the Delaware, then, slowly and deliberately, while his teeth were set, his eyes flashing fire, his brows knit by rage and grief, and, while an unuttered malediction hovered on his lips, he passed his sword-blade twice through the heart of the scout. The latter, for a moment, writhed upward on the steel, like a dying serpent, and then expired.

" Poor Abe Treherne died soon after, for his wounds were mortal.

" So our false Delaware proved, after all, to have been in the American interest, and inspired by some real or imaginary wrongs, to have been the assassin of our sentinels.*

" Fort St. John soon after fell into the hands of the Yankees under General Montgomery ; we were all made prisoners of war, and my poor friend, Charley Halket, died, and (far from his kindred, who lie in the Abbey Kirk of Culross) we buried him amid the snow as we were being marched, under escort, up the lakes, towards Ticonderago."

Such was the major's story of *the advanced picquet.*

* Several sentinels of an outpost were thus actually assas-sinated during the American war. A Scottish periodical of the time gives a Highland regiment—the 74th, I think—the credit of furnishing the victims.

CHAPTER VI.

COSMO JOINS.

" Ye'll try the world soon, my lad,
    And Andrew, dear, believe me,
Ye'll find mankind an unco squad,
    And muckle may they grieve ye.
For care and trouble set your thought,
    Even when your end's attained;
And a' your views may come to nought,
    When every nerve is strained."—BURNS.

AFTER a careful search through some of the old
dog-eared Army Lists, which, with Burns' poems,
Brown's "Self-interpreting Bible," and Abercrombie's "Martial Achievements of the Scots
Nation," formed the chief literary stores in his
snuggery, the old quartermaster discovered that
in the 94th, the famous old Scots brigade, there
was a Captain Richard Warriston. He was the
only one of that name in the service, and doubtless the same officer whom Quentin had mentioned in his letter as having so kindly be-
friended him ; and by Lord Rohallion's direction,
Girvan at once addressed a letter to the officer
commanding the regiment for some information
regarding the runaway.

In due time an answer came from Colonel James Campbell, to state "that no volunteer named Quentin Kennedy had attached himself to the 94th Regiment;" thus the household of the old castle were sorely perplexed what to do, and had to trust to time or to Quentin himself for clearing up the mystery that overhung his actions.

In little more than ten days after Cosmo's name had appeared in the War Office *Gazette,* Quentin received the unwelcome information that the new lieutenant-colonel, his enemy, had arrived at head-quarters, and that a parade in full marching order was to take place on the morrow, when he would formally take over the command of the corps from poor Major Middleton.

Though daily expected, these tidings fell like a knell upon Quentin's heart, and the old sickly emotion that came over him, when Warriston brought the fatal *Gazette* to the mess-room, returned again in all its force.

" I think this Guardsman will prove a thorough Tartar," said Captain Askerne, in whose rooms Quentin first heard Cosmo's arrival canvassed; " and I fear that he wont make himself popular among the Borderers."

" From what do you infer that?" said some one.

" He refused to let the drums beat the ' Point of War' this morning."

" The devil he did !" said Colville.

"That looks ill, damme!" added Monkton.

"I do not understand," said Quentin, as if looking for information.

"It is," said Askerne, "a custom as old as the days of Queen Anne—older, perhaps, for aught that I know—for the drums and fifes of a corps to assemble before the quarters of every officer who is newly appointed to it, and there to honour the king's commission by beating the 'Point of War.' Though dying out now, and frequently 'more honoured in the breach than the observance,' it is a good old custom, peculiar to many of our Scottish regiments. The officer then gives to the drummers a few crowns or guineas, as the case may be, to drink his health; but the Master of Rohallion bluntly and haughtily told the drum-major that he 'would have no such d—d nonsense, and to dismiss!'"

"The deuce! this augurs ill," said Colville, with his affected lisp, as he arranged his hair in Askerne's little camp mirror.

"Perhaps his exchequer is in a bad way."

"Not improbable, Monkton," said Askerne; "he was one of the most lavish fellows in the household brigade, and he played and betted deeply; but there goes the drum for parade; in a few minutes we shall see what like our new man is."

We shall not afflict the reader with details of this most formal parade, during which the regi-

ment marched past Cosmo in slow and quick time
in open column of companies; then followed an
inspection of the men, their clothing, arms,
accoutrements, and everything, from the regimental colours to the pioneers' hand-saws; but thanks
to old Middleton's unwearying zeal and pride in
the Borderers, the somewhat fractious lieutenant-
colonel discovered nothing to find fault with.

Mounted on a fine dark charger, with gold-
laced saddlecloth and holsters, Cosmo, in his new
regimentals, looked every inch a handsome and
stately soldier; and his appearance, together with
his clear, full, mellow voice, when commanding,
impressed the corps favourably. Quentin, from
the rear rank of Askerne's company, surveyed
him earnestly, anxiously, and with secret mis-
givings; for every feature of his cold, keen, and
aristocratic face brought back vividly the morti-
fying and unpleasant passages in which they had
both borne a part at Rohallion, and sadly and
bitterly he felt that the *worst* was yet to come.

The parade over, the regiment was dismissed,
but the orderly bugle summoned the officers to
the front, where they gathered around Cosmo,
who had dismounted and haughtily tossed his
reins to an orderly (Allan Grange, the crest-fallen
and reduced sergeant), his gentleman's gentleman—that town-bred appendage who had excited
alternately the wrath and contempt of sturdy old
Jack Andrews, had resigned, having no fancy for

the chances of war as a camp-follower; so the Master had to content himself with such unfashionable " helps" as soldiers and bâtmen.

Quentin, lingering irresolutely, and half hoping to escape observation, was about to retire to his quarters, when Askerne called to him with a friendly smile—

" Kennedy, come to the front; Middleton is about to introduce the officers, and you must not be omitted."

Poor Quentin felt that his doom had come, and he could feel, too, that as his heart sank, the blood left his cheeks. But honest anger and just indignation came to the rescue, and gave him courage.

" Why should I dread this man—why shrink from one I have never wronged?" he asked of himself. " Of what am I afraid? The sooner this introduction is over, and that I know on what terms we are to be, the better. Perhaps he may be desirous of forgetting the past, of committing to oblivion all that has occurred, and may be the first to hold out a friendly hand. Heaven grant it may be so!"

But this suggestion of his own generous heart was little likely to be realized.

With studied politeness and grace, if not with pure cordiality, Cosmo received each officer as he was presented according to his rank, until the junior ensign, Boyle, was introduced.

"Ah!" said Cosmo, detecting one present *without* epaulettes, "you have a volunteer with you, I see."

"One," said Middleton, "whom I wish especially to introduce to your notice and future care, colonel, as a most promising young soldier, who in a few weeks has passed through all his drills, and is now fit for any duty. Mr. Quentin Kennedy—Colonel Crawford."

The nervous start given by Cosmo, the changing colour of his cheek, the shrinking and dilation of his cat-like eyes, as he raised and almost nervously let fall his eye-glass, were apparent to several; and Quentin saw the whole. Cosmo bowed with marked coldness, and turned so sharply on his heel, that his spurs rasped on the gravel of the barrack-yard.

"Major Middleton," said he, haughtily, before retiring, "tell that young man, Mr.—what's his name——?"

"Mr. Kennedy, sir."

"That when speaking to an officer, he should bring his musket to the *recover*."

And so ended this—to Quentin—most crushing interview.

"What the devil is up now?" said Monkton to Colville; "it is evident that our new bashaw doesn't like gentlemen volunteers."

"Then he is devilishly unjust—that's all,"

said Askerne the Grenadier who had begun his military life as a volunteer.

Quentin could have furnished the clue to all this; but to speak of the friendless childhood which cast him among the household at Rohallion, and, more than all, to speak of Flora Warrender, and to make her name the jest of the heedless or unfeeling, were thoughts that could not be endured. He was silent, and his tongue seemed as if cleaving to the roof of his mouth, while wearily and sadly he turned away to seek the solitude of his bare and scantily-furnished little room.

Middleton, who had followed unobserved, entered after him, and just when Quentin, to relieve his overcharged heart, was on the point of giving way to a paroxysm of rage, even to tears, the worthy old field officer caught his hand kindly, and said with earnestness—

" Don't be cast down, my boy, by what has occurred to-day. He was cold and haughty to every one of us, but it is evidently his way, and may wear off after a time. I hope so, for our Borderers wont stand it. Take courage, lad— take courage, and don't fret about it; Jack Middleton will always be your friend, though a hostile commanding officer is a dangerous rock ahead."

" Oh, major, you are indeed kind and good," said Quentin, as he seated himself at the hard wood table, and covered his burning face with his trembling hands; "but you know not all I have suffered—all I think, and feel, and fear!"

"Chut, Kennedy, look up! 'The English pluck that storms a breach or heads a charge is the very same quality that sustains a man on the long dark road of adverse fortune,' says an author —I forget who—not he of the 'Eighteen Manœuvres,' however; so, Quentin, don't, let Scottish pluck be behind it. To follow the drum is your true road in life, boy, and who but God can tell when that road may end?"

"Major Middleton," said Quentin, bitterly, "the colonel's chilling manner, and *more* than you can ever know, have crushed the heart within me. I never knew my father—of my mother I have barely a memory," he continued in a broken voice—"a memory, a dream! Fate has made me early a victim—a plaything—a toy! Advise me—I feel my condition so desolate, so friendless again. What future can there be for me, if I continue to serve under him; and how can I hope for happiness, for justice, or advancement under such as he?"

"Obey and suffer in silence; bear and forbear, and you will be sure to triumph in the end. 'He that tholes overcomes,' says our Scottish proverb, and the poor soldier has much to *thole* indeed; but do your duty diligently, and you may defy any man—even the king himself."

Quentin strove to take courage from the good major's words, and ultimately did so ; but Middleton knew not the past of those he spoke of, and was ignorant of the secret rivalry and settled hatred that existed between them, especially in the heart of Cosmo ; while Quentin, in his ignorance of military matters, knew not that the Master, if he chose to exert his powers arbitrarily, might dismiss him from the corps at once, unquestioned by any authority for doing so ; and that by the stigma thus attached to his name, the chance of any other commanding officer accepting him as a volunteer would be utterly precluded ; and that Cosmo did *not* do so was, perhaps, only by a lingering emotion of justice or of shame for what his family, and chiefly Flora Warrender and that huge bugbear " the world," would say if the story got abroad.

" Better trust to the *chances* of war," thought Cosmo, grimly, as he lay sullenly at length, smoking, on a luxurious fauteuil in his ample quarters, which were furnished with all the comforts and elegance with which a Jew broker could surround him ; " a brat, a boy, a chick—a d—ned foundling ! With all my conscious superiority of rank, birth, and, what are better, strength of mind and character, why do I dread this Quentin Kennedy ? Why and how does he seem to be so inextricably woven up with me, my fate and fortune—it may be, with the house of Rohal-

lion itself?   Last of all, why the devil do I find
him here?"   (This question he almost shouted
aloud as he kicked away the cushion of the fauteuil.)   "Why do I dread him?   *Dread*—I—
shame! what delusion is this—what depression
is it that his presence—the very idea of his existence—and contact bring upon me?   In all this
there is some strange fate—I know not what;
but I shall trust to the chances of war for a rid-
dance, and to the perilous work I shall cut out
for *him* in particular."

And so he trusted; but with what success we
shall see ere long.

CHAPTER VII.

THE DEPARTURE.

" Our native land—our native vale—
    A long and last adieu;
Farewell to bonny Teviotdale,
    And Cheviot mountains blue!
The battle-mound, the border-tower,
    That Scotia's annals tell;
The martyr's grave—the lover's bower—
    To each, to all—farewell."—PRINGLE.

Cosmo studiously and ungenerously omitted the slightest mention of Quentin's name or existence in the letters which he wrote home to Carrick, well knowing that if he did so, the kind old general, his father, would at once address the authorities at the Horse Guards on the subject of the young volunteer's advancement; and he knew, that if appointed to any other corps than the Borderers, Quentin would be beyond his influence, and free from the wiles and perils in which he had mentally proposed to involve his future career.

At last came the day so long looked forward to by all the regiment—the day of its departure for foreign service, as it proved in the Spanish Peninsula, the land to which, after several useless and bloody expeditions to Holland, Flanders, Sweden, and Italy, the thoughts and hopes and all the sympathies of Britain turned, with the desire of driving out the victorious French, and restoring the Bourbon dynasty—almost an old story now, so remote have the struggles before Sebastopol and the wars of India made the great battles of those days seem to be.

The regiment had been under orders, and in a state of readiness for weeks; but until, for it and for others, the *route* came in the sabretasche of an orderly dragoon who rode spurring in "hot haste" to Colchester Barracks, its members knew not for what country they were destined.

The drums beat the *générale*, the signal for marching, early in the morning of a soft September day, and the four pipers of the regiment played loud and high a piobroch, that rang wildly, in all its various parts, through the calm air, waking every echo of the old barrack square; for the piobroch, we may inform the uninitiated, is a regular piece of music, containing several portions; beginning with an alarm, after which follow the muster, the march, the fury of the charge, the shrill triumph of victory, and the low sad wail for the slain.

With our battalion of the Borderers, there were to march on this morning another of the Gordon Highlanders—the 92nd—one of the most noble of our national corps, together with a

strong detachment of the 94th, under Captain
Warriston, so the enthusiasm of all was at its
height when, in heavy marching order, with great
coats rolled on the knapsacks, blankets folded
behind them, havresacks and wooden canteens
slung, the companies fell in, and there seemed to
be a rivalry between the kilted pipers of the
92nd and the Borderers as to who should excel
most, or (as Cosmo, who was not inspired by
overmuch nationality, said to Middleton) who
should "make the most infernal noise."

Silent and grim, and keeping somewhat
haughtily aloof from all his officers, Cosmo sat
on his black horse, gnawing the chin-strap of his
shako, as if controlling some secret irritation,
while watching the formation of the corps, looking very much the while as if longing to find
fault with some one.

"And so we are destined to reinforce the army
under Sir John Moore?" said Quentin, for lack
of something more important to remark.

"Yes," said Askerne, as he adjusted the
cheek-scales of his tall grenadier cap; "Sir
John is a glorious fellow, and quite the man of
to-day."

"I would rather be the man of *to-morrow,*"
said Monkton, with an air that implied a joke,
though there was something prophetic in the wish.

"I knew Moore when he was serving as a
subaltern with the 82nd in America—he is a

brave, good fellow, and a countryman of our
own, too," said Middleton, whose orderly brought
forward his horse at that moment; " and now,"
he added, putting his foot in the stirrup, " a
long good-bye to the land of roast-beef, and to
poor old Scotland, too! I wonder who among
us here will see her heather hills and grassy glens
again—God bless them all!" And reverentially
the fine old man raised his hand to his cap as he
spoke.

A crowd formed by the soldiers' wives and
children of the regiment, now gathered round
him, for the old major knew all their names and
little necessities, and was adored by them all.
Now he was distributing among them money,
advice, and letters of recommendation to parish
ministers and others, and to none was he more
kind than to the weeping wife of Allan Grange,
who, by his reduction to the ranks, lost nearly
every chance of accompanying the troops abroad.

To the screaming of the bagpipes had now
succeeded the wailing of women, for many soldiers' wives and children were to be left behind,
and to be transferred to their several parishes in
Scotland; many to remote glens that are desolate
wildernesses now; and it was touching to see
these poor creatures, looking so pale and miserable
in the cold grey light of the early morning, each
with her wondering little brood clinging to her
skirts, as she hovered about the company to

which her husband belonged, his quivering lip and glistening eye alone revealing the heart that ached beneath the coarse red coat, amid the monotony of calling rolls and inspecting arms.

On one of the waggons which was piled high with baggage, huge chests of spare arms, iron-bound trunks, camp-beds and folded tents, Quentin tossed the little portmanteau which contained his entire worldly possessions ; then the baggage-guard, looking so serviceable and warlike with their havresacks and canteens slung crosswise, came with bayonets fixed, and the great wains rumbled away through the echoing, and as yet empty streets of Colchester.

None of the officers were married men, fortunately for themselves perhaps, at such a juncture. The colours were brought forth with their black oilskin cases on; the advanced guard marched off, and just as the sun began to gild the church vanes and chimney-tops, and while reiterated cheers rang from the thousands of soldiers who crowded the barrack windows, and whose turn would come anon, the troops moved off, the brass bands of other regiments—the usual courtesy— playing them out, the whole being under the command of the senior officer present, Lieutenant-Colonel Napier of Blackstone, who afterwards fell at the head of the 92nd Highlanders on the field of Corunna.

In the excitement of the scene, Quentin felt all its influences and marched happily on. He forgot his affronts, his piques and jealousies, and as the young blood coursed lightly through his veins, he felt that he could forgive even Cosmo, were it only for Lady Winifred's sake, when he saw him riding with so stately and soldier-like an air between Major Middleton and Buckle the adjutant, at the end of the column, where the splendid grenadiers with their black bearskin caps and braided wings, made a martial show such as no company of the line could do in the shorn uniform of the present day.

All the happy impulses of youth made Quentin's spirit buoyant; thus his light heart beat responsive to the crash of the drums and cymbals, and to every note of the brass band. Thus, when on looking to the rear, he saw so many hundred bayonets and clear barrels (they were not browned in those days) flashing in the sun, with the long array of plumed Highlanders that wound through the streets after his own regiment, he forgot, we say, his grievances, and the cold and haughty Master—we believe he forgot even Flora Warrender—he forgot all but that he was a soldier—one of the old 25th, and bound for the seat of war! Ah, there is something glorious in these emotions—this flushing up of the spirit in a young and generous breast; but alas! the time comes when we look back to the long-

past days with envy, regret, and, it may be—
wonder!

The sorrowful parting, the hurried embraces,
the last kisses, the sad and lingering glances of
farewell being exchanged along the line of march
every moment, by husbands and wives, by parents
and children, as group after group gradually
dropped to the rear of the column they could
but follow with their eyes and hearts, ceased
after a time to impress him by their very number
and frequency; thus he soon laughed with the
gay, and enjoyed all the silly banter of the heedless, as the officers began to group by twos and
threes, after Colchester was left behind, and the
troops were permitted to " march at ease" along
the dusty highway between the meadows and
ploughed fields.

" I have never seen so jolly a morning as
this," said Ensign Boyle, as he trudged along
with the regimental colour crossed on his left
shoulder; " never since first I saw my own name
in print !"

" How in print?" asked Quentin, with simplicity; " you do not mean on the title-page of
a book ?"

" Not at all—nothing so stupid—I mean in
the Army List——"

" Where you have never been tired of con-
templating it since—eh, Pimple ?" asked Monkton; " but I hope you have left your flirting

jacket and best epaulettes with the heavy baggage
—you only need your fighting traps now."

"I say, Pimple," said Colyear, the senior
ensign, who, of course, had the King's colour,
"how much of the ready had that flax-spinner's
daughter, about whom Monkton quizzes you so
much ?"

"Rumour said twenty thousand pounds."

"The devil! You might have done worse—
aw—ch !"

"We're all doing worse, damme, marching for
embarkation on this fine sunny morning," said
Monkton. There goes the band again to the old
air; but, save you, Pimple, few among us leave
' girls behind us' with twenty thousand pounds."

"Adieu to Colchester, its morning drills and
monotonous guards, and that devilish incessant
patter of little drum-boys practising their da-da,
ma-ma, on the drum from sunrise till sunset,"
said Colville, looking back to where the strong
old Saxon castle and the brick steeple of St. Peter
were being shrouded in yellow morning haze
exhaled by the sun from the river Colne.

"Bon voyage," cried a gay staff-officer, lifting
his plumed cocked hat, as he cantered gaily past;
" good-bye, gentlemen."

"Adieu, Conyers," replied Monkton; "can I
do anything for you?"

"Where ?"

"Among the ladies in Lisbon ?"

The officer made no reply, but rode hurriedly on.

"That is the fellow who had to quit Wellesley's staff for eloping with some hidalgo's wife, the night after Vimiera," said Askerne. "Monkton, you hit him hard there."

"Don't you think old Jack Middleton looks dull this morning?" asked some one.

"The colonel is in a devil of a temper, I think," replied Askerne.

"Perhaps he has left his love behind him," suggested Boyle, raising his stupid white eyebrows sentimentally; "don't you think so, Kennedy?"

"Pimple, allow me to rebuke you," said Monkton, with an air of mock severity. An ensign may wear a faded rose next his beating heart; but in a field-officer, such an insane proceeding is not to be thought of."

While this empty talk was in progress, about eight miles from Colchester, a troop of the Scots Greys approached en route for that place; and, as they drew near, the drums and fifes of the Borderers struck up a lively national quick step; the Greys brandished their swords, and gave a hearty cheer on coming abreast of the colours of each regiment, and loud were the hurrahs which responded.

This little episode, and the thoughtless banter which preceded it, had raised Quentin's spirits to a high state of effervescence. Fresh hope had come with all her ruddiest tints to brighten the future and blot out the past, and with all the glorious confidence of youth, he was again building castles in the air, on this morning march, when the sun that shone so joyously on the green English landscape, added to the brilliance of his thoughts and enhanced his joy and happiness.

From his day-dreams, however, he was roughly awakened by the harsh voice of the Master of Rohallion, who half reined in his horse, and turning round with his right hand planted on the crupper, said with great sternness :

"Captain Askerne, I must remind you that, though officers may converse together when the men are marching at case, such a privilege can by no means be accorded to a mere volunteer. Mr. Kennedy, rejoin your section, and keep your place, sir !"

Askerne's dark and handsome face coloured up to the rim of his bearskin cap, and his eyes sparkled with rage at the colonel's petulant wantonness ; while poor Quentin, who, lost in his bright day-dreamings, had certainly, but unconsciously, diverged a few paces from the line of march to converse with his friends, fell sadly back into the ranks, and felt that the dark cloud was enveloping him again.

CHAPTER VIII.

ON THE SEA.

" A varied scene the changeful vision showed,
    For where the ocean mingled with the cloud,
    A gallant navy stemmed the billows broad.
    Blent with the silver cross to Scotland dear,
    From mast and stern, St. George's symbol flow'd,
    Mottling the sea their landward barges row'd,
    And flashed the sun on bayonet, brand, and spear,
    And the wild beach returned the seaman's jovial cheer."
                                Vision of Don Roderick.

THE kingdom of Spain was at this time the great centre of European political interest. France, Prussia, and Russia had scarcely sheathed their swords at Tilsit, when the terrible conspiracy of Ferdinand, the Prince of the Asturias, against his father, Charles IV.—a plot imputed to Michael Godoy, who, from a simple cavalier of the Royal Guard, had, by the queen's too partial favour, obtained the blasphemous title of the Prince of Peace—afforded the Emperor Napoleon, whose creature he was, a pretext for interfering in the affairs of the Spanish Bourbons. He decoyed the royal family to Bayonne, compelled their renunciation of the crown and kingdom of Spain, into which he poured at once his vast armies, and, after the fashion of the cat in the fable, who absorbed the whole matter in dispute. by the monkeys, he solved the problem by seizing the Spanish empire, and gifting it to his brother Joseph, formerly King of Naples.

Portugal, at this juncture, deserted by her government and by her pitiful king, who fled to Rio de Janeiro, in Brazil, fell easily into the power of a French army, under Marshal Junot, who was thereupon created Duke of Abrantes, a town on the Portuguese frontier.

All Europe cried aloud at these lawless proceedings, and the Spaniards, so long our enemies, with our old allies the Portuguese, were alike filled with fury and resentment. The peasantry flew to arms, and the provinces became filled by bands of guerillas, brave but reckless; so the whole peninsula was full of tumult, treason, bloodshed, and crime.

"England," says General Napier, "both at home and abroad, was, in 1808, scorned as a military power, when she possessed (without a frontier to swallow up large armies in expensive fortresses) at least *two hundred thousand* of the best equipped and best disciplined soldiers in the universe, together with an immense recruiting establishment through the medium of the militia."

War, *not* "Peace at any price," was the generous John Bull's motto, and, to aid these patriots, a British army proceeded to the peninsula in June, 1808, under the command of Lieutenant-General Sir Arthur Wellesley. Some sharp fighting ensued along the coast, the prologue to the long and bloody, but glorious drama, that was only to terminate on the plains of Waterloo.

On the 21st of August we fought and won the battle of Vimiera, and nine days after followed the convention of Cintra, by which the French troops were compelled to evacuate the ancient Lusitania, and were conveyed home in British ships; but still the marshals of the empire, with vast armies, the heroes of Jena, Austerlitz, and a hundred other battles so glorious to France, were covering all the provinces of Spain, from the steeps of the Pyrenees to the arid plains of Estremadura.

"Soldiers, I have need of you," says the emperor, in one of his bulletins. "The hideous presence of the leopard contaminates the peninsula of Spain and Portugal. In terror he must fly before you! Let us bear our triumphal eagles to the pillars of Hercules, for there also we have injuries to avenge! Soldiers, you have surpassed the renown of modern armies, but have you yet equalled the glory of those Romans, who, in one and the same campaign, were victorious upon the Rhine and the Euphrates, in Illyria and upon the Tagus? A long peace and lasting prosperity shall be the reward of your labours."

The standard of freedom was first raised among the Asturians, the hardy descendants of the ancient Goths, and in Galicia; then Don José Palafox, by his valiant defence of the crumbling walls of Zaragossa, showed the Spaniards what brave men might do when fighting for their hearths and homes.

"In a few days," said Napoleon, boastfully, in the October of 1808, "I go to put myself at the head of my armies, and, with the aid of God, to crown the King of Spain in Madrid, and plant my eagles on the towers of Lisbon."

The Junta of the Asturias craved the assistance of Britain, even while the shattered wrecks of Trafalgar lay rotting on the sandy coast of Andalusia. Three years had committed those days of strife to oblivion, or nearly so, and arms, ammunition, clothing, and money were freely given to the patriots, while all the Spanish prisoners were sent home. Then, Sir John Moore, who commanded the British forces in Portugal, a small but determined "handful," was ordered to advance into Spain against the vast forces of the Duke of Dalmatia, which brings us now to the exact period of our own humble story, from which we have no intention of diverging again into the history of Europe.

The body of troops among which our hero formed a unit, sailed in transports from Spithead, and in the Channel, and when Portland lights

were twinkling out upon the weather-beam, poor
Quentin endured for the first time the horrors
of sea-sickness, and lay for hours half-stifled in
a close dark berth, unheeded and forgotten, over-
powered by the odour of tar, paint, and bilge,
and by a thirst which he had not the means of
quenching, for he was helpless, unable to move,
and longed only for death.

It was no spacious, airy, and gigantic *Hima-
laya*, no magnificent screw-propeller like the
Urgent, the *Perseverance*, or any other of
our noble steam transports that, on this occasion received the head-quarters of the " King's
Own Borderers," but a clumsy, old, and leaky
tub, bluff-bowed and pinck-built, with her top-
masts stayed forward, and her bowsprit tilted up
at an angle of 45 degrees, and having a jack-
staff rigged thereon. She was a black-painted
bark of some four hundred tons, with the figures
" 200 T."—(signifying Transport No. 200)—of
giant size appearing on her headrails. Between
floors or decks hastily constructed for the purpose, the poor soldiers were stowed in darkness,
discomfort, and filth. The officers were little
better off in the cabin, and hourly their servants
scrambled, quarrelled, and swore in the cooks'
galley, about their several masters' rank and
seniority in the order of boiling kettles and ar-
ranging frying-pans, whilst he hissing spray swept
over them every time the old tub staggered under

her fore course, and shipped a sea instead of riding buoyantly over it.

In the mighty stride taken by civilization of late years, when steam and electricity alike conduce to the annihilation of time and space, the soldiers of the Victorian age know little of what their fathers in the service underwent, when old George III. was King. In stench, uncleanness, and lack of comfort and accommodation, our shipping were then unchanged from those which landed Orange William's Dutchmen at Torbay, or which conveyed our luckless troops in after years to the storming of the Havannah or the bombardment of Bocca Chica.

After Quentin had recovered his strength (got his "sea-legs" as the sailors have it) he presented his pale, wan face on deck one morning, when the whole fleet, with the convoy, a stately 74-gun ship, were scattered, with drenched canvas, like sea-birds with dripping wings, as they scudded before a heavy gale, through the dark grey waters of the Bay of Biscay, the waves of which were rolling in foam, under a cold and cheerless October sky.

On that comfortless voyage to the seat of war, many were the secret heart-burnings he felt; many were the cutting slights put upon him by his cold and hostile commanding officer, who went the tyrannical length of even raising doubts as to whether he should mess in the cabin or among the soldiers; but to Cosmo's ill-concealed rage and confusion, the motion was carried unanimously and emphatically in the poor lad's favour; that the cabin was his place, as a candidate for his Majesty's commission.

Cosmo gave a smile somewhat singular in expression, and unfathomable in meaning, when Major Middleton communicated to him the decision of the officers; but though victorious in this instance, young as he was, the new affront sank deep in Quentin's heart, and he felt that there was " a shadow on his path " there could be no avoiding now.

So rapidly had events succeeded each other since that evening on which the Master had so savagely struck him down in the avenue, that Quentin frequently wondered whether his past or his present life were a dream. His last meeting with Flora Warrender among the old and shady sycamores—Flora so loving, so tender, and true !—his last farewell of old John Girvan (but one of whose guineas remained unchanged) ; that horrid episode of the dead gipsy, when he sought shelter in the ruined vault of Killienzie; the drive in the carrier's waggon; his volunteering at Ayr; the march to Edinburgh, with the voyage to England in the armed smack, and his subsequent military life, all appeared but a long dream, in which events succeeded each other with pantomimic rapidity ; and it was difficult to

believe that only months and *not* years, must
have elapsed since the kind and fatherly quartermaster closed the gate of Rohallion Castle behind him.   And now he was sailing far away
upon the open sea, bound for Spain—a soldier
going to meet the victorious veterans of Napoleon, in England alike the bugbear of the poli-
tician and the truant school-boy; and he was in
the 25th too—that corps of which, from childhood, he had heard so much, and under the orders,
it might be said truly at the mercy, of his personal enemy and bad angel, the cold, proud
Master of Rohallion !

He found it difficult indeed to realize the
whole and disentangle fact from fancy—reality
from imagination; but that the faces of Monkton, Boyle, and the good Captain Warriston,
when he saw him occasionally, were as links in
the chain of events, and gave them coherency.

At times, especially after dreams of home
(for such he could not but consider Rohallion), there came keen longings in his heart to
see Flora once again and hear her voice, which
often came plainly, sweetly, and distinctly to his
ear in sleep. Of her, alas! he had not one
single memento; not a ring, a miniature, a ribbon, a glove—not even a lock of her soft hair—
the hair that had swept his face on that delightful
day when he carried her through the Kelpie's pool
in the Girvan, and which he had kissed and ca-

ressed, in many a delicious hour spent with her
in the yew labyrinth of the old garden, by the
antique arch that spanned the Lollards' Linn,
under the venerable sycamores that cast their
shadows on the haunted gate, or where the honey
bee hummed on the heather braes that sloped so
sweetly in the evening sunshine towards the blue
Firth of Clyde.

From soft day-dreams of those past hours of
happiness he was roused on the evening of the
3rd October by the boom of a heavy gun from
the convoy, and several signals soon fluttered
amid the smoke that curled upward through her
lofty rigging. They were to the effect that *land
was in sight*—the fleet of transports to close in
upon the convoy—the swift sailers to take the
dull in tow; and now from the grey Atlantic
rose a greyer streak, which gradually became
broken and violet-coloured in the sheen of the sun
that was setting in the western waves, as the hills
of Portuguese Estremadura came gradually into
form and tint, on the lee-bow of the transport.

Next morning, when day broke, he found the
whole fleet at anchor in Maciera Bay, and all
the hurry and bustle on board of immediate pre-
parations to land the troops on the open and
sandy beach, where, when the tide meets the
river, a dangerous surf rolls at times, and from
thence they were, without delay, to march to the
front.

It was a glorious day, though in the last month of autumn. The ruddy sun of Lusitania was shining gaily on the hills and valley of Maciera, and on the plain beyond, where already the grass was growing green above the graves of our soldiers, who fell three months before at the battle of Vimiera. But little recked the new-comers of that, as the boats of the fleet covered all the bay, whose surface was churned into foam by hundreds of oars, while clouds of shakos and Highland bonnets were waved in the air, and swords and bayonets were brandished in the sunshine, as with loud hurrahs, that were repeated from the ships, and re-echoed by the rocks and indentations of the shore, the soldiers of the Borderers and the 92nd anticipated a share in the laurels that had been won at Rolica and Vimiera—hopes many were destined never to realize ; for like the thousands who, elsewhere, were marching under Moore and others, towards Castile and Leon, full of youth and health, joy and spirit, many were doomed but to suffer and die, unhonoured and unurned.

Portugal, as we have stated, having been rescued from the grasp of the French by the treaty of Cintra, and Sir John Moore having been ordered to advance into Spain, notification came that a fresh force from Britain, under the orders of Sir David Baird, would land at Corunna, to co-operate with him. Thus the troops on board the little fleet in Maciera Bay were ordered at once to cross the Tagus, traverse Portugal, and join him on the frontiers—a march of more than one hundred and twenty miles, in a land where the art of road-making had died out with the Romans.

At this time the British forces in the Peninsula numbered forty-eight thousand three hundred and forty-one, bayonets and sabres.

On the 15th of the next month the French in Spain, commanded by the Emperor in person, made a grand total of three hundred and thirty-five thousand two hundred and twenty-three men, with upwards of sixty thousand horses; yet, with hearts that knew no fear, our soldiers marched to begin that struggle so perilous and unequal, but so glorious in the end!

CHAPTER IX.

PORTALEGRE.

" You ask what's campaigning ?   As out the truth must,
'Tis a round of complaining, vexation, disgust,
Night marches and day, in pursuit of our foes,
Up hill or down dale, without prog or dry clothes ;
And to add to our pleasure in every shape,
The French give us doses of round shot and grape."
Military Panorama, vol. ii.

ON the evening of the 11th October, the armed
guerillas who hovered on the wooded mountains
which look down on the rough old winding
Roman highway that leads from the dilapidated
citadel of Crato to Portalegre, saw the glitter of
arms in the yellow sunshine, the flashing of
polished barrels and bright bayonets, and the
waving of uncased colours, amid the clouds of
rolling dust that betoken the march of troops ;
and ere long, the same picturesque gentry, in
their mantles, sombreros, and sheepskin zamarras,
might have heard the martial rattle of the British
drum, and the shrill notes of the fife, together
with wilder strain of the Scottish bagpipe, echoing between the green and fertile ranges of the
sierra that there forms the northern boundary of

Alentejo, and the sides of which are clothed in many places by groves of olive, laurel and orange trees; but from the latter the golden fruit had long since been gathered, ere it was quite ripe, to save it alike from the marauding soldiery of friend and foe.

Covered with the dust of a march of twenty miles from the rustic village of Gaviao, they were our old friends of the 25th, the Highlanders, and Warriston's detachment, that were now approaching the head-quarters of the division to which they were to be attached.

On this route from the Bay of Maciera, Quentin had undergone all the misery of a soldier's life during the wet season in Portugal, where the towns were then in ruins and desolate, the country utterly destroyed, and where every one who was not in arms seemed to have fled towards the coast, for, like the breath of a destroying angel, the armies of France had passed over the entire length of the land from Algarve to Galicia, laying all desolate in that wicked spirit of waste which has been so peculiar to the French soldier in all ages.

Each day, in lieu of the old Scottish *réveille* welcoming the morning, Quentin had heard the sharp note of the warning bugle, or of the drummer beating hastily the *générale*, through the ruined streets of Santarem, of Abrantes or elsewhere; through the equally silent lines of tents when

they encamped on the mountains, or the miserable bivouac when they halted in some wild
place where whilom maize or Indian corn grew,
summoning the drowsy and weary soldiers to their
ranks for the monotonous march of another
day.

From the bare boards, the hard-tiled floor, or
perhaps the cold ground, whereon our volunteer
had slept with his knapsack for a pillow, he had
been roused by the voices of the sergeant-major, or
Buckle the adjutant, shouting in the grey morning, " Fall in, 25th—stand to your arms—turn
out the whole!" while the rain that swept in
sheet-like torrents along the desolate streets, and ·
the gale that tore in angry gusts among the
ruined gables and shattered windows, formed no
pleasant prelude to a day's march that was to
be begun without other breakfast, perhaps, than
a ration biscuit soaked in the half-stale fluid
that filled his wooden canteen.

In camp, the tents were made to hold twelve
soldiers each; but some of these were always on
duty. All lay with their feet to the pole and
their heads to the wall or curtain. Each man's
pack was his pillow, and each slept, if he could,
with a blanket half under and half over him.
The rain always sputtered and filtered through
in their faces, till the drenched canvas tightened,
and the water was carried off by a little circular
trench.

Quentin shared Askerne's tent with his two subalterns.

So the night would pass, till the cry of " Rouse !" rang along the lines, and the bugles sounded the assembly, when the blankets were rolled up and strapped to the knapsacks; the wet tents were struck and folded ; the pegs and mallets replaced in their bags, and the troops prepared to march in the grey morning haze, weary, wet, stiff and sore, by reposing on the damp sod.

Quentin had always fancied a bivouac a species of military pic-nic, *minus* the ladies, pink cream, and champagne ; but on the first night he lay in one, when the baggage guard was lagging in the rear and no tents were pitched, as he was drenched in a soaking blanket under the cold October wind that swept down the rocky sierra, he began to have serious doubts whether man was really a warm-blooded animal.

" Ugh !" grumbled Monkton on this night, " who, with brains in his head-piece, would become a soldier ?"

" You remind me," said Askerne, as he shook the water for the twentieth time from his bear-skin cap, " of a story I have heard of Maitland, one of our early colonels who served on the staff of the Duke of Marlborough. It was at Blenheim, I think, when he was riding along the line accompanied by the colonel and another aide-de-camp, whose head was suddenly shattered by a cannon shot from the Bavarian artillery. Perceiving that Maitland looked long and fixedly at the fallen man, Marlborough said angrily—

"'Colonel Maitland, what the devil are you wondering at?'

"'Simply, that how a man possessed of so much brains as our poor friend, ever became a soldier,' replied Maitland, and the phlegmatic victor of Blenheim and Ramilies smiled as he rode on."

Then the dinner during a halt on the march was not tempting, and the *cuisine* was so decidedly bad that even Monkton could not joke about it. The slices of beef fried in a camp-kettle lid, or broiled on an old ramrod—beef that had never been *cold* (the miserable ration bullocks after being goaded in rear of the troops for miles by muleteers and mounted guerillas, being shot, flayed and cut up the moment the drum beat to prepare for dinner) was always tough as india-rubber; while the soup which the soldiers tried to make with a few handfuls of rice and the bones of the said bullocks, lacked only the snails mentioned by Peregrine Pickle, to make it resemble the famous black broth of the Spartans.

A little more of this common-place detail, and then we have done.

For all Quentin suffered, the novelty of treading a new soil and all the varied scenery of Portugal could scarcely make amends; yet there

were times when he could not but view with
interest and pleasure the old arches and aqueducts,
the stony skeletons of departed Rome, the ruined
amphitheatres and temples, especially that of
Diana which Quintus Sertorius built at Evora,
while remains of baths and cisterns, columns,
capitals and cornices of marble and jasper lying
prostrate among the reeds and weeds in wild
places, made him think of Dominic Skaill and
the rapture with which he would have lingered
over them. Then there were the beautiful vine-
yards, the verdant valleys where the lemon and
orange trees grew ; the steep frowning sierras,
wild and barren, but majestic ; the fertile plain
overlooked by the thirteen spires of Santarem ;
and the old Roman bridges, spanning rivers that
rushed in foam down the granite steeps to mingle
with the Tagus.

Little convents perched in solitudes where the
French had failed to penetrate, and where now
the bells rang in welcome to the British ; tiny
wayside chapels and holy wells, presided over by
local saints ; wooden crosses and cairns that
marked where some paisano or guerilla had been
shot by the French—green mounds that marked
where the French, butchered in their turn, had
been buried without coffin or shroud, all seemed
to tell of the new and strange land he traversed.

Though stout and hardy, poor Quentin's powers
of endurance were sorely taxed. In his knap-

sack were all the necessaries of a soldier—to wit, one pair of shoes and long gaiters of black cloth, shirts, socks, and mitts; a forage cap, brushes, black-ball, pipeclay, hair-ribbon, and leather. He had to carry a blanket and great-coat, a canteen of wood for water, and a canvas havresack for provisions was slung over the right shoulder; a pouch with sixty rounds of ball cartridge was over the left; add to these his musket, bayonet, belts, and grenadier cap, and the reader may believe that the poor volunteer felt life a burden before he saw the hill and spires of Portalegre.

Stiff, sore, and weary, on halting he was unable to remove his trappings, or even to take off his cap without the assistance of his servant; and he usually found himself all over livid marks, as if he had been beaten about the back and shoulders with a stick. Not the least of his discomforts was to march under the hot morning sun after a night of rain, with two wet pipeclayed cross-belts smoking upon his chest.

"Ah, if Flora Warrender or Lady Rohallion could see me now!" he would think, when, at the close of each day's march, he lay breathless and powerless on the floor of a billet, or the sod of a camp, or whatever it might chance to be!

Use, however, becomes second nature, and after a time Quentin learned to carry all his harness with ease, or ceased to feel it a burden.

"Châteaux en Espagne!" He was a skilful

builder of such edifices, and had often erected one of great comfort and magnificence for himself; but he found a difficulty in dreaming of them while lying under a drenched blanket, or in a tent on the sides of which the rain was rushing like Rounceval peas, while he had only a knapsack for a pillow, and Brown Bess for a bedfellow.

In the Highland regiments the gentlemen volunteers carried simply a claymore and dirk; in other regiments generally a musket only; but Cosmo was resolved to *grind* Quentin to the utmost; thus he compelled the poor lad to carry all the trappings of the stoutest grenadier.

Rowland Askerne, who loved the lad for his unrepining temper, manly spirit, and gentleness, and who, like the entire regiment, saw how studiously the haughty colonel ignored his existence, was unremitting in kindness to him; and Monkton never ceased to encourage him in his own fashion.

" Well, well," he would say, " it's queer work just now, of course; but some of these fine days you will receive a parchment from the king, greeting you as his ' trusty and well-beloved,' appointing you ensign to that company, whereof, I hope, Richard Monkton, Esquire, is captain; so take courage, Kennedy, my boy !"

He strove to do so, but felt thankful with all his heart for the prospect of a few days' halt, as the regiment approached the western gate of

Portalegre, where a captain's guard of Cazadores
was under arms as the Borderers marched in with
bayonets fixed and colours flying, their band
playing General Leslie's march, " All the Blue
Bonnets are bound for the Border," since 1689
their invariable quick step.   And now its lively
measure woke all the echoes of this singularly
picturesque old Portuguese town, which crowns
the summit of a hill, where its narrow, dark, and
tortuous streets, with quaint mansions overhang-
ing the roadway, are surrounded by an old wall,
among the ruins of which may be traced the
foundations of twelve great towers, and a castle
where, as the monks tell us, dwelt Lysias the
son of Bacchus !

The town was crowded by the regiments com-
posing the division of Sir John Hope; thus, the
deserted convents, the two hospitals, and even
the episcopal palace, had all become temporary
barracks; and now in the stately chambers
where the Bishops of Lisbon and the Counts of
Gaviao, of old the Lords of Portalegre, with their
white-robed prebends, or their steel-clad titulados,
held their chapters and courts, and where a
hundred years before the period of our story,
Philip, Duke of Avignon, received the submission
of the ancient city, the rollicking Irishman sung
" Garryowen" as he pipeclayed his belts or
polished his musket; the grave and stern Scottish
sergeant daily and nightly called the roll, and

John Bull in his shirt sleeves or shell jacket
might be seen cooking his rations under a splendid
marble mantelpiece, which bore the bishop's
mitre and the count's coronet, with the knightly
paete gules of Christ, and the green *fleur de lis*
of St. Avis, while the fuel was supplied by the
cedar wood of fine old cabinets, or gilded furniture that had survived the sojourn of the
Marshal Duke d'Abrantes and his suite in the
same place.

The grenadiers of the Borderers were all bil-
leted in a narrow and antique street, which was
overshadowed by the vast façade of the cathedral;
and there, from the open lattices of their room
(in a house the proprietors of which were either
dead or had fled) Askerne and Quentin sat
smoking cigars and enjoying some of the purple
wine of Oporto, from the cool, vaulted *bodega* of
a neighbouring wine-house, and with their feet
planted on a charcoal *brasero*, they felt, on the evening after their arrival, for the first time, that they
were somewhat at home and could take their
ease, with belts off and coats unbuttoned. And
so they sat and watched, almost in silence, the
swift-coming shadows of the October evening as
they deepened in the quaint vista of the old
Portuguese street, where the costumes were so
striking and singular; the citizen who seemed to
have no lawful occupation but smoking, in his
ragged mantle and broad sombrero; a secular

priest with his ample paunch and shovel-shaped
chapeau; a white-robed Carmelite or grey Franciscan, flitting, ghostlike, amid the masses of
red coats who lounged about the doors and
arcades, most of them smoking, and all chatting
and laughing, till the stars came out, when the
bugles would sound tattoo, and when all loiterers
would have to turn in, save the quarter guards
and inlying picquet.

These were ordered to be of considerable
strength, as a numerous band of homeless and
lawless Spanish and Portuguese guerillas, under
a runaway student of Salamanca, named Baltasar
de Saldos, hovered among the hills. This band
was of somewhat dubious loyalty, as the members
of it, more than once, had scuffles with the
British foraging parties, and even fired on them
—the alliance between this country and Spain
being so recent, that after the long and vexatious
wars of the preceding century, the people could
not understand it.

CHAPTER X.

COSMO'S CRAFT.

" Small occasions in the path of life,
Lie thickly sown, while great are rarely scattered.
*   *   *   *   *
Shame seize me, if I would not rather be
The man thou art, than court-created chief
Known only by the dates of his promotion!"
JOANNA BAILLIE.

THE two first days after Quentin's arrival in
Portalegre, were varied by the flogging of soldiers
for marauding, when they were four months in
arrears of pay. One of these men was flogged
by tap of drum; a measure by which half a
minute was allowed to elapse between each stroke,
greatly enhancing the agony; and this process
went on during more than four hundred lashes,
till the bare muscles were seen to quiver under
the cats, and then he was removed.

On the second day, the troops that had recently arrived from England, together with a
battalion of Cazadores from Lisbon, were paraded
outside the walls of the little mountain city for
the inspection of the lieutenant-general commanding.

Their new uniform and accoutrements contrasted strongly with the ragged, patched, and
war-worn trappings of the corps which had
served during the preceding campaign, and had
so rapidly cleared Portugal of the French.

The Cazadores were active, bustling, and soldier-
like little Portuguese light infantry, all clad in
dark green uniforms of London make, with smart
shakos, having green plumes.   Their ranks were
ever redolent of garlic and tobacco, to all who
had the misfortune to march to leeward of them,
while their snubby round noses, thick lips, and
dark complexions reminded all who saw them
of their Moorish descent.

Prior to the infusion of British officers among
them, the Portuguese soldiery were every way con-
temptible.   Murphy tells us that in the beginning of the war in 1762, "their army was in a
most wretched state, scarcely amounting to ten
thousand men, most of whom were peasants,
without uniform or arms, asking charity, while
the officers served at the tables of their colonels;"
and matters were not much improved when Sir
Arthur Wellesley arrived to uphold the interests
of the House of Braganza, after which he had few
better or braver troops than the Lusitanian Legion.

The general of division, Sir John Hope of
Rankeillour, took particular notice of the Borderers, having been colonel of the regiment
about fifteen years before. He had been wounded

on the Helder, like Cosmo Crawford, and had served in the first campaign of Egypt with great distinction.

He complimented Cosmo in strong terms upon the appearance and discipline of the battalion, both of which high qualities the Master had not the candour or the generosity to say were due to the enthusiasm, exertions, and genuine *esprit de corps* of Major Middleton; and as Sir John rode along the line, wearing a glazed cocked-hat, an old telescope slung across his well-worn red coat, the lace and aiguilette of which were frayed by service and blackened by gunpowder, he looked a thorough soldier. He was tall, well formed, and in the prime of life, being in his forty-second year; and Quentin regarded him with deep interest, for he was informed by Askerne, in a whisper, that " Sir John had joined the army as a volunteer in his fifteenth year, prior to his first commission as a cornet, in the 10th Light Dragoons."

" As we are about to enter Spain by the way of Badajoz," said the general to Cosmo, after the troops had been dismissed to their quarters, " I am particularly anxious to open a communication with El Estudiente."

" Is this a town which lies near it ?" asked Cosmo.

" Oh, no. El Estudiente is a man," replied Sir John, laughing, while the staff joined, as in duty bound, and Cosmo reddened with anger.

"Who, or what is he?" he asked, coldly.

"A guerilla chief—Baltasar de Saldos, a personage of savage character, and very doubtful reputation."

"You recommend him badly, general."

"But truly, though."

"In what way can I assist you in the matter?" asked Cosmo, with increasing coldness of manner, as he began to fear that the unpleasant duty of opening the "communication" in question, was, perhaps, to devolve on him.

"I wish a messenger to convey a despatch from me to him—one of yours—not an officer, whose life would be too valuable; but if you have any private, a troublesome fellow, worthless, frequently in the defaulters' book—you understand me, colonel?"

"I think that I do, Sir John," replied Cosmo, whose green eyes shrunk as he inserted his glass in one, and gazed at the general, keenly; "but is the risk of delivering a message so great in Portugal, after you have cleared it of the French?"

"Stragglers, orderlies, and solitary individuals are at all times liable to be cut off, we scarcely know by whom, the country is so lawless; but this fellow, Baltasar, is somewhere among the mountains near Herreruela, beyond the Spanish frontier; and to say nothing of the wolves that

infest the wild places hereabouts, there are three
chances to one against any messenger returning
alive, even after he has delivered our letter to
Baltasar."

" A lively duty !"

" Portugal and Spain are not without traitors
in the French interest ready to assassinate a red-
coat; others are ready to do it merely to procure
his clothing and arms, and some of the low wayside tabernas are kept by people who would cut
any man's throat for the chance of finding half
a vintin in his pocket. Then there are the hazards
of being hanged as a spy by the French, of
losing one's way among the wild, depopulated
Sierras, and dying there of starvation, or being
devoured by the black wolves, or by those wild
dogs, of which the Duke of Abrantes strove in
vain to clear the country."

" A pleasant country for a sketching tour !"
said Cosmo.

" Yet Sir John Moore has distinctly ordered
me to communicate with these guerillas, to
strengthen us and cover the flank of our advance
towards the Guadiana, as it is not impossible
that the enemy may push forward from Valla-
dolid, and cut off our communication with the
main body of the army, and as scouts and sharp-
shooters, the guerillas are invaluable."

" If your messenger did *not* return, what
proof would you have that he had ever delivered

your letter ?" asked Cosmo, with one of his strange smiles.

" The presence of Baltasar's armed guerillas on our flank as we advance through Spanish Estremadura, would be all the reply I wish. Colonel Napier, of the Highlanders, has said that he would rather go in person than sacrifice one of his men; but——"

" I am not so chivalrous," said Cosmo, laughing, as he shrugged his shoulders and toyed with his gathered reins alternately on each side of his charger's silky mane; " I have a fellow whom I can very well spare, one who is a nuisance to the regiment in general, and to me in particular—one of whom I should like to be handsomely rid; he is clever, sharp, and resolute, too," he added, as he and the general rode slowly side by side into Portalegre.

" He is the very kind of man I require; but," said the worthy general, hesitating and colouring, " it is not a duty on which I should wish to risk a valuable life—you understand me, Colonel Crawford ?"

" Oh, perfectly; when will your letter be ready ?"

" Before sunset; but what is the name of the bearer, for however numerous his chances of failure may be, I must duly accredit him in my mission to the guerilla chief—those Spaniards are so suspicious."

Cosmo took one of his own calling cards, and pencilling on it the name of Quentin Kennedy, handed it to the unsuspecting general.

" His rank ?" asked the latter.

" Volunteer," was the curt reply.

" A volunteer, Colonel Crawford !" exclaimed the general; " I spoke of some private soldier, whose conduct made him worthless. The bearing of a volunteer must be careful—his honour spotless."

" Such are not his," said Cosmo, angrily, for this cross-questioning fretted his fierce and crafty temper; " and I have said that I wish to be handsomely rid of him."

" Very good—you are the best judge of how to handle your command; but if in your place, I should send him back to his friends in Britain."

" The letter," began Cosmo impatiently.

" My orderly will bring it to your quarters within an hour. Adieu, colonel."

" To-night, then, perhaps to-night !" muttered Cosmo, half aloud, through his clenched teeth, and with a sombre smile, as he saluted the general and rode off in search of Buckle, his adjutant. " A volunteer must always be the first man for duty; I swore to work this fellow to an oil, and egad! the game for him is only beginning. Good! to think of the simple general baiting the very trap into which he is to fall. Once handsomely rid of him, I shall

deceive the old folks at home anew, and pretend
that the letters in which I mentioned that he
was serving under me have *miscarried.*"

He cast one of his sinister smiles after Sir
John Hope, and spurred his horse impatiently
up one of the streets of Portalegre, towards the
Bishop's palace, where his quarters were, and
where the colours of the Borderers were lodged
under a sergeant's guard.

Sir John Hope was that distinguished Scottish
officer, who, after Waterloo, was created Lord
Niddry for his many brilliant services, and who,
two years subsequently, succeeded to the old
Earldom of Hopetoun. Concerning him a very
singular story is still current in the French
army.

It is to the effect, that the eldest son of
Marshal Ney challenged the Duke of Wellington
to a mortal duel, for his alleged share in his
father's death—the place of combat to be any
spot in Europe he chose to select. On receiving this cartel, the Duke is said to have
replied :

"My life belongs to my country and must
not be lightly risked in trifles !"

On this, one of his aides-de-camp, the Scottish
Earl of Hopetoun, whom he had alway mentioned with honour in his despatches, accepted
the challenge in his place, and leaving Scotland,
without bidding adieu to his Countess, Louisa

Wedderburn, or their eleven children, repaired straight to Paris, and met young Ney on the Bois de Boulogne, where they fired at once. The story adds, that Hopetoun fell pierced by a ball in the head, in the very place where he had been wounded during the famous sortie from Bayonne in February, 1814, and that as he fell, young Ney flung his pistol in the air, exclaiming—

" Sacré Dieu! the Prince of Moskwa is revenged!"*

* Unfortunately for this story (which contains some strange grains of truth, and which was told me by the Lieutenant of Marshal St. Arnaud's Spahi troop in the Crimea) the gallant Earl of Hopetoun died in his bed, from natural causes, at Paris, on the 27th August, 1823.

CHAPTER XI.

QUENTIN DEPARTS.

" Would ye my death ?   Can that avail you ?
  Or life ? *what* life will ye to give ?
For this existence, grief-embittered,
  Doth hourly die, yet dying live.
My sorrows, if ye fain would slay me,
  Your blows so fierce, so fast to deal,
It needs not : one the least, the lightest,
  Would task endurance strong as steel."
                    Portuguese of Rodriguez Lobo.

On the same evening when Quentin received the despatch from the adjutant, with instructions to start forthwith by the nearest road that led towards the frontier, Monkton was preparing to give a little supper in his billet, and was superintending the cooking thereof in person.

The house he occupied had belonged to some titulado of Portugese Estremadura.   The ceilings were lofty, and the cornices of the heavy and florid Palladian style were elaborately gilded, and everywhere the green fleur-de-lis of St. Avis (an order founded by Alphonso, for defence against the Moors, from whom he took Santarem and Lisbon) was reproduced among the decorations.

The floors were of polished oak; the furniture, in many instances richly gilded, was all of crimson velvet stuffed with down, and the cabinets of ebony were covered with carvings, some representing the past discoveries, victories, and glories, real or imaginary, of the kings of Portugal. · Many fine paintings bore marks of additions received from the French in the shape of bayonet stabs and bullet holes, with finishing touches in burnt cork, by which Venuses and Madonnas were liberally supplied with moustachios and so forth; while the frescoes bore such lovely delineations of fair-skinned, golden-haired, and ripe-lipped goddesses and nymphs, that, as Monkton said, "they made one long for pagan times again." Over a Venus being attired in scanty garments by some completely nude graces, was the motto "*Si non caste tantum modo caute.*"

"Which means?" asked Askerne, who had been trying to make it out.

" In good Portuguese, ' If you can't be chaste, at least be cautious,' an old-fashioned aphorism," said Monkton.

" Poor Portugal !" said Askerne, thoughtfully; " she is left now but with mere traditions of her past; a country without kings, warriors, poets or painters. The land of Camoens, of Rodriguez Lobo, of Antonio Ferreria, Bernardez, the captive of Alcazalquiver, of Andrade de Cominha, cannot *now* produce one patriotic song !"

In one corner of the apartment a dark stain
on the floor showed where blood had been lately
shed, and there were the marks of a woman's
hand upon the wall and oak boards, as if she had
been dragged from place to place, thus telling of
some terrible outrage—an episode of its recent
occupants, the French.

"Now, what the devil is the meaning of
this?" asked Monkton, looking up from his
culinary operations as Buckle entered; "Kennedy
can't be the first man for duty."

"No, he is not," replied Buckle, curtly, for
having on his sword and gorget, he felt and
looked official.

"Then why the——"

"Why select him, you would ask, with the
addition of some unpleasant adjective?"

"Yes."

"Because a volunteer is always the first man
for any duty that is dangerous."

"And is this duty so?" asked Quentin, with
very excusable interest.

"Undoubtedly—there is no use concealing the
fact, as foreknowledge will make you wary; and
if successful, it will be reported favourably to
head-quarters, 'that negotiations with the formidable guerilla chief—what's his infernal name
—have been honourably concluded, through the
courage and diplomatic skill of that very distinguished volunteer, Mr. Quentin Kennedy, now

serving with the 25th Foot, whom I recommend most warmly to your Royal Highness's most earnest and favourable consideration'—that is the sort of thing," added the adjutant, putting aside his sword and belt, as the odour of the cooking reached his olfactory nerves.

"You think, Mr. Buckle, that the colonel will recommend me thus?" asked Quentin, his young heart throbbing with delight.

"And Sir John Hope, too—of course; they can do nothing else," was the confident reply, for the adjutant believed in what he said.

Hope, pride, and enthusiasm swelled up in the poor lad's breast as the adjutant spoke.

"Ah," thought he, "I should have offered my hand to Cosmo, and shall do so when I *return*."

"Congratulate me, major," he exclaimed, hastening to Middleton, who entered at that moment; "I have been chosen for an important duty already."

"So I have heard—so I have heard," he replied, quickly, shaking his head and his pigtail with it.

"And what do you think of it? Here is the despatch, addressed 'Al Senor Don Baltasar de Saldos, Herreruela, *vía* Valencia de Alcantara.'"

"You are particularly to avoid that town," said Buckle, emphatically.

"Why?"

"Because a French garrison occupy it—some of General de Ribeaupierre's brigade."

"It is a little way across the frontier," said Quentin; "so, my dear sir, what do you think of the duty?"

"Think—that the whole affair is a cruelty and a shame!" exclaimed the old major, bluntly. "I've been looking at the map, and see that the place is some miles beyond the frontier—in the enemy's country, in fact."

"Come, major, don't discourage him," said Buckle; "he must go now, and there is an end of it."

"I wish there was. Does he go in uniform?"

"Yes; it is safer."

"How?"

"In mufti he might be taken for a spy."

"Uniform did not protect my poor friend André of the 26th, when taken on a similar mission."

"Come, come, I'll bet you a pony apiece that Kennedy comes off with flying colours," said Monkton. "Some more butter, Askerne—where's the pepper-box?—Quentin is a devilish sharp fellow, and always keeps his weather eye open, as the sailors say."

"What is the distance between this and Herreruela?" asked Askerne, who had hitherto remained silent.

"About thirty British miles, as a crow flies."

"And he is to proceed on foot?"

"But he can do so at leisure—there is no word of breaking up our cantonments here yet."

"But in this country miles seem to vary very

much, Mr. Buckle," said Quentin ; "when am I
supposed to be back ?"

" Back ?" repeated Buckle, rather puzzled.

"Excuse my asking," said the lad, modestly; "but
I am so ignorant of the country, and so forth."

" True, Kennedy. Well, supposing that you
see this Baltasar de Saldos—fine melodramatic
name, isn't it ?—he is doubtless a fellow in a
steeple-crowned hat and seven-league boots, all
stuck over pistols and daggers—supposing you
see him at once, there is nothing to prevent you
being back in six days, at latest."

" So we are about to make a night of it, the
first jolly one we have had since landing at the
mouth of the Maciera, and, damme, here is poor
Quentin going to leave us !" said Monkton, who
in his shirt sleeves was devilling a huge dish of
kidneys over a brasero, for the orthodox fuel of
which (charcoal) he had substituted the shutter
of a window, torn down and broken to pieces.
"One glass more of Oporto for the gravy,
another dash of pepper, and the banquet is complete. You must have supper with us to-night,
ere you go, Quentin."

The same readily found fuel was roasting
on the marble slab of the richly carved fire-
place, a goodly row of sputtering castanos, which
were superintended by Rowland Askerne.

" Where is Pimple to-night ?" he asked,
looking up.

"With Colville, on the quarter guard," said Monkton; "and, rosaries and wrinkles! where do you think they are stationed?"

"By your exclamation, opposite a convent, probably."

"Exactly—el Convento de Santa Engracia; but it hasn't a window to the street, so they might as well have the wall of China to contemplate."

A borrachio skin of Herrera del Duque (the famous wine of the Badajoz district), of which Monkton had somehow become possessed, lay on the beautiful marqueterie table, like a bloated bagpipe, while tin canteens, silver-rimmed drinking-horns, tea-cups, everything but crystal vessels, were ranged round to imbibe the contents from.

The plates and other appurtenances of the table were of the same varied description, and were furnished by the guests themselves, as the French had carried off or destroyed nearly everything in the house. A canteen of brandy and a loaf of fine white bread completed the repast, to which all brought good humour and appetites that were quite startling, better than any they could ever procure for the dainties of the mess-table at Colchester.

Servants were entirely dispensed with; thus the conversation was free and unrestrained, like the jests and laughter.

"I can scarcely assure myself that you are actually going to-night," said the major to Quentin; "the whole arrangement is a black, burning shame; an older man, one of more experience, one who has been longer in the country and had served the campaign in Portugal, should have been sent on this duty."

"But the greater is my chance of honour!" said Quentin, cheerfully.

"And peril too. Your health—and success, boy! This wine is excellent, Monkton—but the service is going to the devil! we have never been the men we were since the abolition of hair-powder and pigtails, brigadier wigs and Nivernois hats! Think of a garrison court-martial according four hundred and odd lashes to a poor devil yesterday, for borrowing a loaf of bread like this, when we are all so far in arrears of pay; and yet, I remember when we ate Jack Andrews' baby in America, men were tucked up to the next tree for just as little."

"Jack Andrews' baby," said Quentin, looking up from his devilled kidneys at the familiar name.

"It is an old regimental story," said the major, laughing, as he filled his horn with wine from the gushing borrachio; "it happened when we were in garrison at Fort St. John on the Richelieu River (a place I have often told you about); provisions were scarce, for the Yankees had intercepted all our supplies, so that at times

we were literally starving, while to conciliate
the colonists, strict orders were issued against
plundering. It was as much as your life was
worth if the provost marshal caught you stealing
anything, even a kiss from a girl in Vermont
or New York, so such a thing as levanting with
a sucking-pig or a turkey-poult, was not to be
thought of even in our wildest dreams; moreover they would not have *sold* a chicken for thrice
its weight in gold, to a red-coat!

"Some weeks passed over thus; we were
getting very lanky and lean, and though our lovely
countenances were ruddied by the American
frost, we were always hungry, always thirsty, and
longed in our day-dreams for a cooper of the
old mess port, or a devilled drumstick; but these
were only to be had at the head-quarters of the
Borderers and Cameronians, then far away in
the Jerseys, in pursuit of the rebels, under Lord
Stirling; and we often shivered with hunger as
well as with cold under the ice-covered roofs of
our wooden barracks at night.

"Lord Rohallion of ours, had a servant named
Jack Andrews, a knowing old file, from his own
place in Carrick, who contrived to make off with
a sheep. How or where Jack did it, the Lord
only knows, and we never enquired; but the
owner, a Pennsylvanian quaker, made an outcry
about it, and the Provost's guard were speedily
on poor Jack's track with the gallows rope.

A stab with a bayonet in the throat soon silenced the sheep, and Jack brought it under his great-coat to our quarters, and while the provost, with Simon Pure, was overhauling the soldiers' bar-rack, we tucked up the spoil in a cradle, with a blanket over it and a muslin cap round its head. We set a piper's wife to rock it, while Jack pretended to make caudle at the fire, and in this occupation they were found, when the provost came in, intent on death, and Broad-brim on retribution.

> " Hush-a-by, baby, on the tree-top,
>   When the wind blows the cradle will rock,"

sung the piper's wife, patting the sheep tenderly.

" ' Hush,' said Jack to the intruders ; ' don't stir for the life that is in you !'

" ' Why—what is the matter with the baby ?'

" ' It's either measles or small-pox ; we don't know which,' said Jack.

" ' Yea verily—aye—ho, hum,' snivelled the Quaker.

" ' All right,' said the provost, as he withdrew with his guard to search elsewhere. The sheep was soon cut up, divided, and a sumptuous supper Major André, Rohallion and a select few of us had that night, and ere morning all traces of it had disappeared, save the skin, which, to the rage of the provost, was found concealed, no one knew by whom, between the sheets of his bed. Long after the fort was taken by the

Yankees, and none had a fear of coming to the
drumhead, the whole story came out, and many
a laugh we had at the provost marshal and
Jack Andrews' baby."

The names mentioned thus incidentally by the
good major recalled so much of home and of
old associations to Quentin, that his warm heart
swelled with kind and affectionate memories;
and now, when on the eve of departing from
friends that he loved so well, and who had a
regard so great for him—departing on a lonely
and decidedly perilous duty—he was on the point
of telling them the story of his earlier life, so
that, if aught occurred to him, his military companions might write to Rohallion; but thoughts
of the haughty Master chilled him, and he
repressed the suddenly-conceived idea.

And now the time came when he was compelled to depart.

He had three days' cooked provisions in his
havresack, and he had still money enough remaining for his wants in a land where he had
to journey almost by stealth, and where the
French had left so little either to buy or to sell.

He took with him his great-coat and forage-
cap; in lieu of his heavy musket, Askerne gave
him a sword, and Middleton a pair of pistols;
and the former accompanied him nearly two
miles on the road from Portalegre.

"You dare danger fearlessly, Quentin," said he.

" I dare it as those who are friendless and alone do! The knowledge that I have few, perhaps none, who would really regret me, renders life of little value."

" Come, Kennedy, egad! this bitterness is ungrateful," said Askerne, in a tone of reproach.

" True, my friend, forgive me! I believe that you, at least, with Middleton and Warriston— he's on duty, remember me to him—Monkton, and a few *others* that are far, far away, have, indeed, a sincere regard for me."

" Well, then, how many more, or what more would you have? The world is not so bad after all," said Askerne, laughing, as he shook his hand warmly and bade him adieu, after giving him much good advice concerning prudence and care of consorting with strangers on the way; for Askerne and his brother officers saw, or suspected that the colonel's selection of the lad was the result of bad feeling; while Quentin deemed it but a part of his hard and venturesome lot as a gentleman volunteer.

Often he turned to wave a farewell to Askerne, whose erect and soldier-like figure was lessening in the distance, as he walked back to Portalegre. At last, a turn of the road, where it wound suddenly between some olive groves, hid him entirely; and, for the first time, an emotion of utter loneliness came over Quentin's heart as he hastened towards the darkening hills.

CHAPTER XII.

ANXIOUS FRIENDS.

" Oh, Leolyn, be obstinately just ;
Indulge no passion and deceive no trust.
Let never man be bold enough to say,
Thus, and no farther, shall my passion stray ;
The first crime past compels us into more,
And guilt grows *fate*, which was but *choice* before."
AARON HILL.

THE third day and the fourth passed away at
Portalegre ; on the fifth and sixth, Major Middleton and others, who felt a friendly interest in
Quentin Kennedy, began to surmise, when they
met on the morning or evening parade, or in
each other's billets, or so forth, that it was time
now he had reported his return, and the good or
bad success of his journey, to the colonel and
general commanding the division.

Other days passed ; it was whispered about
from staff-office officials that ere long the division would leave Portalegre, as the whole
army was about to advance against the enemy ;
and then Captain Askerne, Monkton, Buckle, the
adjutant, and others, became doubly anxious
about the lad, and were interested as much as

men could be under their circumstances, when
human life is deemed of so little value as it is
when on active service and before an enemy.

As for Warriston of the 94th, not being
under the immediate command of Colonel Crawford, he openly and bitterly inveighed against
" the iniquity of having sacrificed a mere youth
in such a manner," and threatened " to bring
the matter prominently before Sir John Moore,"
who commanded the forces in Portugal.

" He has, perhaps, gone over to the enemy—
a despatch is sometimes well paid for," said
Cosmo, in his sneering manner, when some of
these remarks reached him on parade, one
morning.

" Impossible, my dear sir—impossible !" said
Middleton, testily, while spurring and reining in
his horse; " I know the lad as if he were my
own son, and feel assured that he is the soul of
honour; that he was all ardour for the service,
and that he would die rather than disgrace himself."

" Indeed—ah-aw—you think so ?" drawled
Cosmo, with his glass in his sinister eye, as he
surveyed the major with a glance of somewhat
mingled cast.

" I do, colonel," was the emphatic rejoinder.

" He has disappeared at all events—a dubious
phrase. If the fellow has not levanted to the
Duke of Dalmatia with General Hope's despatch,

may his heart not have failed him? may he not have shown the white feather? Better men than he, among the Belem Rangers, have done so ere now."

The imaginary corps referred to contained one of the most offensive imputations to the ears of Peninsula men; thus Captain Askerne exclaimed—

"Cowardice, Colonel Crawford—would you infer cowardice?"

"I infer nothing, gentlemen, but that better men than he have shown the white feather."

"Not in *the Line*, that I am aware of," was the somewhat pointed remark of Middleton; and Cosmo, who had lately come from the Guards, crimsoned with suppressed passion.

"A volunteer is a soldier of fortune, and none such can ever be a coward," said Askerne, stoutly.

"Of course not—the idea is absurd," added Middleton, looking round the group of officers, who glanced their approval.

"You are warm, Major Middleton," said Cosmo, sternly, while his eyes gleamed with their most dangerous expression; "somewhat unnecessarily warm on this trivial subject, I think."

"I am at least honest, colonel, as he must be who defends the absent or the dead."

"We have had enough of this—to your companies—fall in, gentlemen!" said the colonel, sternly and impatiently, as he spurred his horse, unsheathed his sword, and the formula of the parade began, after which he revenged himself by drilling the corps, under a drizzling rain, for nearly two hours, forcing Askerne's grenadiers to skirmish in a swamp, and making old Major Middleton put the battalion twice through the eighteen manœuvres.

About this time a patrol of Portuguese cavalry found near the high road that led through a desert towards the Spanish frontier, the remains of a man, almost reduced to a skeleton, picked, gnawed, and torn asunder, to all appearance recently, by those devouring wolves and wild dogs which infest the mountains of the district.

Terrible surmises of Quentin's fate were now whispered among the Borderers ; the officer in command of the patrol was closely questioned by Middleton, Warriston, and others ; but he constantly stated that the victim had probably been stripped by robbers before being devoured, as nothing had been found near the remains that might lead to their identification, or in any way connect them with the missing Quentin Kennedy. Thus, in default of other proof, as time wore on, the members of the regiment made up their minds to consider the poor bones as his, and concluded that he had perished miserably in the wilderness.

To do Cosmo Crawford justice, there were times when he was not without secret emotions of shame, and even of compunction, for the part he had acted to Quentin. His own conscience, the small still voice that would speak, could not acquit him; but those gleams of the better spirit came only briefly and at intervals, and such unwelcome thoughts were always eventually stifled by the constitutional malignity of his nature, and he would mutter to himself—

" Pshaw! he is well away; what the devil was he to me, or I to him ?"

It was while the troops were lingering at Portalegre and elsewhere along the Spanish frontier, that Lord Castlereagh's despatch, containing the first organized plan of the future campaign, arrived in Lisbon.

In the northern provinces of Spain, thirty-five thousand horse and foot were to be employed; ten thousand of these were to be embarked from British ports, and the rest to be drafted from our army of occupation in Portugal; and these were supposed to be equal to cope with the vast hosts pouring through the many passes of the Pyrenees from France and Germany, and those which already blackened all the plains of Castile and Arragon.

We have elsewhere mentioned the vast strength of the French army, whose head-quarters were at Vittoria.

The brave but ill-fated Sir John Moore was ordered to take the field without delay with the troops that were under his own command. Some fortress or city (unnamed) in Galicia, or on the borders of the kingdom of Leon, was to be the place for concentrating the whole allied armies of Britain, Spain, and Portugal ; and his specific plan of operations was *afterwards* to be concerted with the stupid, jealous, and uncompromising local juntas, and the obstinate and impracticable Spanish generals.

These orders were perilous, loose, and vague ; they promised nothing, but only that war at any hazard was to be waged in Old Castile and on the banks of the Ebro.

And now for a time let us change the scene to a not less tuneful or classic locality—the rocky hills and heather braes of Carrick's western shore.

CHAPTER XIII.

THE PARAGRAPH.

" My kindred are dead, my love is fled ;
    Courage, my heart, thou canst love no more ;
Pale is my cheek, my body is weak ;
    Courage, my heart, 'twill soon be o'er.
Dim are my eyes with tears of sorrow,
They ache for a night without a morrow !"

M. N. S.

It was towards the end of the month—the last days of October, now.

The acorns were falling from the moss-grown oaks, the hollies and hedge-rows were gay with scarlet berries and haws, the grey sea-gulls were often seen mingling with the black gleds and hoodie-crows far afield inshore. The redwing, the fieldfare, and the woodcock had come again to their old haunts on the braes of Rohallion, in the oakwood shaw, in the hawthorn birks that overhang the Girvan, and the deep carse land where the rushes grew and the water flowed of old.

The autumn winds, as they swept through the hollow glen, shook down the last brown leaves of the old sycamores, and the spoils of the past summer lay in rustling heaps about the haunted

gate and the guns of La Bonne Citoyenne on the
battery before the castle-keep. From the tall
square chimneys of the old feudal stronghold on
the storm-beaten bluff, the gudeman of Elsie
Irvine and other fishermen from the coves, saw
the smoke of the rousing fires ascending into the
grey autumn sky, and the evening lights glittering early in the great towers, a land-mark now
to them as it had been to their forefathers long
ages ago, when the Scot and the Saxon found work
nearer home for their swords than fighting for
conquered Spain or ravaged Portugal.

"People now-a-days, with the help of the
penny-post and the telegraph, and the endless
means of communication and of coming and
going, are certainly able to *care for* a greater
number of persons than they could have done a
hundred years ago," says a recent writer in the
"Cornhill;" but he might have said thirty years
ago, so far as the people of Scotland are concerned.

Thus, secluded by her own retiring habits and
personal circumstances, as well as by those incident to the time, content to reside in her narrow
circle, and chiefly among her husband's household
and dependents, Lady Rohallion's heart yearned
with all a mother's love for her lost *protégé*, the
more, perhaps, that the cold and repulsive manner
of her only son Cosmo had cast her warm and
affectionate heart somewhat back, as it were,
upon herself; though the memory of much if not

all his shortcomings in the way of filial reverence and regard were now by her forgotten, or merged in the idea of his absence at the seat of war.

Quentin's memory she cherished chiefly in silence; for, still fostering her hopes or views with regard to Cosmo and the wilful little heiress of Ardgour, she spoke of the lost one but reservedly, and at long intervals, to the latter; though, sooth to say, young Fernie of Fernwoodlee, a neighbouring proprietor, had become so frequent a visitor at the castle, that, so far as good looks, assiduity, and unwearying industry as an admirer might go, he bade fair—gossips said—to supplant both Quentin and the Master of Rohallion, for a lover lost, and another commencing a campaign, were just as satisfactory as no lover at all.

It was about this time that the post-bag brought by John Legate, the running-footman, from Maybole, was opened before Lord Rohallion by his faithful old henchman Jack Andrews, and emptied on the breakfast-table.

One small missive, bearing Fernwoodlee's crest —a fern leaf all proper—he handed to Flora, who coloured slightly and said it referred to a proposed ride as far as the ruins of Kilhenzie, to see the Eglinton hounds throw off, as the keeper had promised to find a leash of foxes in the cover there.

" These fox-hunting fools are beginning their

work betimes—why, this is only October," said his lordship, drily; "they would be better employed riding in the light dragoons against the enemies of Europe."

Pushing the rest of the letters across the table to Lady Rohallion, as if for perusal at her leisure, he opened the latest newspaper, and betook himself, with true military instinct, to the gazette and matters pertaining to the war against France and the Corsican, by land and sea.

Erelong, it was with an exclamation of astonishment that shook the powder from his venerable pigtail, that made Lady Rohallion permit the urn to overrun her teacup, Flora to start nervously, Mr. Spillsby to drop the egg-stand with its contents, and Jack Andrews to spring mechanically to "attention" on his lame leg, that his lordship, raising his voice to an unusually high pitch, read the following paragraph:—

"On the 6th October, the final despatch of the premier reached the general commanding at Lisbon, and by this time the whole army will have been in motion across the Spanish frontier, to chastise the barbarian hordes of the Corsican tyrant, under whose sway the people of France and Spain alike are groaning. We rejoice to say that before marching from Portalegre, Lieutenant-General Sir John Hope of Rankeillour most successfully opened a communication with the famous guerilla, El Estudiente, a matter fully

and finally arranged by the skill and courage of
Mr. Quentin Kennedy, a young volunteer, then
serving with H.M. 25th Regiment, or 'King's
Own Borderers.'"

"Quentin!" exclaimed Flora, rushing behind
Lord Rohallion's chair, her cheeks flushing red,
as she peeped over his shoulder.

"Quentin Kennedy!" said Lady Rohallion, in
a breathless voice, as she grew pale and trembled.

"The boy is found—found at last! There,
read the paragraph for yourselves," said his
lordship, flourishing the paper over his head.

Poor Lady Rohallion made many ineffectual
efforts to do as he bid her; but her eyes were full
of tears, and her spectacles were quite obscured.

"Spillsby—Andrews, send for John Girvan;
zounds! the 25th, too—the blessed old number!
—here's news for him! The lost is found again!
You'll write him, Winny—and Flora, too—
gad, we'll all write!" continued the old Lord, in
a very incoherent way. "The cunning rogue, to
keep us in suspense so long, and to be wearing
the buttons of the old Borderers all the time.
It must be he: there can't be two Quentin Ken-
nedies; oh, no—of course it must be he!"

"There is something strange in this," said
Lady Rohallion, finding relief in tears; "how
many letters, Flora, have we had from Cosmo
since he left us?"

"Five."

" Five letters !"

" One from Colchester; others from Santarem and Abrantes; and two from Portalegre."

"Exactly," said Lord Rohallion, on whose benign brow a cloud gathered; " five letters, and in none of them has one word escaped him concerning the poor lad who joined the corps before him—the dear old 25th, of my earliest memories. It is not generous, Winny; I don't envy Quentin his commanding officer; it shows a bad animus, and I am sorry our boy should behave so."

Lady Winifred was silent, for she felt the truth of what her husband said; and Flora, full of her own joyous thoughts, was silent too.

" Read over the paragraph again, Flora, darling; egad, I must cut it out, and send it over to Earl Hugh, at Eglinton;" and while Flora read, Rohallion walked to and fro, rubbing his hands with intense satisfaction and delight.

" But, good heavens, my lord !" she suddenly exclaimed, while the colour left her face, " what is this that follows ? there is here another paragraph, about—about———"

" About what ?"

" Poor Quentin," she added, faintly.

" Read it !" said Rohallion, impetuously.

" ' We regret to have to add, it is feared that after accomplishing this valuable public service with the guerilla, our enterprising young soldier has fallen a sacrifice to his zeal, or the lawless state of the country, as—as he has not been heard of since.' " . . . . .

Flora's sweet voice died away almost in a tremulous whisper as she read this blighting paragraph, which Lord Rohallion, after hastily snatching the paper from her, read again and again, with his brows deeply knit.

It did not fall upon him with the crushing effect it had upon the two ladies, who sat silently weeping, for the words of the paragraph were, to them, terribly suggestive and vague; and now the old quartermaster, who had been noisily summoned by his veteran comrade the valet, arrived to join the conclave; and truly, had a thirteen-inch bombshell, shot from a mortar of similar diameter, exploded among the breakfast equipage, worthy John Girvan could not have seemed more astonished and bewildered than he did by the whole affair.

Lord Rohallion and he, as old soldiers, endeavoured to explain the matter away, and to speak from past experience of many instances of men reported as "missing" who always turned up again; newspaper paragraphs in general they treated with great contempt, and expressed their certain conviction that "by this time," no doubt, he had rejoined the corps.

Indeed, so certain were they of this that Lord Rohallion desired the quartermaster to write at once; Flora, with charming frankness, offered to enclose a tiny note, and the old general wrote at once by the next mail to the Horse Guards, urging "the immediate promotion of his young friend to the first ensigncy at the disposal of His Royal Highness the Field Marshal Commanding-in-Chief—in the 25th Foot, if practicable."

This done, the male part of the household, though full of the affair, and their innumerable yarns of the corps, which it had called to memory, felt more composed on the subject. The quarter-master furbished up his old red coat, and remained to dinner: Flora's engagement to ride with young Fernwoodlee and the meet at Kilhenzie, were committed to oblivion, and were utterly forgotten, as she sat alone, full of thought, on the old mossgrown garden-seat, with the autumn leaves whirling round her.

Through the branches of the stripped trees on which the rooks were cawing, the sunlight fell aslant upon the copper gnomon of the ancient sun and moon dial, which occupied the centre of the quaint Scoto-French garden, and round the pedestal of which Quentin, to please her, during the last spring, had trained a creeping plant.

The plant was still there, but its tendrils and trailers were dead, withered, and yellow, and sadly Flora felt in her heart that she was lonely, and that Rohallion was now a *broken home*— broken, indeed, as if Death himself had been there !

Lady Winifred was also alone.

The noonday sun was streaming as of old into the yellow damask drawing-room, and the sea-coal fire crackled on the hearth between the delft-lined jambs cheerily and brightly. Before it, on the thick cosy rug, a sleek tom-cat sat wink-ing and purring, and the favourite terrier of Quentin, coiled up round as a ball, was there too, but fast asleep beside the many-spotted Dal-matian dog, which always followed the old-fashioned family carriage.

The antique ormolu clock, that ticked so loudly on the mantelpiece on the night when Quentin was rescued from the wreck, and his father's corpse was cast on the surf-beaten sand, and when he, a wailing child, was brought by Elsie Irvine to Rohallion, was ticking there still, quietly, regularly, and monotonously, and Lady Winifred looked at its quaint dial wistfully, as she might have done in the face of an old and familiar friend.

Now Quentin and her beloved and only son were both far, far away; both were to encounter the perils of war, and she might never see them more! How much and how many things had happened, she thought, and still the old clock ticked there monotonously, even as it had done when, on an evening now many, many years ago, she came a blooming bride to the old castle by the sea; and so it might continue to tick, long

after she, and her comely and affectionate old
Lord, lay side by side among the Crawfords of
past centuries in the Rohallion aisle of the
venerable kirk whose tower she could see ter-
minating the woody vista of yonder lonely glen.

The paragraph of the morning had called up
a multitude of sad thoughts that had long been
buried, and she felt melancholy, almost miserable,
and opening her escritoire, she looked long and
earnestly on the relics of Quentin's father—his
commission in the French service, the letter
in the poor man's pocket-book, and the ring that
was taken from his finger, bearing the name of
Josephine—the boy's mother, doubtless.

The dominie, to whom the quartermaster lost
no time in hastening with the intelligence, like
the old Lord, was stout in his belief that Quentin
would, as he phrased it, " cast up again."

" Disappeared," he repeated two or three
times ; " the bairn no since heard o' ; the thing's
no possible !   He will, he shall return again, be
assured, to receive his reward, for he is worthy
of a crown of gold—worthy of it, yea, as ever
were Manlius Torquatus or Valerius Corvus, ilk
ane o' wham, as we are told in Livy, slew a Gaul
in single combat."

This classic reward did not seem very probable, when a few weeks after, a long official letter
was brought to Rohallion, and added greatly to
the anxiety and perplexity of the inmates thereof.

In this missive the military secretary, by
direction of H.R.H. the Duke of York, "presented his compliments to Major-General Lord
Rohallion, K.C.B., and regretted to acquaint him
that it was impossible to entertain his request
with regard to Mr. Quentin Kennedy, a volunteer with the 25th Foot, as matters had transpired
which might render his clearance before a general
court-martial necessary."

CHAPTER XIV.

THE WAYSIDE CROSS AND WELL.

" If in this exile dark and drear,
  To which my fate has doomed me now,
I should unnoticed die—what tear,
  What tear of sympathy will flow ?
  For I have sought an exile's woe,
And fashioned my own misery ;
Who then will pity me ?"
                    Cancionero de Amberes, 1557.

As Quentin walked on in solitude after Rowland
Askerne left him, he could not help musing, as
he frequently did, on the changes a short time
had wrought in him and in his ideas. It would
seem that from a mere day-dreaming schoolboy,
whose most onerous purposes were to fill his
basket with trout from the Girvan, the Doon, or
the Lollards' Linn ; to supply the cook with an
occasional brace of ptarmigan from the oakwood
shaw, or of blackcock from the Mains of Kilhenzie ; from trying a pad for Flora, or culling
the flowers which he knew she loved most, he
had risen to be a man and a soldier, valued by
his comrades, all officers of bravery and position,
trusted by his superiors, and charged with a great

and confidential duty—a portion of the vast game
of war and politics now played by Britain for
the deliverance of Spain; and yet, withal, he
longed for a companion, and to hear the voice of
a friend, for a sense of intense loneliness gradually stole over him as the twilight deepened,
and the purple shadows grew more sombre on
the hills of Portuguese Estremadura.

To Quentin it seemed that his bodily strength
and bulk had increased, for drill and marching
had developed every muscle to the fullest extent;
thus he was stronger, more active and hardy
than before.

He felt too, that the time had come when
youth was no longer a libel against him; the
time for doing something worthy of being
mentioned in a despatch of the commander-in-
chief, in the government gazette, in general
orders—something gallant, manly, and dashing;
and that he would turn the occasion to its best
account, and achieve something glorious, " or,"
as romances and melo-dramas have it, " perish
in the attempt."

" If I acquit myself well in this, my first
duty, it shall in itself prove a revenge upon
Cosmo!" thought he.

And so he trod manfully and hopefully on,
dreaming of the future, knowing but little of
the path he was at present to pursue, and less
of the perils and pit-falls that were around it.

As the evening deepened into night with great rapidity, for there is very little twilight in those regions—the mighty shadows of the sierra fell eastward in a sombre mass across the valley through which lay the road—a mere bridle path—towards the Spanish frontier, while the ranges of peaks that faced the west were still glowing in ruddy saffron or pale purple against the blue dome of the star-studded sky.

About twelve miles from Portalegre, the road pursued by Quentin enters a narrow gorge or immense chasm or cleft which rends the mountains from their summit to their base. Down the steep wall of rock on one side, a spring trickles for some hundred feet, and at the foot, near the road-way, it is received into the quaintly carved basin of an ancient stone fountain, behind which stands a memorial cross.

A niche in the shaft of the latter contains a little wayside altar. An image of the Madonna was rudely and gaudily painted in the recess, and before it a copper lamp was always kept burning. This shrine, once reputed to be of great sanctity, had been mutilated and its lamp destroyed by the French; but it had been re-placed by another, which was always supplied with wick and oil by the passing muleteers, contrabandistas, guerillas, and others.

The rays of this lamp were burning feebly in the vast rocky solitude, forming a strange and picturesque feature in the deep dark dell, the silence of which was broken only by the plash of the slender thread of liquid that filtered or trickled down the granite face of the dissevered mountain.

This cross and well had been built by Alphonso I., in the year that he achieved his greatest victory over the united arms of five Moorish sovereigns. It had been deemed holy even in those days, for there he had halted and prayed when on the march with his mail-clad knights to the capture of Santarem; and an inscription, frequently renewed, invited the passer to say a prayer for the repose of his soul, and the souls of all the good and true Portuguese who drew their swords against the Moslem.

A long ray of light shed by the rising moon, shone down the cleft at the bottom of which the road lay, casting the shadows of the well and votive cross far along the narrow gorge. The thick foliage of some gigantic Portuguese laurels, which grew in the interstices of the rocks, glittered like bronze gemmed with silver sheen, and offered a resting place for the night; so Quentin, as he felt weary, crept under the branches, which formed a pleasant shelter.

The turf below was soft and dry, and to him, who had slept so often on the bare earth during his march to the frontier, it seemed a comfortable couch enough. The shaft of King

Alphonso's cross on one side and the wall of rock on the other protected him from prowling wolves in the front and rear; the stems of the giant laurels formed barrier on a third side, and the fourth, which was open, he might defend with his weapons if attacked.

He took a draught from his canteen, which was filled with rum and water, and placing it under his head for a pillow, with his sword and loaded pistols ready by his side, he addressed himself to sleep.

The air was filled with a strange but delicious perfume, which came from those little aromatic shrubs that grow wild everywhere throughout Spain and Portugal. The intense stillness of the place, the only sounds there being the trickle of the far-falling water and the croakings of some bull-frogs among the long grass, made him wakeful for a time.

He felt neither alarm nor anxiety, but utterly lonely, and he said over a prayer that in infancy he had often repeated at Lady Rohallion's knee; then something holy and placid stole over his heart; sleep at last closed his eyes and he slumbered peacefully besides the old stone cross of our Lady of Battles.

So passed the first night of his absence from head-quarters.

When Quentin awoke next morning after a long and sound slumber, the result of youth,

high health, and the toil of the past day, though
he had acquired all a soldier's facility for sleeping
in strange places and strange beds, or without
other couch than the bare sod, he was at first
somewhat confused and puzzled on perceiving
the bower of leaves above him, and a minute
elapsed before he could remember where he was,
and how he came to be roosting under those
huge Portuguese laurels.

Then the despatch rushed upon his memory;
he searched his breast pocket, and found the
important document was safe; his weapons were
all right, and he was about to creep forth, when he
suddenly perceived the figure of a man near the
well, and, remembering the reiterated advices of
Askerne and others, he paused to observe him.

His first idea was that the stranger must be
a robber, for, to a Briton, Portuguese and
Spaniards too have usually that unpleasant
character in their aspect.   Their sallow visages,
deep dark eyes, densely black beards and moustaches, with their slouching sombrero, and large,
many-folded cloak of dark brown stuff, together
with a certain fixed scrutiny of expression when
observing strangers, give them all the bravo look
and bearing of the " sensation" ruffian or mysterious bandit of a minor melo-drama; thus, says a
recent writer, " in consequence of the difficulty
of outliving what has been learnt in the nursery,
many of our countrymen have, with the best in-

tentions, set down the bulk of the population of the Peninsula as one gang of robbers."

The Spaniard in question, for such he seemed to be, was a young man of powerful and athletic form ; his face was sallow and colourless, and his hair and eyes were black. He was closely shaven, save a heavy moustache, which had a very ferocious twist across each cheek towards the tip of the ear. His features were very handsome, and his whole appearance was eminently striking.

He had a huge cloak—what Spaniard has *not*, generally to cover his rags rather than his finery —but this he had flung aside, and Quentin could perceive that he had a well-worn zamarra of sheepskin over a gaily embroidered shirt, a pair of crimson pantaloons, which seemed to have belonged to a hussar, and they ended in strong leather *abarcas*, which were laced with thongs from the ankle to the knee. He had a dagger and pair of pistols in his flowing yellow sash, and close by him lay one of those long, old-fashioned travelling staffs, shod with iron and loaded with lead, called by the Portuguese a *cajado*.

Thus, upon the whole, considering the difference of their stature and bodily strength, Quentin prudently thought that the stranger was not a personage to be intruded upon without due consideration.

Reverently removing his black sombrero, which was rather battered and rusty, and had a gilt image of our Lady del Pilar on the gay broad scarlet band thereof, the Spaniard approached the wayside shrine, and kneeling before it, crossed himself three times with great devotion, while muttering a short prayer. Then seating himself on the grassy sward behind the well, he pulled a little book from the pocket of his zamarra, and began to peruse it very leisurely while smoking a cigarito and making his frugal breakfast on a few dry raisins and a crust of hard bread, which he dipped from time to time in the cool water of the gurgling fountain.

" This cannot be a bad kind of fellow," thought Quentin, who felt somewhat ashamed of lurking from one man; so he half-cocked his pistols, placed them in his girdle, and crept forth from behind the stone cross, saying :

" *Buenos dias*, senor."

" Senor, good morrow," replied the Spaniard, with a hand on his dagger, while he surveyed Quentin with a quietly grim, but unmoved countenance, without rising from his recumbent posture ; " are there any more of you under these bushes ?"

" No—I am alone."

" *Por mi vida*, but you chose a strange hiding-place !" said the other, with a glance of distrust.

" A strange sleeping-place, you should say

rather, senor—yet not a bad one," said Quentin, laughing, and willing to conciliate the stranger, who closed his book after quietly turning down a leaf to mark his place; " I crept in over night, and have slept there until now."

" Signs of a good digestion or a clear conscience."

" Of both, I hope, thank Heaven."

" I am indifferently provided with either; yet 1 can breakfast on this poor crust, and be thankful to God and our Blessed Lady for it."

" I can give you something better, Senor Portuguese," said Quentin, unbuttoning his havresack.

" *Muchos gracias*," replied the other; " but remember, senor, that I am a Castilian, and in Spain we have a belief that a bad Spaniard makes a tolerably good Portuguese."

" I beg pardon, senor, but your dress——"

" My dress !" interrupted the other, with a sardonic grin; " oh, *por el vida del Satanos*, the less you say about that the better. I was not wont to sport such a costume when rendering Virgil into Castilian, and Las Comedias de Calderon into Latin, in the Arzobispo College at old Salamanca."

" A student ?"

" Perhaps—it was as might be," replied the other, with sudden reserve; " and you are——"

" What you see me."

Quentin gave a portion of his ration-beef and biscuit to the Spaniard, who took them with many thanks, and with an air that showed he was a man of breeding far above what his present paisano costume seemed to indicate. His hands were strong, white, and muscular, yet seemed never to have been used to work, and a valuable diamond sparkled in a ring on one of his fingers. In the course of conversation, Quentin could gather that he was remarkably well informed of the strength, number, position, and divisions of the British Army, together with the probable movements towards Castile, thus he felt the necessity of acting with the greatest reserve, and getting rid of him as soon as possible; for the most subtle, wily, and dangerous Spaniards were those in the French interest, which, at first, he feared his new friend to be.

" By my life, Senor Inglese," said the Spaniard, laughing, " with all this victual in your wallet, 'tis a miracle of our Lady's Cross that the wolves did not come snuffing about you in the night."

" You are a traveller ?" observed Quentin, after a pause, during which they had been observing each other furtively.

" I hinted that I had been a student among Salamanquinos," replied the Spaniard, coldly.

" And you are now——"

" What the Fiend and the French have made

me!" said he, with a lurid gleam in his fine dark eyes.

"And that is——"

"My secret, senor," said the other, bluntly, adding "*muchos gracias*," as Quentin smilingly proffered his canteen, the contents of which he declined to taste. "The well of our Blessed Lady will suffice for me," he said, and proceeded to twist up another cigarito. "You are very curious about me, senor; but pray what are you?"

"What my uniform declares me," said Quentin, showing the scarlet uniform, which his grey coat had concealed; "a British soldier."

"*Bueno!* Your hand. And whither go you?"

"On duty."

"Where—to whom?"

"That is *my secret*," retorted Quentin, laughing. But a dark expression began to gather in the Spaniard's face, and he looked searchingly at the young volunteer.

"Are you going to the front?" he asked.

"Yes, senor."

"Strange!"

"How so?"

"The British troops have not yet begun to cross the frontier into Spain. They are still in quarters."

"Yes."

"You are not going to the French head-quarters?"

"No."

" Still monosyllables!" said the Spaniard, impetuously. " I must be plain, I find. You are a deserter!"

"I have said that I am going on duty," replied Quentin, haughtily. " You need question me no further. I am not bound to satisfy the curiosity of every wayfarer I may meet."

" *Morte de Dios!*" swore the Spaniard, with a scowl in his deep eye, and a hand on his stiletto.

" I, too, have arms to repress insolence," said Quentin, grasping his sword.

On this the Spaniard laughed, and said—

" Come—don't let us quarrel. You are a brave boy, and your little breakfast came to me most opportunely. Let us enjoy the present without thinking of the future. *Demonio!* Neither of us may be what we seem. We more often look like spits than swords in this world!"

" Senor, excuse me ; but I don't understand your proverb."

" It means simply, that all men are not what they seem. To you I appear a *gitano*, a *mendigo* —it may be, a *ladrone ;* you appear to me a deserter; so our circumstances may change—you prove the spit, and I the sword."

" Spit again!" said Quentin, angrily, as he conceived there was some sarcasm concealed in the word.

" It is a fable. Listen while I read to you what, I suppose, you never heard before."

And, opening his book, which proved to be the little pocket edition of the quaint old literary fables of Don Tomaso de Yriarte, he rapidly read over the story of the " Spit and Espada."

" Once upon a time there was a rapier of Toledo; a better was never seen in the Alcazar, or tempered in the waters of the Tagus. After having been in many battles, and belonging to many brave cavaliers, by one of the vicissitudes of fortune which lay the greatest low, it came at length to lie forgotten in the corner of a scurvy posada.

" There, desirous in vain to breathe a vein and flash once more in battle, it lay long unnoticed and covered with rust, till, by command of her master, a greasy kitchen-wench stuck it through a large capon, and thus forced that which had been a rapier of high renown, arming the hands of the noble and valiant, to degenerate into a mere spit!

" About this time, it likewise chanced that a clownish paisano, by the sport of fortune became a hidalgo at court, and as he must needs have a sword, he repaired to the booth of an espadero, who no sooner saw the kind of customer he had to deal with, than he knew that anything having a hilt and scabbard would do, and so desired him to call next day.

" Against the time of his coming he furbished up an old spit that lay in his kitchen, and sold

it to our courtier as Tisona, the very same blade
with which the Cid Rodrigo of Bivar made the
Arabian Khalifs skip at Cordova, and the Moorish
dogs at Jaen. Hence we see that the innkeeper
was a very great fool, and the espadero a very
great rogue."

"And what am I to understand by all this?"
asked Quentin, who with some impatience had
permitted the Spaniard to read thus far.

"Simply, senor, that though by the vicissitudes of fortune, I seem a spit at present, I may
prove in the end to be a good Toledo blade; for
we should never judge solely by appearances;"
and pointing to a hole in his sheepskin zamarra,
he laughed and added, "Farewell—I go towards
the mountains."

"And I towards Spain: I have but two
wishes—to reach Herreruela, and to avoid the
French in Valencia."

"Truly, they are well and wisely avoided,"
said the Spaniard through his clenched teeth,
while his face became distorted and convulsed by
concentrated hate and passion. "Save myself
and another, my whole family have perished
under their hands. Not even our aged mother
was spared, for she died like my helpless old
father by their bayonets, on the night that
Junot entered Salamanca; and well would it
have been if some of the young had suffered the
same fate *first*. I had three sisters, senor—three

lovelier girls, or three more loving, good, and
gentle, God's blessed sun never shone on. Two
suffered such wrongs on that night of horrors at
Salamanca, that they could not or would not
survive them; the youngest, Isidora, happily
escaped by being in the convent of Santa Engracia,
at Portalegre."

Impressed by the undoubted earnestness of
the Spaniard, Quentin said—

" I am bound to the frontier, bearer of a
secret despatch."

" To whom?"

" Honour ties my tongue for the present,
senor."

" Enough, then; continue to pursue this road
for some miles, you will find a branch to the
left where it runs parallel with the river Figuero,
and leads to Castello de Vide. Proceed straight
on and you will come to Marvao; six miles
further on is Valencia de Alcantara, garrisoned
by the French; cross the river Sever, and a
league or so further brings you to Herrerucla.
Ere long I, too, shall be there, so we may meet
again; but remember that the whole country
swarms with the accursed French, and that
your red coat will ensure your captivity or
death."

" I shall be wary."

" Be so, or, Santos! I would not give a *claco*
for your life! Do you see yonder hill?" asked

the Spaniard, pointing to a lofty peak—the highest of the mountain range.

" Yes—a vapour hovers near it."

" I am going there to see what news the eagles have for the loyal Portuguese."

" The eagles !"

" Exactly—but I forget that you are a stranger and don't understand me," replied the other, laughing.

" Adios, senor," said Quentin, preparing to start.

" Adios, senor soldado—adios, vaya !"

The Spaniard pocketed his book of fables, threw his mantle over his left shoulder, grasped his cajado, and waving his hat, proceeded to ascend with great activity a steep zigzag path up the mountain side, while Quentin Kennedy pursued his solitary way, which opened into a level district covered with green orange, lemon, and olive groves ; and though the warnings of his late acquaintance did not fail to impress him with anxiety, he felt hopeful that he would achieve in safety and with honour the duty assigned him—escaping the perils that might be set him, and the deadly snare into which Cosmo hoped he might fall.

CHAPTER XV.

THE MULETEERS.

" Riper occasions will thy valour claim,
    Danger comes on ; Typhœus-like it comes,
    Whose fabled stature every hour increased."
            AQUILEIA—*Old Tragedy.*

WHILE Quentin travelled onward, thinking over his recent meeting at the well, and puzzling himself about the enigma that was probably concealed by the words of the stranger concerning the eagles having news for Portugal, he was roused from his reverie by the jangling of bells, and ere long a string of mules, all sleek, well-fed, of dapple-colour, and in size larger than any he had ever seen, appeared in view, descending with sure and steady steps a narrow rocky path between the olive and orange groves that covered the steep mountain side.

He paused for a moment to permit the string or line, which consisted of twelve mules, to pass along the road in front ; but the three muleteers in charge, all hardy and sturdy fellows in gaudily braided and embroidered jackets of purple or olive green cloth, smart sombreros, and gay scarfs, accoutred with ivory-hafted knives and brass-butted pistols, hailed him immediately, asked whither he was going, and courteously, with cries of " Viva los Inglesos! viva el Rey!" offered him a draught of wine from the leathern bota that hung at the neck of Madrina, and in a trice he found himself accompanying them on their way.

Perceiving that he belonged to the British army, they were very inquisitive to know what he was doing there alone; but Quentin had heard that some of those muleteers could make their way from the heart of Castile (then swarming with French troops) to the cantonments of the British army, along the Portuguese frontier, evading all infantry outposts and cavalry patrols by their superior knowledge of the country and its secret paths. He had heard also that they frequently acted as spies and traitors on both sides; thus he deemed extreme reserve necessary, and, with a prudence beyond his years and experience, parried their inquiries, and turned the conversation to general subjects, chiefly the various merits of their mules, which were laden with Indian corn, Oporto wine, pulse, flour, and tobacco; and he failed not, in particular, to extol the beauty of Madrina, a stately old mare, nearly sixteen hands in height, which had round her neck and on her gaudy red and yellow worsted head-gear a row of larger bells than the rest of the train.

The clear sound of those bells being known to

them all, they followed her with wonderful instinct, docility, and affection.

So far as he could gather from the conversation, these muleteers were of Old Castile, the principal arriero being Ramon Campillo from Miranda del Ebro; he was a short, thick-set fellow, with a pleasant and sun-burned face, and a beard and head of hair so black and dense that made Quentin think the process of sheep-shearing might, in his instance, have been resorted to with ease and comfort. This shaggy mop he had gathered into a red silk hair-net, over which he wore his hat of coarse brown velvet, adorned by a band and bob of scarlet plush.

These three men carolled and sung as they proceeded along, cracking their whips, indulging in scraps of old warlike ballads, of love-songs and seguidillas, pausing now and then to mutter an *Ave* on passing a cross or a cairn that had some dark story of bloodshed and crime. And many a boast they made of their sunny Castile which France should *never*, NEVER conquer! and many a story they told of the Cid Rodrigo, of our Lady of Zaragosa, the Holy Virgin del Pilar, of miracles and robbers, all pell-mell; but their chief themes were the recent exploits of their guerilla chiefs, then rising into power; of Don Julian Sanchez with the hare lip, and his glorious Castilian lancers; of El Pastor, the shepherd; El Medico, the doctor; El Manco, the cripple; of Don Juan

Martin, the Empecinado, who, when his whole
family had been murdered by the French, after
the ladies of his house had endured horrors worse
than death, in the first outburst of his grief,
smeared himself with pitch, and vowed never to
sheath his sword while a Frenchman remained
alive in Spain; and who, when the French nailed
a number of patriots to the oaks of the Guada-
rama, nailed up thrice that number of French
soldiers in their place, to fill the forest with their
dying groans. With enthusiasm they extolled
all those wild spirits whom the war of invasion
and independence had brought forth, calling it a
Guerra de moros contra estos infideles !

But their local hero of heroes seemed to be
Don Baltasar de Saldos, whom they described as
partly a Cid and partly a devil in his hatred of
France and Frenchmen. The mention of his
name proved of deep interest to Quentin, and
finding him a ready and wondering listener, many
were the stories they told of him and of his band,
which was composed of Spanish deserters, runaway students, ruined nobles, unfrocked friars,
and all manner of wild fellows who loved him
with ardour and obeyed him with devotion.

He was the flower of Castilian guerilla chiefs !

"I have seen and heard enough of French
atrocity in our peregrinations throughout the
kingdoms of Andalusia, Castile, Leon, and Arragon, to make me imbibe somewhat of the same

spirit of vengeance that inspires Baltasar de Saldos—aye, senor, to the full!" said Ramon, in his energy, spitting away the end of his cigarito, and crushing it under his heel.

"In your line one must see much of life," said Quentin.

"Much—maladita! I should think so. I was present in Madrid on the 23rd of last April, when one hundred and twenty defenceless citizens were slaughtered in cold blood by the troops of Murat—shot down by platoons, and for what? Por el Santos de los Santos! only because the epaulettes of his aide-de-camp, the gay Colonel de la Grange, were splashed with mud by some rash students at the gate of Alcala."

"A slight cause, surely."

"But that night, hombre, we had a terrible retribution," said the second muleteer, through his clenched teeth, as he gave a fierce twist to the scarlet silk handkerchief which encircled his head, and the fringed ends of which came from under his sombrero and floated over his shoulders.

"Retribution, Ignacio Noain, I think we had, amigo mio!" replied Ramon, with a bitter laugh; "for it was on that night Baltasar threw off his student's gown and betook him to knife and musket, and rushed through the streets, shouting 'Guerra al cuchillo, Salamanquinos!' and 'Viva el Rey de Espana!' before the head-quarters of Marshal Murat; and sure vengeance he took, for

ere morning the gutters of the Prado were gorged
with the blood of more than seven hundred
Frenchmen, who fell by the muskets and daggers
of the loyal Castilians."

"Then," said the third muleteer, with a
smiling face and in an encomiastic tone, "it was
Baltasar who slew Don Miguel de Saavedra."

"To the devil with him!"

"The traitorous governor of Valencia," added
the other two.

"And it was he," said Ramon, "who with his
namesake, the Padre Baltasar Calvo, for twelve
days and nights followed the fugitive French and
Valencian traitors, the tools and followers of
Godoy, through the streets, knife in hand, slaying
them in cellars, vaults, and bodegas, till the last
who was false to Spain had breathed out his
dog's life, and his heart, reeking on a bayonet,
was thrown on the altar of St. Isidor."

The fiery energy of the speakers, the expression
of their dark flashing eyes, their picturesque
costumes, and the modulation of the grand old
language in which they spoke, made those fierce
and barbarous recitals doubly striking to Quentin
Kennedy, who heard them with something bordering on astonishment, for the English press
had no "own correspondents" *then*, to let the
people at home know what was enacted abroad.

"Then, senor," said Ignacio Noain, "it was
Baltasar de Saldos who suggested the singular

death to which the Spanish regiment of Navarre put the timid Italian, Filangheri."

"And this mode of death?" asked Quentin, whom, sooth to say, the grim energy and sud· denly · developed ferocity of the hitherto jolly muleteers somewhat scared.

"I shall tell you," said Ramon, "for I saw it. You must know, senor soldado, that this Italian was Governor of Corunna and a loyal cavalier to the King; but, terrified or hopeless by the over- whelming power of Bonaparte, he showed some signs of wavering, and refused to issue a pro- clamation of war against the French."

"Might it not have been wisdom to temporize for a time?"

"Santos! this is no time for trifling; so Baltasar rushed among the soldiers of our regi- ment of Navarre, and incited them to seize the governor at Villa Franca-del-Vierzo, a town on the road which leads from Corunna to Madrid, where they dragged him, almost naked, from the Marquis's palace.

"'Muera al Filangheri!' shouted Baltasar to the soldiers; 'unfix your bayonets, plant the ground with them, and toss the traitor in a blanket!'

"With shouts of acclamation at a suggestion so novel, they hastened to do as he suggested. The ground was soon planted thickly with three hundred bayonets, their sockets fixed in the earth, their sharp points upward. The breath-

less governor, pale and imploring mercy, was
tossed thrice into the air from a blanket, as dogs
are tossed on Shrove Tuesday. After the third
toss, the blanket was withdrawn, and the hapless
Filangheri fell crash on the bayonets. He was
impaled in every part of his body at once; after
this, leaving him miserably to die, the soldiers
dispersed to join Baltasar's band of guerillas in
the mountains of Herrcruela; but this destruction
of a king's officer caused Sir John Moore to
deem him false to Ferdinand VII."

"How horrible is all this!" exclaimed Quentin.

"Desperate times and men, require desperate
hearts and stern measures," said the muleteer
Ramon, as he slung his long musket—which no
doubt had a goodly charge of slugs in its barrel—
and took a guitar which hung at the collar of one
of his mules. "But we must not scare you, senor
Inglese, as we shall surely do, if we talk longer
thus; so now for something more cheerful:" and
he began at once to sing, with a very mellow voice,
a little romance, in which his companions joined
with much laughter, and which began thus,—

> "Tiempo es el Caballero,
> The world will all divine;
> Now my girdle is too narrow,
> They'll see my shame—and thine!

> "Tiempo es el Caballero—
> When the maids my garments bring,
> I see them wink and nod their heads,
> I hear them tittering."*

> * Poetry of Spain.

" We have come from Arronches and are going to Castello Branco, in Lower Beira, along the Portuguese frontier," said Ramon, " and yonder is the puebla at which we are to halt," he added, pointing to a few ruined walls that bordered the highway.

" What walled town is that on the hill, with an old castle?" asked Quentin.

" About two leagues beyond?"

" Yes."

" That is Castello de Vide, famous for its cloth factory."

" Castello de Vide—good Heavens, senores arrieros, your pleasant society has lured me out of my proper way."

" I am sorry to hear it," said Ramon, drily.

" I should have gone to the right."

" Madre de Dios!"

" To the right?"

" Towards the French lines?"

Such were the exclamations of the muleteers as their frowns deepened.

" I should have gone somewhat in that direction, at all events," said Quentin, reddening with the annoyance and confusion natural to an honourable person when viewed with mistrust.

" Senor Inglese, in what capacity, or for what purpose are you travelling on foot alone, and in this suspicious fashion, towards the outposts of General de Ribeaupierre, the commander in

Valencia?" asked the muleteer Ramon, sternly, as he drew himself up, and proceeded very deliberately to examine the flint and priming of his long musket.

"By what right do you ask?" demanded Quentin, whose heart beat tumultuously at the prospect of being butchered far from help or justice.

"Take your hand from your pistol—dare you question us, senor—one to three?"

"Yes, I do—by what right do you molest me?"

"The right of loyal and true Castilians," replied the three muleteers, with one voice, as the other two, who had not yet spoken, unslung their bell-mouthed trabucos or blunderbusses, and all their faces assumed that very formidable scowl, which appears nowhere so grimly as in the dark and sallow visages of those sons of old Iberia.

Now ensued a brief, but somewhat unpleasant and exciting pause; and finding that matters had come to this dangerous pass with him, Quentin, on reflection, drew forth his sealed missive, and showing the address to Ramon, said:

"I am the bearer of this despatch from Lieutenant-General Sir John Hope, to Don Baltasar de Saldos, the guerilla chief, and if you are loyal Spaniards, as you say, you will put up those weapons, and direct me by the nearest and safest route to the hills near Herreruela."

"Oh, par todos Santos, but this alters the case entirely!" said Ramon, as they relinquished their weapons, wreathed their grim fronts with sudden smiles, and cordially shook hands with him.

"Why did you not tell us all this at first?" asked the muleteer Ignacio Noain.

"Well, even Madrina, I suppose, does not like to be sharply taken by the bridle," said Quentin, smiling, and feeling considerably relieved in his mind.

"No more does she, the old beauty, she would lash out at her own madre. You have somewhat overshot the way, senor, for a mile or two along the Figuero; however, you shall not leave us yet awhile. Dine with us at the old puebla—the French have not left many stones of it together. Ay de mi! it was a jovial place once; many a bolero and fandango I have danced with the girls here, and where are they all now? We have only bacallao (dried ling) and biscuits, with a mouthful of good wine—real vino de Alicant—to offer you."

"Thanks, senores, but evening is almost at hand."

"It will be nightfall when you reach the base of yonder mountain," said Ramon, pointing to a lofty hill, whose granite brows were all empurpled by the sunshine; "there Gil Llano, a poor vinedresser, lives—a Portuguese, who for my sake, if not for your own, will gladly give you shelter ; be sure, however, to show him this."

With these words, Ramon disengaged from one of the four dozen of brass bell buttons, with which his jacket was adorned, one of the many consecrated copper medals that hung thereat, and placed it in Quentin's hand, just as they entered the ill-fated puebla (village), which was totally roofless and ruined. Fragments of charred furniture, broken crocks, cans, and plates strewed the now untrodden street, where the grass was springing. The broad-leaved vines grew wild about the crumbling walls and open windows ; and a rude cross here and there marked the hastily made graves of the slaughtered villagers.

There, as elsewhere, the wings of the Imperial Eagle, like those of a destroying angel, had spread desolation and death !

" When," asked the poor Portuguese, in one of their manifestoes after the horrors of Coimbra, " did the laws of man authorize the outrage of women, the slaughter of aged and other defenceless inhabitants of places which made no resistance ; the assassination of men who were accounted rich, only because they could not furnish that quantity of treasure of which it was said they were possessed !"

Halting by the old village well, the muleteers attended first to the wants of Madrina and her sleek companions.

" *Arre, arre,* old woman," said Ramon, " thou shalt have a deep cool draught at last ; *arre, arre !* "

This is an old Moorish term (literally gee-up), whence the muleteers are familiarly termed *arrieros.* They then shared with Quentin their dried fish and hard biscuits, with a few olives and luscious oranges, that had become golden among the groves that cast their shadows on the Ebro; and they frequently patted him on the shoulder, and expressed regret for their suspicions, and the mischief these might have led to.

The group around this lonely well, which bubbled through a grotesque stone face, under an old Roman arch, and the scene around, were wonderfully striking and picturesque.

In the immediate foreground were the swarthy Castilian muleteers in their gaudy dress, and their gaily trapped mules, all resting on the bright green sward; close by was the ruined puebla; northward rose Castello de Vide in the distance on its verdant hill, the round towers of its ancient fortress and ruined walls, that had more than once withstood the tide of Moorish and Castilian chivalry; to the east and south rose the great sierras that form the boundary between Spain and Portugal, all crimsoned with the light of the gorgeous sun that was setting in gold and saffron behind the cork tree groves that clothe the hills of St. Mames.

The frugal repast was barely over when the tinkle of a clear and silvery bell that rung in some solitary hermitage, concealed afar off among the chestnut woods in some hollow of the mountains, came at intervals on the evening wind.

"Vespers," said Ramon Campillo, taking off his sombrero; "amigos mios, to prayers."

Then, with a simple devotion that impressed him deeply, Quentin Kennedy saw those sturdy and jovial, but rather reckless fellows, who, but a few minutes before, were (we are compelled to admit it) quite disposed to knock him on the head, kneel down and pray very earnestly for a minute or so.

A few minutes more saw them on their way to Castello de Vide, and him progressing towards the mountains. They waved their hats to him repeatedly, and then as the twilight deepened, the breeze of the valley as it swept over the odorous orange groves brought pleasantly to his ear the jingle of the mule-bells, and the tinkle of Ramon's guitar dying away in the distance, with a verse of the song the three arrieros sung—an old Valencian evening hymn.

> " Thou who all our sins didst bear,
> All our sorrows suffering there,
>   *O Agnus Dei !*
> Lead us where thy promise led
> That poor dying thief who said,
>   *Memento mei !* "

CHAPTER XVI.

GIL LLANO.

" Still, however fate may thwart me,
Unconvinced, unchanged I live;
From those dreams I cannot part me,
That such dear delusions give;
Hoping yet in countless years,
One bright day unstained with tears."
RODRIGUEZ LOBO.

THE outrages of the French invaders in Spain and Portugal were doubtless of the worst description; but those reprisals which the patriots were not slow in making were equal in atrocity. The stories he had heard of these shook Quentin's confidence in his own safety, and in his powers mental and physical; they caused him to regard with something of suspicion, repugnance, and mistrust the dwellers in the land, and to wish himself well out of it, or at least safe once more under the colours of the Old Borderers.

He remembered the intense bitterness, the momentary but clamorous anxiety caused by his late episode, and how keenly the foretasted agony of death entered his soul, when the three muleteers threatened him with their weapons, and when

N 2

there seemed every prospect of his falling by their hand in that mountain solitude, and being left there dead to the wolves; his fate and story alike unknown to all who might feel the slightest interest therein. He remembered all this, we say, and he had no desire to endure such an agony again.

He felt his isolation, his helplessness in many respects, and longed anxiously for the end of his task, and for the society of his comrades and friends, of Askerne, Middleton, and others by whom he was esteemed and trusted.

This very anxiety made him quicken his pace, and thus about an hour after parting from the muleteers at the puebla, he saw a light twinkling on the roadway at the base of the dark green mountain; then, after passing under some half-ruined trellis where the vines were carefully trained and made a leafy tunnel, he reached the dwelling of Gil Llano (pronounced Yano) the vine-dresser, a wayside cottage, with a few smaller adjuncts where the galinas roosted and the porkers snorted.

He knocked at the door, which was slowly opened after some delay, and after he had been reconnoitred by a pair of keen black eyes through an eyelet hole; then the proprietor, a swarthy and stout little Portuguese, black bearded and snub-nosed, appeared with a bare knife clenched between his teeth and a cocked musket in his hands, to demand who was there.

" *Quien es ?*" he asked, angrily.

" *Gente de paez,*" replied Quentin, in a conciliating tone.

" *Pho !* indeed—your dress doesn't say you are a man of peace."

" I am a British soldier travelling on duty," said Quentin.

" How can I assist you, senor?"

" The muleteer, Ramon Campillo, of Miranda del Ebro, who is now on his way to Castello Branco, informed me that you are a loyal Portuguese——"

" None more loyal !" responded the other, slapping the butt of his musket.

" I was to show you this medal, and, if not intruding, remain with you for the night."

" Ramon is my good friend," said the Portuguese, carefully looking at the brass medal, which bore the image of St. Elizabeth, " and this was my gift to him. You are welcome, senor, to such poor accommodation as the French have left me to offer."

The Portuguese conducted Quentin into his cottage, the interior of which, by its squalor and poverty, showed that poor Gil Llano's circumstances had not been improved by the influences of the war.

A candle, in a clay-holder, flickered on the bare table, an iron brasero, full of charcoal and dry leaves, smouldered on the hearth; above the

mantelpiece were a little stucco Madonna and
some gaudy little Lisbon prints of holy person-
ages, such as St. Anthony of Portugal, with his
beloved pig; St. Elizabeth the queen, who died
at Estremoz in 1336; St. Ignatius Loyola, and
others in scarlet and blue drapery, with golden
halos, all pasted on the whitewashed wall.

The cottage appeared to consist of three or
four small apartments, all roofed with large red
tiles, through the holes in which Quentin could
see the stars shining, and suggesting an idea of
umbrellas in case of rain. The rafters were
thickly hung with bunches of dried raisins, by the
sale of which to the passing muleteers and contrabandistas, Gil and his family subsisted. But
even this humble place bore traces of the retreat-
ing French. One of the little windows had been
dashed to pieces by a musket-butt, and most of
the woodwork had gone for fuel when Junot's
voltigeurs bivouacked among the vine trellis,
half of which they tore down and destroyed.

Poor Gil Llano, whose whole attire consisted
of a zamarra, a pair of red cotton breeches, a
yellow sash, and the net which confined his hair.
made Quentin Kennedy heartily welcome, and
spoke with enthusiasm and gratitude of the
British, who had swept Portugal of the French;
and he exulted about the recent battle of Vimiera,
which he had witnessed from the Torres Vedras,
where, he frankly admitted, he had hovered

among the cork-trees, and, with his musket, had "potted" successfully some of Ribeaupierre's dragoons as they fell back in disorder before the furious advance of General Anstruther's column.

Quentin soon felt himself at home, and shared with Llano's family the supper of ham and eggs, cooked in a crock between the brasero and one of the stones of Antas, which are supposed, when once heated, to continue so for two days. He might have excused the flavour of garlic, but found an Abrantes melon sliced with sugar, and a flask of Oporto wine, very acceptable.

The half-clad mother and her meagre, dark-skinned brood, with their large black eyes, he could perceive regarded him as a heretic and soldier, doubtfully, even fearfully, and askance— an English heretic being always associated, in the minds of Peninsula people, with priestly denunciations and the *autos de fé* of the Holy Office in its palmy days. However, after a time, as he manifested no desire to eat any of the children, but bestowed upon them all he could afford—a handful of half-vintins, part of the poor quarter-master's parting gift—confidence became established, and little bare-legged Pedrillo crept close to his knee ; Babieta peeped slily at him from behind her mother's skirts, and, when he hung Ramon's brass medal round the tawny neck of Gil, the nursling, the goodwoman Llano's heart opened to him at once.

Perceiving that Quentin was so young, she asked, while her dark eyes filled with a tender expression, if his mother sorrowed for him, and if she had many other sons, that she could spare him; adding that, after all she had seen of war, she would rather die than permit either of her boys to become soldiers, even to fight for Portugal.

"Ere long Portugal shall have stronger hands than we could furnish to fight for her," said Gil, confidently. "No miracle the blessed saints of heaven have ever worked has been half so wonderful as these marvellous and prophetic eggs that have been found by Don Julian Sanchez, by El Pastor, the Alcalde of Portalegre and others, in the nests among the mountains. True it is, senor," he continued, on perceiving Quentin's glance of inquiry and surprise, "that eggs have been found laid in the mountains by the birds of the air—eggs bearing inscriptions which foretell that as Portugal has been deserted at her utmost need by the House of Braganza, our brave old king, Don Sebastian, of pious and glorious memory, will come to protect and rule over us again."

"Don Sebastian," said Quentin, who had heard this farrago of words with some wonder; "how long is it ago since he was king?"

Gil reckoned on his brown fingers, and then said—

"About two hundred and thirty years."

"How—what?" exclaimed Quentin, thinking that he had not heard aright.

"Exactly, senor; he was taken—some say killed—in battle by the Moorish dogs at the battle of Alcazal-quiver, on the coast of Fez, in 1578; but his restoration to us is certain now."

"And *eggs*, do you say, have prophesied this?"

"By the soul of St. Anthony of Lisbon, yes! The miraculous legends written on their shells told us so. I saw one with my own eyes as it lay on the altar of the Estrella convent, where it had been brought by the Marquis d'Almeida, who found it on the mountain of Cintra."

"And you read the legend?"

"No, senor—I cannot read; moreover, it was written in old Latin."

"By whom, Senor Gil?"

"God and St. Anthony only know," replied Gil, crossing himself after dipping his fingers in a little clay font of *agua-bendita* that hung beside the mantelpiece.

Now Quentin remembered the words of the stranger whom he had met by the wayside cross, and whom he had last seen toiling up the mountain with the aid of his staff, as he alleged, in search of eagles' nests. He had some trouble to preserve his gravity, and probably nothing enabled him to do so but his wonder at the perfect simplicity and the good faith of this Por-

tuguese peasant in the return of Lusitania's long-
lost hero.

On inquiring further, he learned, for the first
time, that there still existed in Portugal the sect
called of old " Sebastianists," fondly cherishing a
belief that their crusader king (who fell in battle
against Muley Moloc) was detained in an enchanted island, where he was supernaturally pre-
served; and that they also cherished a belief that
he would reappear with all his paladins to
deliver Lusitania when at her utmost need!

Portugal's utmost need had come and gone;
Roleia and Vimiera had been fought and won by
Sir Arthur Wellesley; but still the Sebastianists
believed in the ultimate return and intervention
of their favourite hero, and eggs marked by the
more cunning with some chemical agency, bearing
legends foretelling the event, were opportunely
found and exhibited: a puerile trick, which
Marshal Junot, General de Ribeaupierre, and
others soon contrived to turn against the inven-
tors; for *other* eggs bearing mottoes of very
different import were frequently found in the
same places.

A belief similar to that of the Sebastianists
long lingered among the Scots relative to their
beloved James IV., who fell at Flodden; among
the Germans, regarding Frederick Barbarossa,
who filled all Asia with the terror of his name,
and died on the banks of the Cydnus; among

the Britons concerning their fabulous Arthur of the Round Table; and among the ancient Irish concerning some now unknown warrior named Dharra Dheeling. But it was left for the poor Portuguese to be among the last to console themselves under defeat and disaster with such delusive hopes; and thus in the year of Vimiera, " many people," says General Napier, " and those not of the most uneducated classes, were often observed upon the highest points of the hills, casting earnest looks towards the ocean, in the hopes of descrying the enchanted island in which their long-lost hero was detained."

CHAPTER XVII.

DANGER IN THE PATH.

" Beloved of glory, Spain ! hail, holy ground !
All hail ! thou chosen scene of deeds renown'd,
By warriors wrought in each progressive age,
Who struggled to repel th' oppressor's rage.
Tell thou the world how on thy favoured coast,
Our Wellesley fought, and Gaul her sceptre lost."
Roncevalles—a Poem.

PROCEEDING eastward next morning, Quentin
was guided by Gil Llano for some miles towards
the Spanish frontier. To avoid all chance of
being seen by cavalry or foraging parties, the
officers commanding which were sometimes
really ignorant rather than oblivious of the
actual line of demarcation between Spain and
Portugal, the worthy vinedresser conducted him
by unfrequented but steep and devious mountain
paths, which left far on their right flank the little
town and fortress of Marvao, that lies in the
Comarca of Portalegre, and as they were now
within six miles of Valencia de Alcantara, which
was the head-quarters of Ribeaupierre's cavalry
brigade, the utmost circumspection was necessary.

The morning was one of singular loveliness ;

the white mists were rolling up the green mountain sides from the greener valleys below, and
there was a peculiar freshness and fragrance in
the atmosphere which made Quentin feel buoyant and happy, for a time at least; the sun was
high in heaven, the dew was glittering on every
herb and tree, and the mountain scenery looked
bright and glorious.

The blood of our soldiers who fell at Rolcia
and Vimiera had not been shed in vain for
Portugal. Already signs of peace were visible
in her valleys and towns, and all was in repose
along her frontier. Thus Quentin could hear
the lowing of oxen and the bleating of sheep
come pleasantly on the morning wind that passed
over the green sierra, bearing with it the odour
of the orange groves in the valley and of the
flowering arbutus that bordered the way.

In a hollow of the hills, Llano showed Quentin
a lake, on the borders of which some of the
miraculous eggs had been found by Baltasar de
Saldos in a cypress grove; and he alleged that
its waters had the power of swallowing or
sucking into the bowels of the earth whatever was thrown therein, consequently not a
leaf, or reed, or lotus were to be seen floating
there.

"But its power, senor, is a mere joke when
compared with that of the lake of Cedima, which
lies about eight leagues from Coimbra, and which

instantly swallows up the largest logs and trees, if cast therein."

"Is there a whirlpool in the centre?" asked Quentin.

"Saints and angels only know what is in the centre; but in my father's days—he was a farmer, senor, in the Quinta das Lagrimas—there came a Danish cavalier who refused to credit the story, and offered, mockingly, to cross the lake on horseback, in presence of the Juiz-de-fora, the Reformator of the University, the Alcalde of the city, and all the great lords of Coimbra.

"After hearing the bishop (who is always Conde de Arganuil) say mass in the church of Santa Cruz, and after partaking of the Holy Communion before the altar there, he mounted his horse, and, in presence of a vast multitude, proceeded to the lake of Cedima. Then when he saw its black and ominous water that lay without a ripple in the sunshine, his heart somewhat failed him, and lest the story of the lake might be true, and lest his life might indeed be lost, on perceiving a great stake, or the trunk of an old chestnut tree near the edge, he tied a thick rope to it, securing the other end to his right leg. Another rope of similar strength he tied to the neck of his horse, a fine Spanish gennet, and giving him the spur, he uttered a shout and plunged headlong into the water.

"A little way the horse swam snorting, and then began to sink; ere long his ears alone were visible! Then they too disappeared; the water bubbled above his nostrils as his head went down; then the dark water flowed over the rider's shoulders—then over his head, and while a cry of dismay rose from the terrified people, the steed and the stranger vanished together and were seen no more."

"So the ropes proved of no service?" said Quentin.

"The one that was about the neck of the horse was snapped right through the centre; but at the end of the other was found the right leg of the unfortunate Dane, torn off by the thigh, doubtless as the downward current whirled him into the vortex; and so from that day a belief in the waters of Cedima has been stronger than ever in Portugal."

"After the marvellous eggs and the enchanted island, I can easily think so," said Quentin.

When worthy Gil Llano (who expressed a hope to see him again if he returned that way) had left him, with the information that from the top of the next hill he would see Spain and the spires of Valencia de Alcantara, Quentin proceeded all the more rapidly that he was now alone, and his steps kept pace with the busy current of his thoughts.

His whole ideas of the duty on which he

had been sent were somewhat vague. He had but three instructions given him : first, to avoid Valencia (which the reader must not confound with the capital of the kingdom of the same name) ; second, to reach Hereruela how he best could ; third, to deliver his despatch ; and for the execution of this he had been sent from Portalegre unsupplied either with money or credentials to any Alcalde, Juiz-de-fora, or other civil or military authority, in case of any difficulty arising.

There were times—and this was one—when Quentin felt as if he were again at Rohallion—at his home, for such he felt it to be—relating all these adventures to those who were now there ; to the kind and soldier-like old Lord ; to the courteous and gentle Lady Winifred ; to the old quartermaster, with his kind red face and yellow wig, while Mr. Spillsby the butler and Jack Andrews loitered near to listen ; to the dominie, with his rusty blacks, his square shoe-buckles, and his musty memories of the classics ; and more than all, to Flora Warrender !

And then, with these thoughts, there seemed to come to his ears the pleasant rustle of the aged sycamores as the west wind shook their branches, the cawing of the black rooks on the old grey keep, the rush of the Lollards' Linn pouring under its arch and over its ledge of rock ; and to his fancy's eye the sierras of Portugal gave place to the brown hills of

Carrick, the distant Craigs of Kyle, and "the bonnie blooming heather," or the waves of the Clyde as they boiled in foam over the Partan Craig and climbed the dark headland of Rohallion.

So the past returned and the present fled!

Amid those cherished scenes he had long since left his happy boyhood. Now he felt himself, as we have said, every inch a soldier and a man, inspired by a sense of duty, of trust, and not a little by the love of adventure natural to youth. The inborn ambition which the solid weight of his knapsack and accoutrements, and all his sufferings when on the march from Maciera Bay, had somewhat chilled; the high spirit that Cosmo's hatred and cutting coldness had striven to crush, both sprung up anew in his buoyant heart, and he felt it glowing with hope, energy, and enthusiasm; and now, when he had reached the summit of the mountain over which the road passed, and on issuing from a narrow rocky defile, saw a vast extent of open country beyond, a glorious and fertile landscape, all vibrating apparently in the rays of the cloudless sun, he waved his cap and almost cried "hurrah!" for he knew that he looked down on——Spain!

Before him, as on a map, he saw the vast extent of Spanish Estremadura stretching into distance far away, all steeped in a lovely golden glow, the almost universal verdure of the land-

scape relieved here and there by the water of
the Salor and other minor tributaries of the
Tagus, winding like blue silk threads through
velvet of emerald green, dotted by thickets of
chestnut, orange, and cork trees; and there, too,
were the strong embattled towers and the spires
of Valencia de Alcantara, with the tricolour on
its greatest bastion; and in the distance, half
hid in saffron haze, through which they loomed
in purple tint, the ramparts of Albuquerque, on
its steep hill, the heritage of the Condes de
Ledesma.   Between these cities lay a little
puebla, which he knew must be San Vincente,
near, but not through which, lay his path
to the hills that overlooked the plain.

Thoughts of the poetry, of the beauty, and
romance of Spain came thronging on his memory, and we must confess they formed an odd
chaos of cloaked cavaliers with guitars and
rapiers; dark eyed donnas in balconies, fluttering
fans and veils; lurking rivals, with mask and
dagger; mountain robbers in high-crowned hats,
with their legs swathed in red bandages, after
the orthodox fashion of all melodramatic banditti.
These, together with the solid splendour and
wonderful stories of the Alhambra, the wars of
the high-spirited Moors of Granada, ending so
sadly in *el suspiro del Moro*, when the warriors
of Ferdinand and Isabella rent the banner of the
Prophet from the weak hand of Boabdil el Chico,

not unnaturally made up his stock ideas of the sunny land he looked upon.

But it was the land of the Cid Campeador— he at whose name the eyes of even the most unlettered Spaniard will lighten—for he was the veritable and redoubtable Wallace of Castile against the enemies of Christianity and the Christian's God. Such memories as these rushed on Quentin's mind as he looked down on Estremadura; nor could he forget, though last not least, that it was the native land of him " who laughed Spain's chivalry away"—the illustrious Cervantes, the one-handed soldier of Lepanto.

A distant but unmistakeable sound of musketry reverberating among the mountain peaks on his left, roused him somewhat unpleasantly from his dream, bringing him all at once from the romance of the past to the reality of present Spanish life.

Several shots he heard distinctly pealing through the air; others followed, and after an interval, two dropping shots, but at a greater distance, as if they proceeded from some flying skirmishers. Then all became still, and he heard only the voices of the birds as they wheeled aloft in the sunshine or twittered among the arbutus leaves.

The road, a narrow and rugged path now as it descended, passed through a dark grove of wild pines; on issuing from which, Quentin's nerves received somewhat of a shock on seeing a French light dragoon, in pale green uniform, lying on his back quite dead, with the foam of past agony on his lips, and the blood of a recent wound still oozing from his left temple, through which a musket shot had passed. Crushed, apparently by a horse's hoof, his light brass helmet lay beside him. A few yards off lay another *Chasseur à cheval*, and further off still lay a third, who seemed to have been dragged some distance by his horse ere his foot had been disengaged from the stirrup, for a bloody and dusty track was visible from where Quentin stood to where the Chasseur lay.

Quentin paused, for his heart beat wildly, and instinctively he looked to the flints and pans of his pistols, his hands trembling as he did so— with an excitement justifiable in one so young— but *not* with fear.

These three unfortunates were the first Frenchmen—the first slain—and, in fact (save the dead gipsy in the vault of Kilhenzie) they were the *first* dead men he had looked upon; thus he glanced timidly, and while his heart swelled with pity, from one to the other.

There they were, three smart and handsome young men, clad in showy light cavalry uniforms, each perhaps a mother's pride and father's hope, left dead and abandoned to the ravens, in that wild place, with their white faces and glazed

eyes staring stonily at the glorious noonday sun,
while the little birds came hopping and twitter-
ing about them.

Quentin's gentle soul was stirred within him;
he was new to this butcherly work, and war
seemed wicked indeed! Those three rigid figures
—those three pale faces with fallen jaws, and
those bloody wounds, made a scaring and terrible
impression upon him; but as he continued
hastily to descend the hill, and left them behind,
he foresaw not the callous heart and time that
use and wont would bring.

CHAPTER XVIII.

THE CHASSEUR À CHEVAL.

" The soldier little quiet finds,
    But is exposed to stormy winds,
    And weather."—L'ESTRANGE.

AFTER proceeding a little way, the sound of
voices, as if engaged in fierce altercation, made
him pause and look round warily, pistol in hand.
He drew behind a gigantic Portuguese cypress
that overshadowed the way, and on reconnoitring,
discovered two men engaged in a fierce and
deadly struggle. They were a French cavalry
officer and a Spanish guerilla.

The Frenchman was almost in rags, for his
silver epaulettes and green uniform, covered with
elaborate braiding, had been torn in his conflict
with the Spaniard, for, as they grappled, they
rolled over each other down a gravelly bank into
the dry bed of a mountain stream, where they
only paused to draw breath before renewing the
contest, in which the guerilla was apparently
getting the mastery. He had a broadbladed
dagger in his sash; but, as the Frenchman held his
wrists with a death-clutch, he was unable to use it.

" Ah, sacré Dieu !" cried the officer, on whose
breast the knees of the guerilla were pressed
without mercy ; " I will yield on the promise of
quarter—even from you."

"Dog of a Frenchman ! May thy foot be
heavy on my neck if I spare thee !" was the
hoarse and fierce response of the Spaniard, in
whom Quentin, with considerable interest, recognised his friend of the wayside cross, whom he
last saw going bird-nesting up the mountains in
search of the miraculous eggs.

" Espanole," said the Frenchman, in tones of
rage and entreaty mingled, " would you kill a
defenceless and unarmed man ?"

" Why not, if he is French ? Who slew my
aged father ? Who slew my mother—my sisters—
all—all ? Who deluged our home with blood,
and desolated it with fire ?"

" Not I—not I—spare me," exclaimed the
Frenchman, as he felt his strength failing him
fast ; " my mother, Spaniard—hound !—ah, ma
mère—ma mère—mon Dieu !" he added, with a
hopeless groan ; and these two French words
stirred some deep, keen chord, some long-for·
gotten memory in the heart of Quentin, who
felt his temples throbbing.

" Maledita ! the strife of our forefathers is but
renewed," continued the Spaniard, in his noble
and forcible Castilian, through his clenched
teeth, while his eyes flashed fire, and his mous-

taches seemed to bristle; "it is a war to the knife against dogs and infidels, for what are Frenchmen but dogs and infidels, even as the Moors were of old?"

Again, without avail, the hapless Chasseur pleaded for his life; but the more powerful conqueror heard him to an end, and then laughed exultingly.

"I am guiltless of all, of everything but doing my duty," he urged.

"Duty!" repeated the other; "shall I tell you of our pillaged altars and desecrated churches, of ruined cities and desolated villages; shall I tell you of our slaughtered brethren, our outraged wives, sisters, and ladies of the holy orders, some of whom have been bound to gun-carriages, stripped, and exposed in the common streets and plazas? Par Dios! these things are enough to call down Heaven's thunder on the head of your accursed Corsican!"

"Ah, morbleu!" gasped the Frenchman, "what a devil of a savage it is! Peste! I assure you, monsieur, I have never touched even the tip of a woman's hand since I had the misfortune to cross the Pyrenees. Tudieu! the Emperor finds us other work and other things to think of."

By a violent wrench the Spaniard now got his right hand free, and in an instant, like a gleam of light, his long knife glittered as he upheld it

at arm's length above the poor young Frenchman, whose pale face and dark eyes assumed a
most despairing aspect.

Quentin could no longer look on unmoved.

" Hold—hold !" he exclaimed, and sprang towards them threateningly.

" Oho, amigo mio," said the Spaniard, looking
round with a saturnine smile ; " 'tis my friend
of the laurel bushes—the spit that looked like a
sword."

" Hold, I say, Spaniard—would you murder
him in cold blood ?"

" Demonio, yes ; and you, too, if you would
protect a soldier of the false Corsican. Begone,
and leave us, or it may be worse for you."

" I shall not."

" Maladita !" said the Spaniard, grinding his
teeth, and clutching the throat of the fallen man

" Release him, I say," demanded Quentin,
resolutely.

" Vaya usted con cien mill demonios," (Begone, with a hundred thousand devils), said the
Spaniard, absolutely, gnashing his strong white
teeth, which glistened beneath his black moustache.

" Oh, sauvez moi, mon camarade," implored
the poor Frenchman.

" Thus, then, die—die en el santo nombre de
Dios !"

With this impious shout, the furious guerrilla,

or whatever he was, raised the dagger which he had lowered for a moment; but ere it could descend, Quentin, with lightning speed, snatched up the heavy cajado which lay at his feet, and, loth to use a more deadly weapon against a Spaniard, struck the guerilla a blow on the head and rolled him over. A heavy malediction escaped him, and then he lay motionless and still, completely stunned.

Breathless with his recent struggle and its terrors, the French officer lost no time in springing to his feet.

"A thousand thanks to you, monsieur! But for you—there—there had been a vacancy in my troop to-night. But here—come this way; we have not a moment to lose, for the hills are full of these guerillas. Peste! they are as thick as bees hereabout; and believe me, the men of Baltasar de Saldos are not to be trifled with."

As the Frenchman spoke, he seized Quentin by the sleeve, and half led, half dragged him through the grove of pines; after which, they ran down hill for more than a mile, till they reached the main-road that led directly to Valencia the lesser, when Quentin paused, and began to reflect that he was going very oddly about the deliverance of Sir John Hope's despatch, a document that probably announced the day on which the entire army would break up from its cantonments and advance into Spain!

CHAPTER XIX.

EUGENE DE RIBEAUPIERRE.

"*Ford.* Well, he's not here I seek for.
Page. No, nor nowhere else but in your brain.
Ford. Help me to search my house this one time: if I
find not what I seek, show me no colour for my extremity,
let me for ever be your table sport; let them say of me, 'As
jealous as Ford, that searched hollow walnuts for his wife's
leman.' "—*Merry Wives of Windsor.*

QUENTIN KENNEDY was only master of a certain
amount of the Spanish language, which he had
rapidly acquired through the medium of his
friend the dominie's sonorous Scottish latinity;
but fortunately the young Frenchman, who
seemed to be highly accomplished, spoke English
with remarkable fluency.

His uniform, we have said, was in rags; his
epaulettes had gone in the recent struggle, the
straps of lace for retaining them on the shoulders
alone remained. A hole in the breast of his
light green jacket showed where the gold cross
of the Legion had been rent away by some
guerilla's hand, and the state of his scarlet
pantaloons made one see the advantage of wearing

a kilt for pugnacious casualties, as they were now reduced to mere shreds.

He was a slender young man, in appearance only a year or two older than Quentin, though really many years his senior in experience of the world and of life generally. His hair, which he wore in profusion, was dark brown and silky, and his hands, on one of which sparkled a splendid ring, were white and almost ladylike. An incipient moustache shaded his short upper lip; his features were very regular, and he was so decidedly good-looking, that Quentin could not help thinking that if he had a sister like him, she must be charming!

They quitted the highway and entered a dense thicket by the wayside, where breathless, hot, and weary, they cast themselves on the cool deep grass that grew under the leafy shade, and the last of the contents of Quentin's canteen, divided between them, proved very acceptable to both.

"I perceive that you are a French officer," said Quentin; "may I ask whom I have had the honour of succouring?"

"Certainly, mon camarade; I am a sous-lieutenant of my father's regiment, the 24th Chasseurs à Cheval—my name is Eugene de Ribeaupierre."

"Any relation of the general who commands in Valencia?"

"A very near one," said he, laughing; "I am his son, and monsieur's very obedient servant. Come! let us rest ourselves and talk a little. The tap on the head you gave that Spaniard was most critical and serviceable to me."

"True--it only came just in time!"

"I hope it may have despatched him outright."

"I trust not, now that the end was accomplished."

"Now that we have breathing time, you will perhaps excuse my little curiosity, and say how you came to be here, within two or three miles of our sentinels?"

"The country is quite open," said Quentin, evasively, with a smile.

"Your troops, we have heard, are closing up from Lisbon and elsewhere; but have *not* as yet been rash enough to enter Spain, the territories of King Joseph."

"Rash, monsieur?"

"Peste! I suppose your generals have not forgotten the sharp lessons we taught them at Rolcia and Vimicra?"

Quentin laughed to hear the pleasant tone in which the Frenchman spoke of two very important defeats of the Emperor's troops as "lessons" to the British, but he said plainly enough,

"I am here because I was sent on duty."

"To whom, monsieur?"

Quentin hesitated.

" Nay, out with it, man—trust me, on my
honour—I may well pledge it to one who has
saved me from a barbarous death within this
hour, and earned my warmest gratitude."

" Well, then, I go to Don Baltasar de Saldos."

" Diable! the man's a guerilla chief, and we
have just had a severe brush with his people.
My patrol, consisting of a sergeant, a corporal,
and twelve chasseurs, were riding leisurely along
the road from San Vincente towards the summit
of yonder mountain, when, from a grove of cork
and cypress trees, there flashed out some twenty
muskets. It was an ambush; the leading section of them fell dead; the rest broke through,
sabre à la main, and fled, pursued by the
guerillas, who sprang after them with the yells
of fiends and the activity of squirrels, leaping
from bank to rock, and from rock to tree, firing
and reloading so long as we were in range.
Struck by a ball in the counter, my horse reared
wildly up, and threw me; for some minutes I
was insensible, and on recovering, found myself
in the paws of yonder Spanish bear, who was
thrice my bulk and strength. You know the
rest. I thought it was all up with me. As
Francis said at Pavia, ' tout est perdu, sauf
l'honneur!' Baltasar's head-quarters are in a
mountain puebla near Herrerucla, where he successfully defies my father's cavalry. Am I
right in supposing that you have been sent to

invite his co-operation in some projected movement?"

"My orders were simply to deliver to him a
despatch and rejoin my regiment."

"It is a dangerous and desperate errand, my
friend," said the young Frenchman, while regarding Quentin with some interest; "I mean desperate to be undertaken by one alone. It looks
almost like a sacrifice of you!"

"A sacrifice?" repeated Quentin, as his
thoughts naturally wandered to Cosmo.

"Parbleu, yes—to the exigencies of the service."

"Some of my friends were not slow in saying
as much," replied Quentin; "but then I—I am
only a volunteer, and as such, must take any
hazardous duty, I have been told."

"Well, here we must lurk till nightfall—you
to avoid our patrols, which are usually withdrawn
for a few hours after the evening gun fires, when
the inlying picquet gets under arms; I to avoid
those pestilent guerillas. The shade here is cool,
and if we had a bottle of wine, a sliced melon,
and a little ice, our pleasure would be complete."

"And you think I must conceal myself here?"

"Undoubtedly, mon ami; our people are
scouring all the highways, and would be sure to
cut you off. Then there is that devilish Spaniard
—ah, the brigand!—he will not be in haste to
forget the knock you gave him on the head, and

should he or his comrades fall in with you, I would not give you a sou for your safety!"

" Strange, is it not, that the first man I have struck on Spanish ground should be a Spaniard?"

" These dons have unpleasant memories for such little attentions, and here the secret shot or stab usually settles everything; but before we separate, I shall have the honour of showing you the direct path to the head-quarters of De Saldos, after which, you must look to your pistols and put your trust in Providence. I shall keep your secret, and if there is any other way in which I can serve you, command me."

" I thank you; but I hope that to-night, or to-morrow morning at latest, will see my face turned towards Portugal, for I long to rejoin my corps."

" The fugitives of my party will spread a calamitous report concerning me in Valencia, and my father, the poor old general, will suppose that I am lying shot on the mountains, instead of holding this pleasant *tête-à-tête* with one of the sacré Anglais over the comfortable contents of his canteen," said Ribeaupierre, laughing. " What a droll world it is!"

" And your mother—I think I heard you mention your mother. She——"

" Happily will know nothing about it, as she is with Joseph's court. She is a gentle and loving creature, with a heart all tenderness.

Ah, the seat of war, would never do for her, and, ma foi! it doesn't suit me either. It was not willingly I became a soldier, be assured; and yet, now that I am fairly in for it, and have won my epaulettes and cross, I should not like to find myself a mere citizen again. Peste! I shall not in a hurry forget the night on which, by a great malheur, a great mistake, I was forced to become a soldier."

"Mistake—how?" asked Quentin, smiling at the young Frenchman's gestures and energy.

"Mon camarade, a man says more when under the influences of eau-de-vie, or champagne, than he ever does under those of vin-ordinaire, cold water, or a bowl of gruel; and, as your remarkably potent rum-and-water has put me in that condition when a man reveals his loves and hates, and, more foolish still, sometimes his private history, I don't care if I tell you how I became a soldier.

"My father," began the garrulous chasseur, "is an officer of the old days of the monarchy, and held his first commission, like the Emperor himself, from Louis XVI., the Most Christian King, and they were brother subalterns in the regiment of La Fere. To the friendship that grew up between them there, the old gentleman owes his brigade and the Grand Cross of the Legion, quite as much as to his own bravery in Germany, Italy, and Flanders. My mother (or she at least whom I have been taught to call my mother, for she is his second wife,) was a widow of rank, who lost her whole possessions in the stormy days of the Revolution. She was without children, and when my father was assisting the Little Corporal to play the devil at Toulon, Arcola, Lodi, Marengo, and elsewhere, she most affectionately took charge of me, and of my education in Paris.

" As we were not rich, it was proposed to make a doctor of me, and so I was duly matriculated at the Ecole de Médecine, and commenced my studies there, not with much enthusiasm or industry either ; but in the vague hope, nevertheless, that I might some day cut a figure and have my portrait hung among the full lengths of Ambrose Paré, Marechal, La Peyronnie, and others in the school.

" I look back with no small repugnance to the daily tasks I performed there, and to the horrors of the dissecting-room, after boyish curiosity grew satiated. My brain became addled by lectures on the maxillary sinus, on diseases of the stomach, of the pylorus, the hepatic and abdominal viscera ; elephantiasis, aortic aneurism, the lacteal and glandular system, and Heaven alone knows all what more, till I imagined that I had alternately in my own person every ailment peculiar to man. We had plenty of subjects, for daily the guillotine was slicing away in the Place de la Grève, and I have seen the loveliest women and the noblest men in France laid on those tables to be stripped and dissected by the knife of the demonstrator.

" I was soon voted the worst if not the most stupid student that ever put his foot within the college walls. The professors were in despair. They could make nothing of me ; and to muddle my poor brain more, about this time I must needs fall in love. Ah ! I perceive that you now become interested. I was not much over seventeen, and my first love——"

" First ?" said Quentin.

" *Oui—ma foi !* I have had a dozen—was Madame Lisette Thiebault, a friend of my mother."

" A widow, of course ?"

" Not at all. She was unfortunately the wife of one of our doctors in the Rue de l'Ecole de Médecine," replied the *étourdi* young Frenchman.

" Married !" said poor Quentin, somewhat aghast.

" *Peste !* of course she was ; but we don't care for such little obstacles in Paris. Well, Lisette, for so I must name her, was nearly ten years my senior, and so had what she called a motherly interest in me. She was a very handsome woman, somewhat inclined to *embonpoint,* with a clear pale complexion and laughing eyes, exactly the colour of her hair, which was a rich deep brown. She was always gay, laughing and smiling, except when her husband, the doctor, was present, and one could no more make fun with him, than with old Bébé."

" Who, or what was he ?"

" The mummy of the King of Poland's dwarf —*Ouf!* what a horror it is !—which we have in the School of the Faculty at Paris. Lisette was very fond of me, and, being a little addicted to literature—she was fond of poetry, too—so we read much together.

"Ere long, monsieur, the doctor began to think all this very improper, so he rudely and abruptly put a stop to our studies ; he locked Ovid up, and me out. *Tudieu!* here was an outrage ! I thought of inviting him to breathe the morning air on the Bois de Boulogne ; but a duel between a first-year's student and an old doctor was not to be thought of. Madame had a tender heart, so she pitied me. She considered her husband's conduct cruel, ungrateful, out-rageous, barbarous ; so, as it was necessary that my classical studies should not be neglected, we arranged a little code of signals. Thus, Lisette, by simply keeping a drawing-room window open or shut, or a muslin curtain festooned or closely drawn, could inform me when Bluebeard was at home or abroad ; whether the breach was practi-cable or not ; and thus we circumvented our tyrant for a time, and I returned with ardour to the study of classical poetry ; but as for the dissecting-room, diable! it saw no more of me.

"Of the doctor I had always a wholesome dread, as he was a *Septembriseur.*"

"What is that?" asked Quentin, perceiving a dark expression shade the face of Ribeaupierre.

"'Tis a name we have in Paris for those who were concerned as aiders or abettors of the horrible September massacres—he would have thought no more of slily putting a bullet into me, than of killing a wasp; thus, you see, I pursued the acquisition of knowledge under difficulties.

"Now came out the edict issued about eight years ago, for raising two hundred thousand men for the army and marine, and every young man in France had to inscribe his name for the conscription. I omitted—we shall call it delayed—to inscribe mine; but my learned friend, M. le Docteur Thiebault, unknown to me, performed that little service in my behalf. He was extremely loth that the Republic—it was the glorious indivisible Republic of liberty, equality, fraternity, and tyranny then—should be deprived of my valuable aid by land or sea.

"About the time when he usually returned from visiting his patients, I had bidden adieu to madame, for our studies were over, and in the dusk of the evening was on my way home when surprised by a patrol of the police under a commissaire, at the corner of the Rue Ecole de Médecine. To avoid them I shrunk into a porch, but they invited me rather authoritatively to come forth, and on my doing so, a sergeant passed his lantern scrutinizingly across my face.

"'A young man,' said the commissaire, who was new in the quartier; 'who are you?'

"'I am not obliged to say,' said I.

"'Ah—we shall see that; what are you?'

"'A student of the Faculty of Médecine. Vive la République! War to the cottage—peace to the castle!' I replied, waving my hat.

"'Is your name inscribed for the levy, blunderer? You quote oddly for a student!'

"'Of course my name is inscribed,' said I, boldly, though I little knew that it was so.

"'Show me your card which certifies this.'

"'Mon Dieu!' I exclaimed, as a brilliant thought occurred to me; 'do not speak so loud, monsieur.'

"'Diable; may we not raise our voices in the streets of Paris?' he asked.

"'Not if you knew the mischief an alarm would do me.'

"'Tête Dieu! 'tis an odd fellow, this!'

"'Monsieur, pity me!' said I, in a voice full of entreaty. 'I throw myself upon your generosity—I perceive that I melt your heart. I have not my card; it is with my wife——'

"'Morbleu! you are very young to have a

wife, my friend, with a chin like an apple,' said
the grim old sergeant, as he passed his lantern
across my face again; 'I hope she is fully
grown; but to the point, my fine fellow, or we
shall have to march you to the Conciergerie, and
they have an unpleasant mode of pressing ques-
tions there.'

"'Where is this wife of yours, my little
friend?'

"'In her house, M. le Commissaire, where
you see that light above the lamp with the scarlet
bottle. Ah, the perfidious! There she awaits
a lover for whom I am watching.'

" I acted my part to the life, though jealousy
is *not* a peculiarity of French husbands.

"'And this lover?' said the commissaire,
becoming suddenly interested, perhaps from some
fellow-feeling.

"'He is a young brother student of mine.'

"'His name?' said the commissaire, pro-
ducing a note-book.

"'Eugène de Ribeaupierre.'

"'We know him,' said the other, 'for the
greatest young rascal in all Paris. He destroyed
a tree of liberty in the Palais Royal, and painted
the nose of Equality red in the Jardin des
Plantes.'

"'The same, monsieur,' said I, in a whining
voice; 'he will come here disguised in a grey
wig and spectacles to delude you, M. le Commis-

saire, and me too, unhappy that I am. Ah, mon Dieu, there he is! there he is! Seize him, in the name of morality and justice, of the République Démocratique et Sociale!'

"The patrol instantly laid violent hands on the person of Doctor Thiebault, who, to do him justice, made a violent resistance, and broke the sergeant's lantern, to the tune of twenty francs, before he was borne off to the Conciergerie, where he passed three days and nights in a horrid vault among thieves and malefactors, before he was brought up for examination, when it was discovered that it was not a young student, but an old professor of the healing art, standing high in the estimation of all Paris, who had been maltreated and carried off by the watch.

"So the whole story came out, and on the fourth day I found myself off *en route* to join my father's corps of Chasseurs à Cheval, then serving against the Austrians. My good mother shed abundance of tears at my departure; the Abbé Lebrun gave me abundance of good advice and a handful of louis d'or, which I considered of more value, and in a month after I found myself face to face with the white coats in the forest of Frisenheim, on the left bank of the Rhine.

"As a parting gift my dear friend Lisette had given me a holy medal to save me from bullets and so forth; but, diable! it nearly cost me my

life, for one of the first balls fired near Oggers-
heim beat it into my ribs ; the ball came out,
but the blessed medal stuck fast, and all the skill
of our three doctors was required to extract it,
so after three months I found myself again in
my beloved Paris on sick leave."

CHAPTER XX.

THE GALIOTE OF ST. CLOUD.

"To be generous, guiltless, and of free disposition, is to
take those things for bird-bolts that you deem cannon-bullets.
There is no slander in an allowed fool, though he do nothing
but rail; nor no railing in a known discreet man, though he
do nothing but reprove."—*Twelfth Night*.

"So," resumed Ribeaupierre, "this was the way
in which I became one of the 24th Chasseurs à
Cheval, in the service of the Republic one and
indivisible, as it boasted to be, as well as demo-
cratic and social; and how I now find myself a
sous-lieutenant, under the Emperor, whom God
long preserve!"

"And Lisette?——"

"Bah! in my absence I found that she had
taken to study poetry with M. Grobbin, a grenadier of the Consular Guard, the same who was
the cause of the First Consul issuing his remarkable order of the day, concerning that Parisian
weakness for destroying oneself, in the passion
named love.   Did you never hear of it?"

"No."

"Ma foi! You English know nothing that is acted out of your foggy little island."

"And this order——"

"Stated that as the Grenadier Grobbin had destroyed himself in despair, for his dismissal by Madame de Thiebault, the First Consul directed that it should be inserted in the order of the day for the Consular Guard, 'that a soldier ought to know how to subdue sorrow and the agitation of the passions; that there is as much courage in enduring with firmness the pains of the heart as remaining steady under the grape-shot of a battery; and to abandon oneself to grief without resistance, to kill oneself in order to escape from it, is to fly from the field of battle before one is conquered!' The order was signed by Bonaparte, as First Consul, and countersigned by Jean Baptiste Bessières."

"Have you ever seen the Emperor?" asked Quentin?

"Once, mon ami—only once."

"In the field?"

"No; but nearer than I ever wish to see him again, under the same circumstances at least. Shall I tell you how it was?"

"If you please."

"Well, monsieur, it happened in this way. I had just been appointed a sous-lieutenant in the 24th Chasseurs à Cheval; we had returned from service in Italy, and were quartered at St.

Cloud, where we were soon tired of the gardens, cafés, waterworks, and so forth. A few of us had been on leave in Paris for some days, where our spare cash and prize money were soon spent among the theatres, operas, feasting, and other means of emptying one's purse, so we were returning cheaply to barracks by the galiote, which then used to traverse the great bend of the Seine every morning, leaving the Pont Royal about ten o'clock for St. Cloud; the voyage usually lasted about two hours, and cost us only sixteen sous each.

"On this occasion, as the morning was very wet, the canvas covering was drawn close, and as we had the galiote all to ourselves—save one person, a stranger—we were very merry, very noisy, and very much at home indeed, proceeding to smoke without the ceremony of asking this person's permission, for which, indeed, we cared very little, as he appeared to be a plain little citizen some five feet high, about thirty-six years of age, and possessing a very sombre cast of face, over which he wore a rather shabby hat drawn well down, a grey greatcoat with a queer cape, and long boots; and he appeared to be completely immersed in the columns of his newspaper.

"We were conversing with great freedom concerning the consulate, which was just on the point of expanding into an empire, and our senior lieutenant, Jules de Marbœuf (now our lieutenant-colonel) was named by us 'Monseigneur le Maréchal Duc de Marbœuf, and master of the horse to Pepin le Bref.' Then we ridiculed unmercifully the proposal of the Tribune Citizen Curée, that the First Consul should be proclaimed *Emperor*, and in this quality continue the government of the French *Republic*.

" ' Peste ! what a paradox it is !' exclaimed Jules, emitting a mighty puff of smoke, as he lounged at length upon the cushioned seat of the galiote.

" ' And the Imperial dignity is to be declared hereditary in his family,' I added, impudently, reclosing one of the openings in the awning, which the quiet stranger had opened, as our smoking evidently annoyed him.

" ' In three days *the pear will be ripe ;* France will become an appanage of Corsica, and I shall obtain my diploma as peer and marshal of France,' exclaimed Jules with loud voice ; ' and you, Eugene———'

" ' Oh, I shall be Minister of War to the Little Corporal.'

" ' Bravo !' said the others, clapping their hands ; ' we shall all pick up something among the ruins of this vulgar and tiresome Republic.'

" ' M. le Citoyen,' said Jules, with affected courtesy, ' I perceive the smoke annoys you— you don't like it—eh ?'

" ' No, monsieur,' replied the other briefly and sternly.

" ' Then M. le Citoyen had better land, for before we reach St. Cloud, he will be smoked like a Westphalian ham.'

" ' Take care, Jules,' said I, ' the citizen may be a fire-cater—some devil of a fellow who spends half his days in a shooting gallery.'

" ' *Parbleu*, he doesn't look much like a fire-cater; but perhaps monsieur is an editor—an author ?' suggested Jules, with another long puff.

" ' Exactly,' said I; ' he is an author.'

" ' Of what ?'

" ' The famous *Voyage à Saint Cloud par mer, et retour par terre*, taking notes for a new edition.'

" This sally produced a roar of laughter, on which the citizen suddenly folded his paper and prepared to rise, as we were now close to St. Cloud.

" ' Don't forget to record, M. l'Editeur, that last week I pulled a charming young girl out of the river close by.'

" ' Trust you didn't pull her hair up by the roots, Jules,' said one.

" ' Or rumple her dress ?' said another.

" ' Fie !' I exclaimed; ' but you will give us each a copy, M. l'Editeur ?'

" ' On receiving your cards, messieurs,' replied the other with a grim smile.

" ' Here is mine—and mine—and mine,' said we, thrusting them upon him.

" ' And here is *mine*,' said he, presenting to Jules an embossed card, on· which was engraved ' Napoleon Bonaparte, First Consul.'

" We remained as if paralysed, unable either to speak or move ; but the justly incensed First Consul, after quitting the galiote, which was now moored alongside the quay, said to a gentleman whose uniform proclaimed him a general officer, and who seemed to be waiting there,—

" ' Bessières, take the swords of these gentlemen, who are to be placed under close arrest, and send the colonel of the 24th Chasseurs to me instantly.'

" His massive features were pale as marble ; his keen dark eyes shot forth a lurid glare ; his lips were compressed with concealed fury, and we all trembled before the terrible glance of this little man in long boots. Ah, mon Dieu ! what a moment it was ! How foolish, how triste, how crestfallen we all looked.

" ' Your name, monsieur ?' said he suddenly to me.

" ' Eugene de Ribeaupierre,' said I, with a profound salute.

" ' Any relation to the officer who bears that name, and who was captain-lieutenant in the Regiment de La Fere ?'

" ' I am his only son, monseigneur.'

"'That reply has saved you and your companions from degradation and imprisonment; but still you must be taught, messieurs, that to protect, and not to insult the citizen, is the first duty of a soldier. To your quarters, messieurs, and report yourselves under arrest until further orders!'

"The authoritative wave of his hand was enough, and we slunk away with terrible forebodings of the future. A severe reprimand was administered through Bessières; but whether it was that our political opinions had been uttered too freely, or that the First Consul had no wish to see the 24th figure in the forthcoming pageant of his coronation as Emperor, I know not, but on the day following our precious voyage to St. Cloud, we got the route for Genoa, so that was my first and last meeting with our glorious Emperor, whose name I have made a *cri de guerre* in many a battle and skirmish, and for whom I am ready to die!" he added, with genuine enthusiasm. "Sunset! there goes the gun in Valencia," he exclaimed, as the boom of a cannon pealed through the still air. "The evening is advancing, monsieur, and we must part, unless you will accompany me to Valencia."

"Impossible!" said Quentin.

"I will gage my word of honour for your safety there and safe-conduct to the mountains," said he, as they issued cautiously from the thicket upon the highway.

" I thank you, but I am most anxious to complete my task."

" *Très bien*—so be it; then we part at yonder cypress-tree. Hola! what have we here—a dead horse—the charger of one of my men?" exclaimed Ribeaupierre, as they came suddenly upon a cavalry-horse lying dead, with all his housings and trappings on, by the wayside. " It is the horse of Corporal Raoul, one of the three men who fell in the ambuscade—several bullets have struck the poor nag, and it has galloped here only to bleed to death. Raoul was a devil of a fellow for plunder; I know that he always carried something else than pistols in his holsters —let us see."

Unbuttoning the flaps of the holsters, Ribeaupierre drew forth a pistol from each, and these, as they were loaded, he retained; but at the bottom of one holster-pipe he found a canvas bag.

" *Parbleu*, look here! Raoul, poor devil, thought no doubt to spend these among the girls in Paris. Plunder, every sou of it," he added, tumbling among the grass a heap of gold moidores, which are Portuguese coins, each worth twenty-seven shillings sterling. " This is Raoul's share of the sacking of Coimbra, which the Portuguese permitted themselves to make such a hideous bawling about. It was the plunder of the living, so you may as well have a share of it *now* that it is the spoil of the dead."

" Who—I ?" said Quentin, hesitating.

" Take it—*ma foi !*"

" Can I do so ?"

" I should think so; what—would you leave it here to fall into Spanish hands, or be buried with a dead horse?" said Ribeaupierre, as he rapidly divided the money, which amounted to one hundred and sixty pieces in all. " 'Tis eighty moidores each ; a sum like that is not to be found often by the wayside."

He almost thrust his share into Quentin's pocket, and a few minutes after, they bade each other warmly adieu, with little expectation of ever meeting again.

Ribeaupierre pursued his way towards Valencia de Alcantara, while, following his direction, Quentin proceeded towards the hills near Herreruela, the rocky peaks of which were yet gleaming in crimson light, though the sun had set.

He seemed still to hear the pleasant voice, and to see the dark and expressive face of his recent companion as he trod lightly on, clinking his moidores, happy that he was now master of a sum amounting to more than a hundred pounds sterling, which would enable him to repay his dear old friend the quartermaster, and would amply supply his own wants while on service, for some time at least.

It was a remarkable stroke of good fortune, and he reflected that but for his meeting with Ribeau-

pierre, he might have passed without examining
the dead troop-horse that lay by the wayside;
he reflected further, that but for the turn taken
happily by the episodes of the day, he might
have fallen into the hands of a French patrol,
and been now, with his despatch, in safe keeping
within the walls of Valencia.

CHAPTER XXI.

THE GUERILLA HEAD-QUARTERS.

"I made a mountain brook my guide,
    Through a wild Spanish glen,
And wandered, on its grassy side,
    Far from the homes of men.
It lured me with a singing tone,
    And many a sunny glance,
To a green spot of beauty lone,
    A haunt for old romance."—MRS. HEMANS.

SAVE in the west, where the hues of crimson and gold predominated, the sunset sky was all of a pale violet.   Though the mountain peaks were rough and barren, and the plains of Estremadura, long abandoned and for ages uncultivated, were waste and wild in general, the road by which Quentin proceeded towards Herreruela lay through rich scenery and land that was fertile.

The tall Indian corn had been reaped, but its thick brown stubble remained.   In some places it had too evidently been destroyed by fire to keep it from the French, or by them to harass and distress the Spaniards.   The olive and the vine grew wild by the wayside; the orange tree and the leafy lime, the fig, and the prickly

pear were frequently mingled in the same place
with the variegated holly, while the myrtle and
the lavender flower loaded the air with sweet
perfume.

Darkness came rapidly on ; the reddened summits of the sierra grew sombre, the western
flush of light died away, and ere long Quentin
found himself traversing a steep and gloomy road,
that led right into the heart of the mountains.

A sound that came on the night wind made
him pause and listen.

It was the great bell of Valencia de Alcantara
—the same that had rung so joyously when the
Christian cavaliers of Salamanca defended the
wild gorge through which the Tagus rolls at Al-
Kantarah (*the bridge* of the Moors)—and it was
now tolling the hour of ten.

Ribeaupierre was now with his friends and
comrades, doubtless recounting his adventures
and his escape, by the aid of a British soldier.
A knowledge of this caused Quentin some anxiety, lest among the listeners, there might be
some who had neither the gratitude nor the
chivalry of the young chasseur, and who might
take means to cut off his return to Portugal, for
he was now fully aware of the risk he ran on
the Spanish side, and began to see something of
the snare into which he had fallen.

As the last stroke of the bell died away on
the wind, a sense of intense loneliness came over

Quentin's heart; the sound seemed to come from a vast distance, and the narrow road he was traversing penetrated into the mountains, which seemed to become darker and steeper on each side of it; but there is something intoxicating in the idea of peril to a gallant soul. It kindles a glorious enthusiasm at times, and thus he marched manfully on till a voice in Spanish, loud, sonorous, and ringing, demanded in a military manner—

"*Quien esta ahi?*" (Who comes there?)

"*Gente de paez,*" replied Quentin, while the rattle of a musket and the click of the lock as it was cocked came to his ear, and he saw the dark outline of a human figure appear suddenly in the centre of the path.

"*Estere ahi* (Stay there), and say from whence you come," said the challenger again.

Quentin naturally paused before replying, as he knew not by whom he was confronted, and could only make out a tall figure wearing a slouched sombrero, by the pale light of the stars.

"Presto—quick!" continued the stranger, slapping the butt of his musket; "from whence come you?"

"The British cantonments," replied Quentin, conceiving the truth to be the wisest answer to a Spaniard.

"*Bueno!* why didn't you say so at once?" exclaimed the other; "but what seek you here?"

" I am bearer of a despatch for Don Baltasar
de Saldos. Am I right in supposing you are one
of his people ?"

" Si, senor ; this is his head-quarters."

By this time Quentin had come close to the
questioner, who still kept his bayonet at the
charge, and who seemed to be a Spanish peasant,
accoutred with crossbelts and cartridge-box. He
was posted on the summit of a hastily-constructed
earthwork, which was formed across the road in
a kind of gorge through which it passed ; and
there, too, were in position three brass field-
pieces, French apparently, loaded no doubt with
grape or canister to sweep the steep and narrow
approach.

Beside them lounged a guard of some forty
men or so, muffled in their cloaks, smoking
or sleeping, but all of whom sprang to their feet
and to their weapons as Quentin approached.
He had now taken off his grey coat to display
his scarlet uniform, and, when one of the guard
held up a lantern to take a survey of him, loud
vivas and mutterings of satisfaction and welcome
greeted him on all sides.

" Senors, where shall I find Don Baltasar ?" he
inquired.

" At his quarters in the puebla, senor. Lazarillo, conduct the senor to De Soldas," said one
who seemed to exercise some authority over the
rest ; " but I fear you will find him busy at

present. At what time are those French prisoners
to be despatched ?"

"Midnight, Senor Conde," replied he whom he
had named Lazarillo.

" It wants but half an hour to that," said
the guerilla officer, who was no other than the
Conde de Maciera, as he looked at his watch ;
and it was with emotions of intense pleasure and
satisfaction that Quentin found himself proceeding towards the mountain village which formed
the head-quarters of the formidable guerilla chief,
and thus acting, as he hoped, the last scene in the
task assigned him ; but he knew little of the
people among whom he was thrown, for in
character they are unlike all the rest of Europe.

" Nature and the natives," says a traveller,
" have long combined to isolate still more their
peninsula, which is already moated round by the
unsocial sea. The Inquisition all but reduced the
Spanish man to the condition of a monk in a
wall-enclosed convent, by standing sentinel and
keeping watch and ward against the foreigner
and his perilous novelties. Spain, thus unvisited
and unvisiting, became arranged for *Spaniards
only*, and has scarcely required conveniences
which are more suited to the curious wants of
other Europeans and strangers, who here are
neither liked, wished for, or even thought of—
natives who never travel except on compulsion, and
never for amusement—why, indeed, should they?"

Late though the hour, the guerillas, a loose and, of course, disorderly force at all times, seemed all astir in their quarters. By the clear starlight Quentin could see that the street consisted of humble cottages bordering the way, with red-tiled roofs, over nearly every one of which a huge old knotty vine was straggling. At one end rose a strong old archway, " old," Lazarillo said, " as the days of King Bomba," and there, when the puebla had been a place of greater pretension, a gate had closed the thoroughfare by night.

Now there was no barrier save a bank of earth and rubbish, hastily thrown up, and a couple of field-pieces mounted thereon seemed to hint the rigour with which intruders would be prosecuted; in short, it prevented any sudden surprise in that direction. There were lights— pine-torches or candles—burning in all the houses, and, as he passed the windows, Quentin could perceive the dark-bearded faces, the striking figures, and varied costumes of the guerillas. Various groups of them thronged the little street, and a company of them were parading, under arms, before the largest house in the puebla.

"That is the posada, senor," said Quentin's guide. "There Don Baltasar resides; but we have come too late to speak with him, at least until his work is done."

"His work," repeated Quentin, inquiringly;
"what is about to be done?"

"*Por Dios!* you shall soon see," he replied
with a grin, as a number of men bearing blazing
pine torches issued from the large house, which
the guide styled the posada, and, by the united
light of these, Quentin was enabled to behold a
strange, a wild, and very awful scene.

As a drum only half braced was hoarsely
beaten, the guerillas came swarming out of the
wayside cottages in hundreds, and a singularly
savage but picturesque set of fellows they were.
All were strong and hardy Castilians; many were
exceedingly handsome both in face and form, and
there was scarcely one among them that might
not have served as a model for a sculptor or a
study for an artist.

Their Spanish peasant costumes, in some instances were sombre and tattered, in others new
and gay; the jackets, olive or claret colour, being
gaudily embroidered, and worn over the scarlet
or yellow sashes which girt the short, loose
trousers. Many were bare-legged and bare-footed,
and many wore long leather abarcas. Not a few
wore fanciful uniforms of all colours, among
which Quentin recognised the brown coats of the
Spanish line, and a few scarlet, which had no
doubt been stripped from the dead at Roleia and
Vimiera, as they seemed to have belonged to the
29th regiment, and the Argyleshire Highlanders.

Most of them wore the native sombreros;
many had their coal-black locks gathered in a
net of scarlet twine, or bound by a large yellow
handkerchief, the fringed end of which floated
on the left shoulder, while others sported regimental shakos and staff cocked-hats. All were
armed with long Spanish guns, sabres, pistols,
and daggers, and all nearly were cross-belted
with cartridge-box and bayonet.

In one or two instances the closely-shaven
chin and the tonsure, but ill-concealed by the
half-grown hair, indicated the unfrocked friar,
who had taken up arms inspired by patriotism or
revenge against the destroyers of convents, or
it might be to have a turn once more in the
world, while the state of Spain loosed all ties,
divine as well as human.

Half hidden in the shadow of the starlight
night, and half thrown forward into the strong
red glare of the upheld pine torches that
streamed in the wind, the figures of those in the
foreground and those flitting about in the rear—
the varied colours of their costumes, their black
beards and glittering eyes, their flashing weapons,
together with the rude mountain village, with its
old and time-worn archway, made altogether a
strangely wild and picturesque scene.

But its darker and more terrible features are
yet to be described.

CHAPTER XXII.

A REPRISAL.

" Proud of the favours mighty Jove has shown,
  On certain dangers we too rashly run ;
  If 'tis His will our haughty foes to tame,
  Oh, may this instant end the Grecian name !
  Here far from Argos let their heroes fall,
  And one great day destroy and bury all !"
                                        Iliad xiii.

QUENTIN's nerves received something like an
electric shock when, on proceeding a little further forward, he saw a line consisting of sixteen
poor French prisoners, partly bound by ropes,
standing in front of the rudely-formed rampart
which closed up the archway, and in front of
them were four large pits, whose appalling shape
and aspect left no doubt that they were to be
the premature graves of the unfortunate men
who now stood in health and strength beside
them.

Those sixteen persons were of various ranks,
as four at least seemed by their silver epaulettes
to be officers, and medals and crosses glittered
on the breasts of several. Their uniform was
dark blue, lapelled with red, and all the privates

wore large shoulder-knots of scarlet worsted. They were all French infantry men, taken in some recent skirmish. Bareheaded, they stood a sad-looking line, and in their pale but war-bronzed faces, on which the flickering glare of the torches fell with weird and wavering gleams, there seemed to be no ray of hope for mercy or reprieve at the hands of their captors, who were about to sacrifice them in the horrid spirit of reprisal which then existed between the Spanish guerillas and the French invaders.

"Good heavens!" said Quentin, in an agitated whisper; "are these men about to be shot?"

"Si, senor—every one of them!"

"For what reason?"

"Being on the wrong side of the Pyrences," replied the Spaniard, with a cruel grin.

"Shot—and without mercy?"

"Precisely so, senor."

"By whose order?"

"One who does not like his orders questioned —Don Baltasar de Saldos."

"Is he capable of such an act?"

"Capable! Santiago! The French have made his heart as hard as if it had been dipped in the well of Estremoz (beyond the mountains), which turns everything to flinty rock."

As if to enhance the torture of their anticipated doom, the Spaniards went slowly and deliberately about the selection of a firing party, which consisted of no less than sixty men, who loaded in a very irregular manner, and, as their steel ramrods flashed in the torch-light and went home with a dull *thud* on the ball cartridges, a thrill seemed to pass through the prisoners.

One, a grim-visaged and grey-moustached old captain of grenadiers, folded his arms, shrugged his shoulders, and smiled in scorn and defiance. Doubtless, since the fall of the Bastile and the days of the barricades, he had seen human lives lavished with a recklessness that hardened him ; but there was another officer who covered his face with his handkerchief and wept; not in cowardice, for his gallant breast was covered with the medals of many an honourable field ; but perhaps his heart at that moment was far away with his wife and little ones in some sunny vale of Languedoc, or by the banks of the silvery Garonne.

Some had their teeth clenched, and their eyes wearing a wild glare of hate, of fear, and defiance mingled ; some there were who seemed scarcely conscious of the awful doom prepared for them, and some glanced wistfully and fearfully at the newly-dug pits which were to receive them when all was over.

Some were occupied by external objects, and the eyes of one followed earnestly the course of a falling star of great beauty and brilliance, which vanished behind the hills of Albuquerque.

A guerilla, clad in somewhat tattered black velvet, now took off his sombrero, and in doing so, displayed, by a pretty plain tonsure, that he was an unfrocked or degraded priest; but now inspired by something of his former holy office, he held up a small crucifix, and exclaimed—

"Frenchmen, if any man among you is a true son of the Church, I pray God and the Blessed Madonna to receive him, and have mercy on his soul !"

"That is the Padre Trevino, our second in command," whispered Lazarillo; "and he is the best shot among us."

As Trevino spoke, the sixteen prisoners and all the onlookers, crossed themselves very devoutly. Some of the doomed closed their eyes, and by their muttering, seemed to be praying very earnestly. Intensity of emotion seemed to render them all more or less athirst, as they were seen to moisten their pale lips with their tongues.

The stern grey-haired captain on the right alone seemed unmoved; he had neither a prayer to give to Heaven or to earth, and thus stood gazing stonily and grimly at his destroyers.

"On your knees, senors! on your knees !" said Trevino.

"Never to Spaniards !" replied the old captain.

"Are they really in earnest, M. le Capitaine ?" asked the prisoner next him, a mere youth.

" Earnest—ma foi! I should think so, Louis."

" Ah, mon Dieu—to be shot thus—it is terrible !" he exclaimed, in a piercing voice.

" On your knees, Frenchmen," repeated the militant friar, " not to us, but to God !"

" To the blessed God, then," said the old captain ; " kneel, comrades ; 'tis the last word of command you will ever hear from me."

They all knelt, and now the firing party came forward three paces—

> —— " a death-determined band,
> Hell in their face and horror in their hand."

And forming line about twenty paces from the prisoners, shouldered arms. Then Quentin felt his excited heart beating painfully in his breast, and he held his breath as if suffocating. From the shoulder the muskets were cast to the " ready," and then followed the terrible clicking of the sixty locks, a sound that made the youngest victim, who had been named Louis, a fair-haired lad (some poor conscript, torn from his mother's arms, perhaps), to shudder very perceptibly and close his eyes ; and now came the three fatal and final words of command from the unfrocked friar.

" Camaradas, preparen las armas !"

" Apunten !"

(" Vive la France ! Vive l'Empereur !" cried the old captain, defiantly.)

" Fuego !"

The straggling volley of musketry broke like a thunder peal upon the silence of the night, and echoed with a hundred reverberations among the mountains, till it was heard, perhaps, by the sentinels in Valencia. Red blood spirted from the wounds of the victims, some of whom leaped wildly up and fell heavily on the ground. The grey smoke rolled over them in the torch-light, and when it was lifted upward like a vapoury curtain by the midnight wind, Quentin could see the sixteen hapless Frenchmen all lying upon the earth. Six were screaming in agony, imploring the Spaniards to end it—to finish the vile work they had begun—writhing in blood and beating the ground with their heels; but then there were ten, who, alas! lay still enough, with red currents streaming from the wounds in their yet quivering corpses.

Half killed and gasping painfully, the old French captain struggled into a sitting posture, but fell back again, as another volley poured in at ten paces ended the butchery.

In a few minutes more they were stripped, even to their boots, and flung quite nude and scarcely cold into the pits at the foot of the breastwork, four being cast into each.

In the pocket of the poor officer who had wept there was found a lady's miniature, and three locks of fair hair that had evidently belonged to

little children. The loose earth was heaped over
the dead, the torches were extinguished, and,
like a dissolving view or some horrible phantas-
magoria, the whole affair passed away and was
over.

In the horror excited by the scene and all its
details, Quentin forgot his mission, his despatch,
almost his own identity; a sickness and giddi-
ness came over him, till he was roused by the
voice of Lazarillo, his guide, who said in the
most matter-of-fact way—

"Follow me, senor—perhaps Don Baltasar can
receive you now."

The house to which he was conducted was the
most important in the place, and had been for
ages its chief posada or caravanserie, where the
muleteers passing between Oporto, Lisbon, and
the southern and eastern provinces of Spain, had
been wont to halt and refresh. It was said to
have been for a time the residence of the Scoto-
Spaniard Don Iago Stuart, who, with the *Sabrina*
and *Ceres*, two Spanish frigates, fought Lord
Nelson for three hours in the Mediterranean, in
1796, with the loss of one hundred and sixty
men.

The under story was appropriated to the
stabling of horses, mules, and burros, and from
thence a rickety wooden stair led to the upper
floor, the walls of which were cleanly whitewashed,
and the floors covered, not with carpets, which in

Spain would soon become intolerable with insects, but with thin matting made of the esparto grass or wild rush.

Military arms and household utensils were hung upon the walls or placed on the wooden shelves; the stiff-backed chairs and sofas were already occupied by some of the before-mentioned picturesque and motley actors in the late scene, and a large branch candlestick, that whilom had evidently figured on the altar of some stately church, with its cluster of sputtering candles, gave light to the long apartment, and enabled Quentin to examine it, and to see seated at the upper end, a man in a kind of uniform, writing, occasionally consulting an old and coarsely engraved map of Alentejo, and referring from time to time to the Padre Trevino and others, who leaned on their muskets, and who, lounging and laughing, smoked their cigaritos about his chair.

This personage wore a black velvet jacket fancifully embroidered with silver; a pair of British Light Infantry wings, also of silver, probably stripped from some poor 29th man who fell at Roleia, were on his shoulders. He wore a gorgeous Spanish sash, with a buff cavalry waist-belt and heavy Toledo sabre in a steel scabbard. His sombrero, adorned by a gold band and large scarlet plume, was stuck very much on one side of his head, as if he were somewhat of a dandy; but underneath it was tied a handkerchief, deeply saturated with the blood of a recent wound.

"Senor Don Baltasar," said Lazarillo very respectfully, "a messenger from the British cantonments on the frontier."

He of the silver wings and Toledo sabre looked up, and Quentin was thunderstruck on finding himself face to face with the stranger of the wayside well, the same personage from whom he had rescued Eugene de Ribeaupierre, and whom he had stunned like an ox by a blow of the cajado!

CHAPTER XXIII.

DON BALTASAR DE SALDOS.

" We must not fail, we must not fail,
However fraud or force assail;
By honour, pride, or policy,
By Heaven itself! we must be free.
We spurned the thought, our prison burst,
And dared the despot to the worst;
Renewed the strife of centuries,
And flung our banner to the breeze."—DAVIS.

A START of extreme astonishment deepening into
a black scowl, which anon changed to something
of a scornful smile in the Spaniard's sallow
visage, was Quentin Kennedy's first greeting from
the Guerilla Chief, who then bowed haughtily,
and said with an unpleasant emphasis—

" Oho, senor; so *you* are the messenger!
Santos—why didn't you tell me your errand
on the day we met by the cross of King
Alphonso? You would thus have saved yourself a devil of a journey and me this knock
on the head."

" It would have been unwise to reveal my
mission to the first stranger I met; I deplore
the result of our second interview, senor; but

I would not stand by and see an unarmed man killed without interfering."

"A Frenchman!" said Baltasar with intense scorn.

"Maledito," said the Padre Trevino, a man with a pair of quiet and deeply set, but the most treacherous looking dark eyes that ever glanced out of a human head. "Maledito!" he repeated, while playing with the knife in his sash, "so this is the fellow who wounded you and rescued the French officer?"

"Yes, Padre; but that is *my* affair, not yours," said Baltasar, haughtily.

"And your precious Frenchman—you conducted him no doubt to Valencia?" said the Padre, anxious apparently to make mischief.

"I left him very near it—indeed, he was my guide part of the way here," replied Quentin with composure.

"Very accommodating of him, certainly," said Baltasar, in whose face the scowl returned; it was evident, apart from his indignation at Quentin, that he had found some of the *wrong eggs*, the legends on which foretold the early abandonment of the entire Peninsula by the British, for his mind was full of ill-concealed anger and apprehension. "You see now, senor," he resumed with a malevolent grimace, "you see now that the spit has become a sword, and the sword only a spit. Por vida del demonio!

but Don Tomaso Yriarte was right after all, for we must never take men or things for what they may appear."

While Quentin was pondering what reply to make to this strange speech, a drop of blood fell from the wound in Baltasar's head, and made a large scarlet spot on the open map of Alentejo. On seeing this the eyes of the Spaniard flashed fire, his nostrils seemed to dilate, and, striking the table with the haft of his dagger, he exclaimed—

" But that the fact of shooting the bearer of a British despatch—a messenger of Don Juan Hope, as Lazarillo says you are—might compromise me with the Junta of Castile as well as with your general, and thus injure the budding Spanish cause, by the Holy Face of Jaen! I would send you to keep company with those sixteen dogs whom Trevino shot to-night!"

" Senor, I was innocent of intending evil against *you*," urged poor Quentin.

" And this despatch which you bring, if it be as my soul forebodes, a notification that I am only to cover the retreat of the British when falling back upon Lisbon and the sea, *then* say over any prayer your heretic mother may have taught you, for you, Inglese, shall not see the sun of to-morrow rise. I never forgive an insult—a word or a blow !"

Though Quentin had been told at Portalegre

somewhat of the contents of the despatch, he knew so little of the great game of war and politics about to be played in Spain that his mind misgave him, and he trembled in his heart lest the treasured paper which he now handed to this ferocious Spaniard, might indeed prove his death-warrant, and seal his doom! He thought of his pistols, and cast a glance around him—escape was hopeless, and a cruel smile wreathed the thin wicked lips of the Padre Trevino.

Baltasar tore open the long official sheet of paper, and when his piercing eyes had run rapidly over the contents, to Quentin's great relief of mind, a smile that was almost pleasant spread over his sallow visage, like sunshine on a lake.

" Hombres," he exclaimed to those around him, " listen! There are none here but true Castilians, so all may share my joy. On the second day of the ensuing November, the first division of the British army which is to rescue Spain will enter Castile by the Badajoz road, led by Sir John Hope, whose advance we are to cover by a collateral movement along the mountains by the hill of Albuera. Long live Ferdinand the Seventh!"

" Viva el Rey de Espana !"

" Viva el nombre de Jesus !"

Such were the kind of shouts that were raised by a hundred voices, while sundry faces, erewhile darkened by hostile and suspicious scowls, were now wreathed with broad smiles, and many a battered sombrero and greasy bandanna were flourished aloft, while to the triumphant vivas the musket-butts clattered an accompaniment on the esparto-covered floor; and many a somewhat dingy hand shook Quentin's with energy, while, in token of friendship and alliance, wine, cigaritos, and tobacco pouches were proffered him on all sides.

When the hubbub was somewhat over, Quentin (with some anxiety for his departure, as the atmosphere of the guerilla head-quarters seemed a dangerous one) said to the chief—

" Don Baltasar, my orders were and my most earnest wishes are to join my regiment at Porta-legre, so I should wish to set out by daybreak to-morrow."

" But the army will soon be advancing—why not remain with us till it comes up?"

" Impossible !" said Quentin, whose heart sank at the suggestion.

" Perhaps you think that you have seen enough of us; but in a war of independence, the invaded must not be too tender-hearted."

" Nay, senor; but if it would please you to give me to-night your reply to the general commanding our division, it would favour me greatly."

This simple question seemed to raise some

undefinable suspicion, or recall something unpleasant to the Spaniard's mind, for, knitting his thick black brows over his deeply-set and lynx-like eyes, he regarded Quentin with a steady scrutiny, and said :

"You are not an officer, it would seem? (How often had this remark stung poor Quentin.) You have no sash, gorget, or epaulettes?"

"No, senor," replied Quentin, with a sigh; "I have not the good fortune."

"What are you then—a simple soldado?"

"Senor," replied Quentin, with growing irritation, for, in truth, he was very weary of his long day's journey, and its exciting episodes; "the letter you have just read, I believe, tells you what you require to know."

"Santos ! you are a bold fellow to bear yourself thus to *me*."

"I am a British soldier on military duty," replied Quentin, loftily, as he saw that hardihood was the only quality appreciated by his new acquaintances.

"What is this? You are styled, *voluntario del Regimiento Viente y Cinco—Fronteros del Rey* —is that it?"

"A volunteer of the King's Own Borderers— yes."

"An English corps, of course, by your uniform?" remarked Baltasar, while twisting up a cigarito.

" No, senor."

" *Maledito*—what then ?" he asked, pausing, as he lit it.

" Escotos."

" *Demonio !* I saw them at Vimiera, and thought all the Escotos were bare-legged, and wore Biscayner's bonnets with great plumes. But you shall have the answer you wish this instant. I am not a man for delay."

" A guide also, senor, will be necessary, so that I may avoid the French patrols."

" You made your way here without one," said the Spaniard, with one of his keen and suspicious glances ; " moreover, I suppose you are not without at least *one* French friend in Valencia ; but a guide you shall have, if we can spare one," he added, dipping a pen in an ink-horn, and, drawing before him a sheet of paper, he wrote hastily the following brief despatch, for El Estudiente, as he was sometimes named, had been well educated by his father, a professor at the University of Salamanca.

"SENOR GENERAL,—I have had the high honour of receiving your despatch announcing the day of your march into Castile, and, with the help of God, Madonna, and the saints, I shall be in motion at the same time towards the hill of Albuera, with my guerilla force, now two thousand strong, with five 12-pounders, to cover your

flank, if necessary, from the cavalry of Ribeaupierre, who occupy all the district in and about
Valencia. With the most profound esteem, I
have the honour to be, illustrious Senor and
General, &c. &c.—

        "BALTASAR DE SALDOS Y SALAMANCA."

While addressing this letter, which he handed
to Quentin, he turned to the Padre Trevino, who
had stood all the while leaning on his long
musket, and said, with a sombre expression on
his dark face :—

"Padre, now that I have a moment to spare,
I shall be glad to learn how your plan for ridding
us of General de Ribeaupierre has failed, and
what has become of your remarkably luxuriant
beard and whiskers, which were ample enough to
have frightened Murillo himself? You are now
shaven as bare——"

"As when I threw my gown and sandals over
the Dominican gate at Salamanca," interrupted
the ex-friar, with a grin.

"Exactly so."

"Well, Baltasar, *amigo mio*, when I entered
Valencia this morning, I had, as you know, a
goodly natural crop of black beard and whiskers,
with a wig that for length of matted locks
rivalled those of Lazarillo here. Over these I
had a high-crowned sombrero, with a tricoloured
cockade, emblematical of my zealous loyalty to

Joseph, the Corsican. Clad in an old brown mantle, I assumed the character of a poor, meek man, the bearer of a petition to the French general, De Ribeaupierre, whom I meant to stab to the heart as he read it—aye, *por Dios!* though surrounded by all his staff and quarter-guard, for I was well mounted, and they never would have overtaken or stopped me, save by closing the city gate.

" I reached the head-quarters just as the whole staff were turning out, for tidings had come that the guerillas of that devil of a fellow Baltasar the Salamanquino, had cut off a cavalry patrol, and shot the general's only son, a lieutenant of chasseurs. The excitement was great in the garrison, where there was such mounting and spurring, drumming and so forth, that I was almost unheeded, while noisily importuning the staff-officers that I had a petition for the general.

" ' Here, Spaniard, give it to me,' said one who was covered with orders, pausing, as with his foot in the stirrup, he was just about to mount his horse.

" I measured him with a glance—I looked stealthily all round me to see that the streets were clear for a start, as he opened my petition and read it.

" I drew closer; the red cloud I have seemed to see on *former occasions*, came before my eyes ; my heart beat wildly, my hand, hot and feverish, was on my knife. Another moment it was buried in his heart, and I was spurring along the street towards the southern gate, which I reached only to find it shut !"

" A thousand devils !" said Baltasar.

" *Por Baccho !*" muttered the listeners, with their eyes dilated.

Dismounting, I quitted my horse, rushed down an alley, where I saw the door of a bodega open, and plunged down into it unseen, scrambled over the borrachio skins into a dark corner and crept behind a heap of them. There I lay panting and breathless, dreading the proprietor (but he had been hanged that morning as a spy), and also the French, armed parties of whom passed and repassed, swearing and threatening ; and from what they said, I learned that I had not killed the general——"

" *Not* killed him ? what the devil, Padre !— I thought you always struck home !"

" So I do, and so I *did*, but the knife had reached only the heart of his military secretary."

" Well, then, 'tis one more Frenchman gone the downward road, the way we hope to send them all. And you——"

" I lay for some time in the cool wine vault, among the cobwebs and dirty borrachio skins. One of them—for the temptation was too great—I pierced with my yet bloody knife, and a long, long draught of the vino de

Alicante, cold, dry, mellow, delicious, golden-
coloured——"

" Ha, ha, ha! Bravo Padre Trevino!" chorussed
all the laughing listeners, as they clattered away
with their musket-butts in applause of his atro-
cious narrative.

" Thou wert revived, no doubt?" said Baltasar,
impatiently.

" *Amigo mio*, I should think so ; it brightened
my intellects ; it gave me new ideas—I drew
inspiration from that beloved borrachio skin. I
cast away my ample wig, drew from my wallet
shaving apparatus, and in a trice I was shaven
to the eyes, as you see me. Abandoning my
cloak, I concealed my dagger in my left sleeve,
took a wine skin under my arm, and walking
deliberately to the officer in command of the
guard at the south gate, offered the wine for sale
at half its value, seeming to all appearance a very
quiet citizen, anxious in these hard times to do
a little business, even with the enemy. He
took the skin from me, bid me go to the devil
for payment ; the sentinel opened the wicket,
and I was thrust out of Valencia—the very thing
I wanted. I said nothing about my poor wife
or starving little ones, lest their hearts might
relent, but turned my face to the mountains, and
I am here."

This savage story met, we have said, with
great applause, and Quentin, after the scene he

had witnessed in the street of the puebla, felt no surprise that it did so ; but his horror of the Padre was great, and he felt his repugnance for the guerillas increase every moment.

Policy and necessity forced him to dissemble ; yet, in that mountain village there seemed such an atmosphere of blood, dishonourable warfare, and patriotism gone mad, that he longed intensely to be out of it, and once again in the more congenial and civilized society he had left.

"Supper, senor," said Don Baltasar, rising from the table and gathering up his papers ; " let us rest now, for you must be weary, and in truth so am I ; and then to bed, for the hour is late, and we have both work to do upon the morrow. Trevino, who has the quarter-guard ?"

" El Conde de Maciera, senor," replied the Padre.

" Good—not a bat will stir between this and Valencia without his hearing of it. This way, then," added Baltasar, ushering them into an inner apartment, where a very different face from any Quentin had yet seen in the Peninsula shed a light upon the scene.

CHAPTER XXIV.

DONNA ISIDORA.

" She sung of love—while o'er her lyre
The rosy rays of evening fell,
As if to feed with their soft fire
The soul within that trembling shell.
The same rich light hung o'er her cheek,
And played around those lips that sung,
And spoke as flowers would sing and speak,
If love could lend their leaves a tongue."

MOORE.

UNPLEASANT though his new acquaintances were
in many ways, Quentin felt a certain sense of
lofty satisfaction that he was a successful though
humble actor in the great European drama. His
mission was achieved! The junction with the
first division would doubtless be effected by the
guerillas, and as he thought of the castle of
Rohallion and those who were there, of gentle
Flora Warrender and his boyish love, he began
to hope—indeed to believe—that he was actually
destined for great things after all.

In such a mind as Quentin's there was much
of chivalry, nobility, and enthusiasm that mingled
with his deep love for a pure and beautiful
young girl like Flora.

In some respects, the companionship, aspect, equipment, and bearing of those half-lawless, but wholly patriotic soldiers, seemed a realization of those day-dreams or imaginary adventures his romance reading had led him to weave and fashion; but the awful episode of the night, though fully illustrative of the Spanish character, and of the mode in which the patriots were disposed to carry on the war, was a feature in guerilla life never to be forgotten!

"My sister, the Senora Donna Isidora," said Baltasar, assuming much of the courtly bearing of a true Spanish gentleman, while introducing Quentin to a very handsome girl; "Donna Ximena, the mother of our comrade Trevino," he added, with a deeper reverence, on presenting him to a woman, so old, little, dark, and hideous, that, after bowing, he hastened to look again at the younger lady.

"The senor will kiss your hand, Isidora," said Don Baltasar.

Quentin did so, just touching with his lip a very lovely little hand, but, happily for him, the leathern paw of the venerable Trevino was not presented. Then the party, which consisted of Baltasar, Trevino, two other Spaniards, whose names are of no consequence, the two ladies, and their youthful guest, seated themselves at table.

The mother of the ungodly Trevino was a deaf

old crone who seldom spoke, but always crossed herself with great devotion when Quentin looked her way, having a proper horror of all heretics, whom she believed to be the children of the devil, and all to be more or less possessed of the evil eye.

Beauty belongs to no particular country, and is to be found, more or less, everywhere, yet most travellers now begin to admit that Spanish beauty is somewhat of a delusion or a dream, which poets and novelists think it proper or necessary to indulge in and rave about; and some of the aforesaid travellers begin to assert that, beyond a pair of dark eyes and a set of regular teeth, it cannot be honestly said that the women of Spain have much to boast of.

Be that as it may, Isidora de Saldos was a singularly lovely girl, in somewhere about her eighteenth year, a very ripe age in the sunny land of Castile. Her eyes indeed were marvellous, they were so soft and dark, and alternately so sparkling, languishing, and expressive of earnestness, all the more striking from the pale complexion of her little face. In their deep setting and with their long thick upper and lower lashes, those seductive eyes seemed to be black, while, in reality, they were of the darkest grey. Her dark brown hair was long, rich in colour, and unrivalled in softness. It was of that texture which, unhappily, never lasts long, and which often, ere five-and-twenty comes, has lost alike its length and profusion.

Her Spanish dress became her blooming years, her figure (which was rather *petite*), and the piquant character of her beauty. It consisted of a scarlet velvet corset, and short but ample skirts of alternate black and scarlet flounces, all very full; slippers of Cordovan leather, with high heels, and scarlet stockings, clocked almost to the knee, over the tightest of ankles.

A white muslin handkerchief, prettily disposed over her bosom, a high comb at the back of her head, round which her magnificent dark hair was gathered and fastened by a long gold pin, that looked unpleasantly like a poniard (indeed, it could be used as such), with silver bracelets on her slender wrists, long pendants that glittered at her tiny ears, a large medal bearing the image of the Madonna hung round her neck, and a black lace mantilla, depending from the comb and flowing over all, completed her attire.

The medal was of pure gold, and bore the inscription, "*O Marie, conçue sans péché, priez pour nous qui avons recours à vous,*" and was, as she afterwards informed Quentin, the gift of the Padre Trevino, who found it on the body of a Frenchman whom he had shot near Albuquerque.

"Did you ever taste a real Spanish olla, senor?" asked Baltasar, as the covers were removed, and the odour of a steaming and savoury dish pervaded the apartment.

Quentin declared that he had not.

" Then thou shalt taste it to-night. My sister is a famous cook," said Baltasar; " an olla she excels in—it was the favourite dish of our old father, the professor at Salamanca, and is the most noble dish in the world !"

" If Spanish, it must be," said Quentin, flatteringly.

" True," said Baltasar, gravely, while giving each of his enormous moustaches an upward twist; " we consider everything Spanish supremely good."

" We are rather a proud people, you see, senor," said Donna Isidora, laughing; " and so far is pride carried, that to touch royalty is to die."

" Manuel Godoy touched royalty pretty often," said Trevino, with a grim smile, " and we never heard that Her Majesty of Spain resented it particularly."

" Did you ever hear of the escape of the sister of Philip III., senor ?"

" I regret to say, Don Baltasar, that I never heard of Philip himself," replied Quentin.

" About two hundred years ago our royal family were residing at Aranjuez," said Baltasar, while filling his own and Quentin's glass with wine ; " it is a country palace twenty miles south of Madrid, and is remarkable for its size and beauty. One night it caught fire; the court and all the attendants took to flight, leaving the youngest sister of Don Philip to perish. She was seen at one of the windows wringing her hands and imploring the saints to succour her, but a young arquebusier of the royal guard proved of more avail. He bravely dashed through the flames, raised her in his arms, and bore her forth in safety. But Spanish etiquette was shocked that the hand of a subject—of a man especially—had touched royalty; nay, worse, that he should have entered her bed-chamber, so the soldier was cast into a dungeon, chained to a heavy bar, and condemned to *die!* But the princess graciously pardoned him, and he was sent away to fight the Flemings under the Duke of Alva. His name was De Saldos, and from him we are descended."

Spanish etiquette made Donna Isidora rather silent and reserved; she somewhat uselessly addressed the old crone Donna Ximena from time to time, and that worthy matron only responded by mutterings, shaking her palsied head, or signing the cross beneath the table. At other times Isidora made an occasional remark to Trevino, by whom she was evidently greatly admired, for his keen stealthy eyes were seldom off her face, and a malevolent gleam shot from them whenever, in dispensing the courtesies of the table, she addressed Quentin Kennedy.

The past day's skirmish among the mountains, the capture and slaughter of the sixteen French prisoners, had appetized Baltasar and his three companions; and though Spanish cookery is seldom very excellent, Quentin was quite hungry enough to enjoy the olla podrida of beef, chicken, and bacon, boiled with sliced gourd, carrots, beans, red sausages, and heaven knows what more, well peppered and spiced.

A few strings of rusks, a dish of raisins, with plenty of good Valdepenas in jolly flasks, closed the repast, after which the invariable cigars were resorted to, prior to repose.

As the whitewashed room, though scantily furnished, was close and warm, and as fighting was over for the night, Baltasar and his comrades unbuttoned their jackets, and each disencumbered himself of a *peto* or wadded stuffing, which was supposed to turn a bullet, all the better that there was pasted thereon a coloured print of some local saint.

The conversation ran chiefly on the new war about to be waged by the allies in Spain, the various routes likely to be taken by the several divisions, the probable points of concentration, and so forth. These were chiefly discussed by Baltasar and his three companions, all of whom had already seen much service against the French. The extreme youth of Quentin, and his total ignorance of the country, made them somewhat ignore his presence, notwithstanding the important despatch he had brought, the scarlet coat he wore, and that he was the herald of that great strife that was not to cease, even at the Hill of Toulouse!

He sedulously avoided addressing or coming in contact in any way with the Padre Trevino, of whom he naturally had a proper horror, as an apostate priest who, exceeding his duty as a guerilla, became an assassin, and so coolly avowed his deadly design upon the father of Ribeaupierre.

The youth, the fair complexion, the gentleness of voice and eye the donna saw in Quentin, together with certain unmistakeable signs of good breeding, when contrasted with the dark, fierce aspect and brusque bearing of those about her now, failed not to interest her deeply.

The solitary mission on which he had come; the distance from his own country, of the exact situation of which, in her strange Spanish notions of geography (though passably educated for a Castilian), she had not the slightest idea, for in those points her countrymen are not much improved since Vasco de Lobiera wrote of the fair Olinda taking ship in Norway, and sailing to the King of England's "Island of Windsor;" the knowledge that Quentin was come to fight, it might be to *die,* for her beloved Spain, all served to present him in a most favourable light

to her very lovely eyes, which rested on him so
frequently that the sharp-sighted Trevino more
than once bit his ugly nether lip with suppressed
irritation, while Quentin felt his pulses quicken
with pleasure, for the dark little beauty, in her
picturesque national costume, was a delightful
object to gaze upon; thus, a longer residence
than he intended in that mountain puebla might
perhaps have led we are not prepared to say to
what species of mischief.

As the wine circulated, and the conversation
still turned on the war, Quentin ventured the
remark—a perilous one amid such gentry—that
he thought the scene he had recently witnessed
was not favourable to the good success of the
Spanish cause.

Every brow loured as he said this, and the
gentle donna looked uneasy.

"Madre divina! you don't know what you
talk about, senor," said Baltasar, gravely; "had
you seen your countrymen, as I have mine, shot
down in poor defenceless groups of thirty or
forty at a time, on the open Prado of Madrid,
you would think less harshly of us."

"And, senor," urged Isidora, in her soft and
musical tones, "the poor people of the city were
forced to illuminate their houses in honour of
the sacrifice. Was not such cruelty horrible?"

"Horrible indeed, senora," replied Quentin,
feeling that it really was so, though sooth to

say he would have agreed with anything she might have advanced, for there was no withstanding those earnest eyes and that seductive voice.

"Light as noonday were the streets on that awful night," said Baltasar, as the fierce gleam came into his eyes and the pallor of passion passed over each of his sallow cheeks; "ten thousand lamps and candles shed their glare upon the heaps of slain, where women were searching for their husbands, children for parents and parents for children, while the cannon thundered from the Retiro, and the volleying musketry rang in many a street and square. What says the Junta of Seville in its address to the people of Madrid? 'We, all Spain, exclaim—the Spanish blood shed in Madrid cries aloud for revenge! Comfort yourselves, we are your brethren: we will fight like you until the last of us perish in defence of our king and country!' Senor, the massacres of the 2nd of May were a sight to shudder at—to treasure in the heart and to remember!"

"And by our holy Lady of Battles and of Covadonga, we are not likely to forget!" swore Trevino, striking the table with the hilt of his knife.

"The spirits of the Cid Rodrigo, of Pelayo the Asturian, and all the loyal and brave men of old, are among us again," said Baltasar, with enthusiasm, " and we shall crush the slaves of the Corsican to whom Manuel Godoy betrayed us !"

"Godoy," said a guerilla who had scarcely yet spoken, but who seemed inspired by the same ferocious spirit; "oh that I may yet some day despatch him as Pinto Ribiero slew that similar traitor, Vasconcella the false Portuguese."

"Always blood !" thought Quentin, beginning to fear that from indulging in bluster and rodomontade, they might fall on him, were it for nothing more but to keep their hands in practice.

" I perceive you look frequently at my guitar," said Donna Isidora, on seeing that Quentin evidently disliked the ferocious tone adopted by her brother and his companions; "do you sing, senor ?"

" No, senora."

" Or play ?"

" The guitar is scarcely known in my country; but if you would favour us——"

" With pleasure, senor," said she, with a charming smile.

" Bueno, Dora," said her brother, taking from its peg the guitar and handing it to her; on which she threw its broad scarlet riband over her shoulder, ran her white and slender fingers through the strings, and then a lovely Spanish picture, that Phillips might have doted on, was complete.

" What shall it be, Baltasar ?" she asked;

adding with a swift glance at Quentin's scarlet coat, ' *Mia Madre no caro soldados aqui*'—eh ?"

" Nay, Dora, that would scarcely be courteous to our guest, who is a soldier."

" What then, mi hermano ?"

" Give us one of Lope de Vega's songs. There is that ballad which compliments the English king who came to seek a wife in Spain."

Then with great sweetness she sang Lope's verses, which begin—

> " Carlos Stuardo soy,
>   Qui siendo amor mi guia,
> Al cielo de Espana voy,
>   Por ver mi estrella Maria."

While she sang, Quentin thought of the old Jacobite enthusiasm of Lady Winifred and Lord Rohallion, and how they would have admired alike the song and the singer; and while his eyes were fixed on her soft pale face and thick downcast eyelashes, he neither heard the accompaniment Baltasar beat with a pair of castanets, or by the Padre Trevino with the haft of a remarkably ugly knife, which seemed alike his favourite weapon and plaything.

In a few minutes after this they had all separated for the night, and Quentin, without undressing, as he proposed to start early on the following morning, stretched on a hard pallet and muffled in his great coat, with his sabre and pistols under his head, soon sank into slumber, the sound, deep slumber induced by intense fatigue; and from this not even the horrors of the recent massacre, the louring visage of the suspicious Trevino, the voice, the eyes, of the lovely young donna, or any other memory, could disturb him.

CHAPTER XXV.

THE JOURNEY.

"Meanwhile the gathering clouds obscure the skies,
From pole to pole the forky lightning flies,
The rattling thunders roll, and Juno pours
A wintry deluge down and sounding showers;
The company dispersed to coverts ride,
And seek the homely cots or mountain side."

Æneis iv.

FROM this long and dreamless sleep Quentin Kennedy started and awoke next morning, but not betimes, as the sun's altitude, when shining on the whitewashed walls of the posada, informed him. He sprang up and proceeded to make a hasty toilet.

"Breakfast, a guide, and then to be gone!" thought he, joyfully.

On issuing from his scantily-furnished chamber into the large room of the posada, or rather what was once the posada, he found a number of the guerillas busy making up ball-cartridges. Heaps of loose powder lay on the oak table, and the nonchalant makers were smoking their cigars over it as coolly as if it were only brickdust or oatmeal.

The guitar that hung by its broad scarlet ri-band from a peg on the wall, brought to memory all the episodes of last night, and Quentin sighed when reflecting that a girl so lovely as its owner should be lost among such society, for to him, those patriot volunteers of his Majesty Ferdinand VII. had very much the air and aspect of banditti.

He looked forth from the open windows into the street of the puebla; the morning was a lovely one. The unclouded sun shone joyously on the bright green mountain sides, while a pleasant breeze shook the autumnal foliage of the woods, and tossed the large and now yellow leaves of the ancient vines that covered all the walls of the old posada, growing in at each door and opening; but Quentin could not repress a shudder when he saw the four large graves at the foot of the archway, for the faces and forms of the poor victims came before his eye in fancy with painful distinctness—the rigid figure of the grey-haired captain, the other officer who wept for his wife and children, the conscript whom they named Louis—the manly and unflinching courage of all!

Baltasar de Saldos twisted up his enormous whiskerando-like moustaches, and smiled grimly as only a taciturn Spaniard can smile, when he perceived this, as he conceived it to be, childish emotion of his guest.

" The ladies await us, senor," said Baltasar ; and Quentin, on turning, found the dark and deeply-lashed eyes of Isidora bent on his, as she smilingly presented her plump little hand to be kissed, and then the same party who had met last night again seated themselves at table, and a slight breakfast of thick chocolate, eggs, and white bread, was rapidly discussed. As soon as it was over, the brilliant young donna and the withered old one withdrew, bidding Quentin farewell, and adding that as he was to depart so soon, they should see him no more.

Quentin, with a heart full of pleasure, belted on his sabre and assumed his forage cap ; he also drew the charges of his pistols and loaded them anew.

"And now, Don Baltasar, with a thousand thanks for your kindness, I shall take my departure," said he. " But how about a guide to avoid the main road, and escape the enemy's patrols ?"

" As we are so soon to leave this, and commence active and desperate operations, the end or extent of which none of us can foresee, the Padre Trevino, who is the very model and mirror of sons, has decided on sending that excellent lady his mother (a slight smile spread over the Spaniard's sombre visage as he spoke) across the frontier for safety. She goes to the convent of Engracia, at Portalegre ; and, as she knows the whole country hereabouts as if it were her own inheritance, she shall be your guide."

" She—Donna Trevino?" exclaimed Quentin, who was by no means enchanted by the offer of such an encumbrance.

" Si, senor. You will be sure to take great care of her."

" But—but, Don Baltasar, that old dame! (devil he had nearly said)—why not send one of your band?"

" I cannot spare a single man. Spain will need them all. The senora is very deaf and old, you need scarcely ever address her, and, as she is taciturn, she will not incommode you. Besides our Spanish mistrust of strangers, she has—excuse me, senor—a horror of all who are beyond the pale of the Church."

" But, senor," urged poor Quentin, " to travel for two or three days with a deaf old lady!"

" What are you speaking of, senor? We are only a little more than thirty miles from Portalegre as a bird flies. You lost your way, and rambled sadly in coming here; but I shall mount her on a mule, and you on a horse, and you may easily be there, even though proceeding by the most steep and devious route, before the sun sets."

" To-night!"

" Exactly. There is, as you are aware, a vast difference in travelling on horseback with a guide, and a-foot, in a strange country, without one."

" I thank you, senor," said Quentin, considerably relieved, " and shall commit myself to the guidance of the old lady, though I fear that she views me with no favourable eye."

" Here come your cattle."

" A noble horse, by Jove !"

" I have filled your canteen with aguardiente."

" Thanks, senor."

" I know that you Inglesos can neither march nor fight, as we Spaniards do, on mere cold water, with the whiff of a cigar."

They were now at the door of the posada, where a group of dark, idle, slouching, and somewhat villanous-looking guerillas were loitering, to witness the departure.

" Ah, if these fellows only knew that my pockets were so well lined with moidores !" thought Quentin.

Lazarillo held the horse (which had evidently been a French cavalry charger) and the mule by their bridles. The former had a fine switch tail, which was now tied or doubled up in the Spanish fashion, as he had to perform a journey. The latter was a tall, sleek, and handsome animal, whose figure indicated great speed and strength.

The saddles were Moorish (the fashion still in Spain), made with high peak and croup behind ; the stirrup-irons were triangular boxes, and the bridles, bridoons, and cruppers, with their brass bosses, scarlet fringes, tassels, and trumpery ornaments, closely resembled the harness of the circus.

At the pommel of the horse's saddle, hung a leather bottle of wine, and behind was a handsome alforja, or travelling bag, ornamented with an infinity of tassels, and containing bread, sausages, a boiled fowl, and other edibles to be consumed on the journey. Nothing was forgotten, and as Quentin mounted his horse, the old lady was led forth by Trevino, who, with Baltasar's assistance, lifted her into the mule's saddle.

The venerable donna was muffled up in a large loose garment of striped stuff, purple and white; it covered her from head to foot, and but for her thick veil, which entirely concealed her withered visage, she might have passed for an old Bedouin in a burnous.

"Senor, this lady is one in whom I am so deeply interested," said Trevino, with the keen, fierce, and impressive glance peculiar to him, and with a hand, by force of habit, perhaps, on his knife; "I say, one in whom I am so deeply interested, that I trust to your care and honour in seeing her, without hindrance or delay, safe to Portalegre."

"I shall see her safe to the gate of the Engracia convent," said Quentin; "and how about returning the cattle, Don Baltasar?"

"Leave them there, too—my free gift to the convent. And now, adios," said he, with a low bow; "doubtless we shall meet again when the army is in motion."

"I hope not," muttered Quentin. "Adios, senores."

A few minutes more and they had left the puebla, with its lawless garrison, its cannon, and eathern bastions, on which the scarlet and yellow ensign of Castile and Leon was waving, far behind them, and were riding at a rapid trot down the green mountain path which Quentin had travelled alone last night.

Soon he saw the place where the road branched off to Valencia, and where he had parted from Ribeaupierre; and, ere long, he passed the dead horse, already torn and disembowelled by the wolves or the wandering dogs which infested all the wild parts of Estremadura.

How changed were the scene, the circumstances, and the companionship since he had last been in the saddle, cantering along the road to Maybole, escorting Flora Warrender!

Leaving this path, and striking off to the left, Donna Ximena, to whose guidance he silently and implicitly committed himself, and who rode a little way in front, managing her mule with ease, and, considering her years, with undoubted grace, conducted him up a steep and narrow track that led into the wildest part of the mountains, where the summits of slaty granite were already beginning to be powdered by frost and snow in the early hours of morning, and where the valleys, which the industry of the Moors made gardens that teemed with fertility and beauty, are now desert wastes, abounding only in rank pasturage.

Their cattle soon became blown, and, as the pleasant breeze that fanned the foliage in the forenoon, had already died away, and been succeeded by an oppressive and sultry closeness, they proceeded slowly, and now Quentin thought he might venture to converse a little with his silent companion, for the monotony of travelling thus became tiresome in the extreme.

"Donna Ximena," said he, as their nags walked slowly up the mountain path. "Donna Ximena!" he repeated, in a louder key, before she said, without turning her head—

"Well, senor?"

"It surprises me much that Don Baltasar permits a girl so lovely as his sister to reside among those dangerous guerillas."

To this remark the haughty old lady made no response, so, raising his voice, he added—

"He may now be without a home to leave her in; but, certainly, Isidora is, without exception, the most beautiful and winning girl I ever saw—in her own style, at least," he concluded, as he thought of Flora Warrender.

He had to shout this remark at the utmost pitch of his voice before the old lady replied, with a gloved hand at her right ear,—

"Yes, senor—she put a large and beautiful sausage into the alforja."

"Bother the old frump!" said Quentin; then shouting louder still, he added, "Your head, senora, is so muffled in that mantle and veil, that it is quite impossible you can hear me."

"Were you speaking, senor?"

"The devil! I should think so—yes!"

"Speak louder."

"I cannot possibly speak louder, senora; but I was remarking the danger that might accrue to a girl of such wonderful beauty as Donna Isidora among the companions of her brother."

"It is Valdepenas, senor."

"*What* is Valdepenas?"

"The wine in the bota—taste it if you wish—I filled it for you."

Quentin relinquished in despair any further attempt to make himself heard or understood, and for some miles they proceeded, as before, in total silence, while the gathering of the clouds betokened a storm, and Quentin was certain he heard thunder at a distance; but a few minutes after, the sound proved to be that of a brass drum reverberating between the mountain slopes! As these drums were then used by the French alone, he instinctively reined up, and his silent guide, to whom he did not deem

it worth while to communicate his alarm, did
so too.

"Ah—you heard that, my venerable friend,"
said he aloud.

The sound now became continuous and steady,
and his horse, an old trooper we have said,
snorted and pricked up his ears intelligently.
It was the regular but monotonous beating of
a single drummer, who was timing the quickstep
for the troops in the old fashion still retained
by the French, when on the line of march, as
it proves an excellent method, in lieu of other
music, for getting soldiers rapidly on.

Desirous of reconnoitring, Quentin somewhat unceremoniously pushed his horse past the
mule of his fair, but exceedingly tiresome companion, and dismounting, led it forward by the
bridle.

The path, rugged and narrow, here went right
over the steep crest of a hill between some
volcanic rocks that were covered with dark-
green clumps of the Portuguese laurel and wild
olive tree; and from thence it dipped abruptly
down into a little green valley where stood a
farm house in ruins.

There by the wayside was a human skull,
white and bleached, stuck upon the summit of
a pole, the grim memorial of some act of retri-
butive justice for murder and robbery.

Proceeding slowly and listening intently as he

went, for the sound of the drum was coming every moment nearer, Quentin peeped over the eminence and found himself almost face to face with the first section of the advanced guard of a French regiment of infantry; they were scarcely a hundred yards distant, and were toiling up the steep ascent.

In heavy marching order, with their blankets and blue great-coats rolled, they were clad in long white tunics of coarse linen, with large red epaulettes, high bearskin caps, each with a scarlet plume on the left side; the legs of their scarlet trousers were rolled up above the ankles; all had their muskets slung, and they were chatting, laughing, smoking, and marching, some with their hands in their pockets, and others arm-in-arm, in that slouching and free manner peculiar to all troops when "marching at ease," but more especially to the French.

On seeing the alarming sight, Quentin leaped on his horse, and cried—

"Away, Donna Ximena for your life—here are a body of the enemy—we shall be either shot or taken prisoners!"

And very ungallantly caring little whether his venerable friend, the mother of the worthy Trevino, fell into the hands of the French, provided that *he* escaped them, Quentin goaded the sides of his horse with his Spanish stirrup-irons, and lashed its flanks with a switch which he had torn from an olive tree.

It sprung off with a wild bound; the lady's mule also struck out, and away they went headlong down the mountain side together at a break-neck pace, followed by shouts from the French, the first section of whom were now on the crest of the eminence, and who unslung their muskets and opened a fire upon them.

Every shot rung with a hundred reverberations between the mountain peaks; Quentin, however, never looked back, but rode recklessly and breathlessly on, thinking as the old lady scoured after him on her mule, and as he lashed his horse without mercy, that he somewhat resembled Tam o' Shanter pursued by Cuttie Sark.

There was no contingency of war of which he had a greater horror than that of becoming a prisoner. If taken by the enemy, years might pass on and still find him in their hands, and when released or exchanged, he would be little better than a private soldier—not so good, in fact. His time for promotion would be irrevocably past, and all the stories he had heard of the sufferings to which the French Republican and Imperial officers subjected our troops when prisoners in the impregnable citadel of Bitche, the fortress of Verdun, and elsewhere, crowded on his mind, with a consciousness of the beggared and hopeless life to which the event might ultimately consign him, even if he survived the captivity, which, in his restless and irritable horror of all restraint, he very much doubted.

Fortunately for him the long-barrelled muskets of the French infantry were very dissimilar to Enfield rifles in the precision of their fire; thus, he and his companion were soon beyond all range, and an opaque vapour, alternating between purple and brown in its tint, that descended on the mountains, while a storm of blinding rain and bellowing wind broke forth, put an end to all chance of pursuit; but they rode on fully ten miles without knowing in what direction, when the fury of the storm compelled them to take refuge in a thicket.

Dismounting, Quentin was too breathless and blown to attempt to outbellow the wind in making excuses to old Donna Ximena; he simply lifted that good lady off her mule, and conducted her under the stately chestnut trees, which gave them shelter. He then unslung the bota and the alforja from his crusader-like demipique, and was proceeding to secure the bridles of their nags to a branch, when there burst a shriek from his companion, with the exclamation—

"Madre divina! O Madre de Dios!"

At that instant there shot forth a terrific glare which seemed to envelop them, and to fill the whole thicket with dazzling light, showing every knot and twisted branch, and every gnarled stem.

Then there was a tremendous crash, as a thunder-
bolt ground a giant chestnut to pieces, literally
splitting its solid trunk from top to bottom;
next rang the roar of the thunder peal as it rolled
away over the vapour-hidden mountain peaks,
leaving the dense and murky air full of sulphur-
ous heat and odour.

Stunned by the torrent of sound, and half
blinded by the lurid glare, more than a minute
elapsed before Quentin discovered that, startled
alike by the flash and the thunder-clap, the
horse and mule had torn their bridles from his
hands and galloped madly away, he knew not
whither.

Even the faintest sound of their hoofs could
no longer be heard amid the ceaseless hiss of the
descending rain, every drop of which was nearly
the size of a walnut; so now, there were he and
old Donna Ximena (who crept closer to him than
he cared for) left a-foot he knew not where, in
that gloomy thicket, evening coming on and
night to follow, a storm raging, and the French
in motion in the neighbourhood!

"Here's a devil of a mess!" sighed poor
Quentin.

CHAPTER XXVI.

A SURPRISE.

" *Preciosa.* Is this a dream ?   O, if it be a dream,
Let me sleep on, and do not wake me yet !
Repeat thy story ! say I'm not deceived !
Say that I do not dream ! I am awake ;
This is the gipsy camp ; and this Victorian."
                                   The Spanish Student.

To address or to consult his old and deaf companion would have been worse than useless, so
Quentin angrily sat down to reflect, and, unfortunately, in sitting down, did so on a prickly
pear.   Now, there are more pleasant sensations
in the world than to sit upon such an esculent,
or a Scots thistle (when one is inclined to ponder
and to " chew the cud of sweet and bitter fancy"),
with their bristling stamens, especially if one
wears the stockingweb regimental pantaloons
then worn ; so Quentin sprang up, and issuing
from the thicket, perceived with great satisfaction, that though the rain was then falling, the
clouds were rising and the wind abating ; in fact
that the storm, which had most probably concealed their flight from the French, was gradually passing away ; but whether or not, one fact

was evident—that the donna and he must pass the night in the thicket.

It was fortunate that he had rendered the flight of their cattle of less consequence, by previously securing the bota of wine and the bag of provisions, and also that he had ridden with his pistols at his girdle, and not in holsters.

As the light increased a little when the clouds dispersed, he perceived a ruined arch, the use or origin of which it would be difficult to determine. It seemed to be a portion of a small aqueduct or vault, Roman, Gothic, or Moorish perhaps—anything but Spanish. It stood amid the great old trees of the chestnut grove, and was half hidden by the luxuriant grass, the gorgeous wild flowers, and odoriferous creepers. It was about six feet in height, but several more in depth, and heaps of fallen masonry, covered with moss and lavender-flowers, enclosed it on one side.

Quentin examined the ruin, and finding it strewed with dry and withered leaves, blown thither by the wind, he led in his trembling companion, who seated herself near him, and with muttered thanks drank a mouthful of wine from the bota, while he drew forth the contents of the alforja, to wit, a huge loaf of fine white bread, a boiled fowl, and a red sausage, that, of course, smelt villanously of garlic. It was in vain, however, that he pressed Donna Ximena to partake of the guerillas' good cheer. The old lady had evidently no objection to a comforting drop of the generous Valdepenas, but when he offered her food she only buried her head in her veil and rocked herself to-and-fro, as if overcome by weariness or alarm.

Placing his mouth near her ear, Quentin endeavoured, by roaring as if he were in a gale of wind at sea, to discover if she knew whereabouts they were—whether near Valencia de Alcantara or Albuquerque; whether near Marvao or San Vincente; whether on the Spanish or Portuguese side of the frontier; but she only shook her head, and made signs of the cross, as the twilight deepened.

Quentin thought that Don Baltasar had certainly selected his guide, as the Dean of St. Patrick counselled all housemaids should be, for their years and lack of personal charms.

" By Jove—the plot thickens !" said he, as he tugged away at a drumstick of the boiled galina and consoled himself with a hearty pull at the bota, while his companion laid her old muffled head on a heap of leaves, and appeared to fall sound asleep ; at least Quentin never cared to enquire whether she was so or not.

There were moments when he seriously considered whether he was not justified in marching off quietly without beat of drum, and leaving this venerable bore to shift for herself, while he made the best of his way to Portalegre, as he had left it, a-foot; but there seemed to be something so ungallant and ungenerous in leaving an elderly female (not that the fact of her being the maternal parent of Padre Trevino enhanced her value) alone, in such a place and at night too, that he resolved to wait till morning dawned, and then he would see what a night might bring forth; and this resolution he formed all the more readily that the rain was still pouring in a ceaseless torrent.

Hour after hour passed in silence, no sound coming to his ear save the monotonous patter of the rain falling on the brown autumnal leaves; to Quentin it proved alike a weary and dreary time, until the shower began to abate, and for the first time in his life he heard a nightingale pouring its plaintive and varying notes upon the air.

Quentin placed their provender and his pistols in a dry place, gathered a heap of leaves for a pillow, and coiling himself up at the other end of the ruin, *i.e.*, as far away as possible from old Donna Ximena, he followed her example and courted sleep.

With the first blink of the day he started from his nest of leaves. Grey dawn was stealing between the great rough stems of the chestnut wood. The rain and the wind were over; the vapours of the night had dispersed, and no trace remained of the past storm save the scathed and thunder-riven tree, the ruins of which were scattered around its root.

The green slopes of the distant hills were visible, dotted by the drenched merino sheep, thousands of which are annually driven into Estremadura, to fatten on the rich wild grass of its pastures. In the distance, and darkly defined against the increasing pink and violet tints of the sky, were two windmills, quaint and old, like those which the Knight of La Mancha assailed; their wheels were broken, and the fans hung motionless and in tatters.

A herd of wild swine rushed through the grove, snorting and grunting in their headlong career, but the Donna Trevino still slept soundly, if Quentin might judge by her breathing, which was low and regular. After stepping forth to reconnoitre, and finding the whole vicinity of the thicket silent, and no appearance of either friend or foe on the roads in any direction, he deemed this the wisest and safest time to set forth, and returned to wake his companion, whom he really began to wish—we shall not say where, or with whom—but safe at least with her son, the Padre Trevino.

On approaching he perceived that the loose and ample garment of alternate white and purple stripes in which she was enveloped, was partly deranged, and the thick black lace veil which covered her head was open in front, for now one half of it floated over her right shoulder. Then, on drawing nearer, how great was his astonishment to behold in the sleeper, *not* the wrinkled and withered visage of the deaf old woman, whom all yesterday and all last night he supposed to be his bore and companion, whom he had left to shift for herself when the French appeared, and from whom he had crept as far away as possible in the singular den they tenanted—not the faded visage, we say, of Donna Ximena, but the pale and delicately cut features, the wondrously long black eyelashes, and the lovely little face of Donna Isidora !

The red pouting lips were parted, and the pearly teeth below were visible, imparting to her expression a charming air of child-like innocence and repose. Ungloved now, one white and slender hand, grasping her gathered veil, was pressed upon her bosom ; her left cheek reposed upon her outstretched arm, and the partial disarrangement of her picturesque costume, as she had turned in her sleep, left visible rather more than her short Spanish skirts usually revealed of two remarkably pretty ankles, cased in their tight scarlet stockings.

The hardships to which her brother's recent guerilla life had subjected her, evidently enabled the adventurous girl to " rough it," as soldiers say ; thus she still slept soundly, while Quentin, half kneeling down, surveyed with wonder, perplexity, and pleasure, the beauties thus suddenly revealed by the open veil.

Touching her hand, he awoke her.

She started up with an exclamation of alarm, and her hand seemed instinctively to feel for the bodkin which confined her hair. Aware that she was discovered now, she assumed a sitting posture, threw back her thick veil, and a singular expression, half angry and half droll, came into her dark eyes, as she said—

"You have been looking at me as I slept! Was it proper to penetrate my disguise, senor?"

"Pardon me, senora; I did not, indeed; I came but to wake you, and found your veil open; could I refrain from looking—from admiring?"

"And you have discovered me—— "

"To be young and beautiful—— "

"When you thought me old and hideous—is it not so?" she asked, laughing.

"I confess it, and with pleasure, senora. This is very enchanting—but what romance is it— what absurd comedy is this you are acting?"

"Absurd?"

"Pardon me again; but though it is a game or drama that charms me very much, it is not without peril."

"To whom?"

"To both—perhaps most of all to you, senora."

She replied only by a haughty smile, so Quentin continued—

" Now we shall make our way together de-
lightfully to Portalegre, and there can be no
more deafness; or can it be that you and Donna
Ximena changed places here in the night? Oh,
tell me what does all this mean?"

" I shall tell you, senor," said the now blush-
ing girl; " it means simply that my brother was
most anxious that I, and not Donna Ximena,
should reach the St. Engracia convent, as a
place of permanent safety till these wars and
tumults are over. He also wished to supply you
with a guide to Portalegre, where, but for the
loss of our horses, we should have been last
night. Thus my brother——"

" Deemed that as old Donna Ximena you
would be safer with me than in your own character?"

" Exactly," she replied, laughing; " we
thought there would be little chance of your
attentions annoying her."

" Do you imagine that when the French appeared I would have turned my horse's head and
left *you* without thought or ceremony, as I left
her—she whom I considered an old, deaf bore
and encumbrance? You have acted well your
part, senora. How you made me roar and
shout, as if I was commanding a whole brigade!"

" And now, senor, that you know I am *not*
Donna Ximena, will you respect me the less?"

" On the contrary, I shall respect you a great

deal more," said Quentin with enthusiasm, as he took her hand in his; but she withdrew it as if to adjust her veil.

"Then, am I to understand that in your country, youth is more honourable than age?"

"Nay, it is not, but youth is more pleasing, certainly."

"You have been most kind to me, senor."

"Kind, senora?" Quentin thought she was quizzing him.

"Yes; I cannot forget how, even as old Ximena, you lifted me from my mule, conveyed me in here, made a couch and pillow for me, and so forth. *Beso usted la mano, caballero* (I kiss your hand, sir)," she added, taking his hand in hers.

"Oh, Donna Isidora, I cannot permit you to do this—unless——"

"Do you not know the customs of Castile? Well, unless what?"

"You permit me to kiss yours."

"How simple! there, senor," she added, presenting a very lovely little hand, which he pressed to his lips.

"Your cheek now—ah, you will permit me?" urged Quentin, becoming a little bewildered by the whole situation, and by the clear dark eyes that looked so softly into his.

"Do so, senor."

Quentin was promptly pressing forward, when

the point of a very unpleasant looking little
stiletto met his cheek!

"Senora," he exclaimed, "what do you mean?"

"That I shall stab you to the heart if you
molest me—that is all!" said she, as a gleam
came into her dark eyes that vividly reminded
Quentin of Baltasar.

"So, so, senora," said Quentin, with an air
of pique, "you are certainly able to take care of
yourself."

"I live in times when it is necessary I should
be so," was the dry retort.

Quentin surveyed her with growing interest,
for her beauty was very remarkable in its deli-
cacy and darkness. She had a short crimson
upper lip, that seemed to quiver with every
passing thought, for she was an impressionable,
enthusiastic, and high-spirited girl. After a pause,

"Now that you have done admiring me, I
suppose," said she, "you will kindly say what
we are to do?"

"How?"

"We cannot remain here among the leaves,
like a couple of gitanos, or two rooks in search
of a nest."

"We shall continue our journey to Portalegre,
with your permission, senora; and now that you
have recovered your hearing, and that I am not
obliged to bellow like a madman, you will perhaps, if in your power, tell me where we are?"

Donna Isidora laughed and presented her hand; Quentin assisted her to rise, and on issuing from the ruined arch, she looked about her for some time.

" By those two windmills," said she, " I know that we are not far from Salorino."

" A town, senora?"

" Yes; it lies at the base of yonder lofty mountain, on the left bank of the river Salor."

" Is it large ?"

" A considerable place for manufactures. This purple and white striped woollen stuff is made there; but the town must be avoided, as it is occupied by a troop of Polish Lancers."

" Then did we ride the wrong way in the rain last night ?"

" Yes; we are still fully thirty miles from Portalegre."

" Thirty miles yet, senora !"

" Yes, and Valencia de Alcantara, where the French Light Cavalry are, lies exactly midway, on the main road, between us and it."

Quentin's heart sunk at this information.

" You are certain of all this, senora ?" said he, laying his hand lightly on her arm.

" Quite, senor."

" We cannot—you, at least, cannot—proceed thirty miles on foot; so what in heaven's name shall we do?" said Quentin in great perplexity.

" The Conde de Maciera, who serves in my

brother's band of guerillas as captain of a hundred lancers, has a villa at the foot of yonder
hill near the Salor; I remember that the wildest
bull we ever had in the arena at Salamanca
came from thence. The place is scarcely two
miles distant from this, and could we but reach it,
doubtless some of his domestics might assist us."

"The idea is excellent; let us set out at
once!"

"Be advised by me, senor, and take some
breakfast first," said the Spanish girl, laughing;
"it is a custom we guerillas have, always to eat
when provisions can be had, lest we halt where
there are none."

Quentin at once assented, and opening the
alforja produced the fowl and other edibles, on
which they made a slight repast before setting
forth.

Seating herself within the ruined arch, her
head reclined upon her left hand, Isidora displayed to perfection a lovely rounded arm, and
a pair of taper ankles and little feet, towards
which Quentin's eyes wandered from time to
time.

"You look at me very earnestly, senora," said
he, while his cheek reddened and his heart fluttered on finding the dark searching eyes of the
young donna fixed on him more than once.

"There is, I can see, a sad expression in your
eyes, senor."

" Do you think so ?" asked Quentin, smiling.

" Yes."

" But how, or why do you suppose so ?"

" I don't know; I perceive that you are a mere boy (muchacho), and yet—and yet——"

" What, senora ?"

" Ave Maria purissima ! I can't say—there is something that speaks to me of thought, reflection, care beyond your years."

" It may well be so, dear senora ; I have never known a relative in the world ; I have been an orphan from infancy, and——"

" And now," said she, presenting him with her hand, "you are a soldier who comes to fight for Spain !"

" And for *you*, too, senora," he added, as he touched her fingers with his lips, and with a devotion that somewhat surprised himself. " But are you afraid of me, as old Donna Ximena was ?"

" No—why do you think I am ?"

" You sign the cross so often."

" Because, senor—excuse me, but the morning air is excessively chilly here, and I yawn frequently."

" And you do so?——"

" For fear Satanas should dart down my throat unseen and unfelt. It is a belief— superstition you may deem it—that we have in Castile; though you, perhaps, who have, unfor-

tunately, been educated among heretics, may
know neither the dread nor the holy sign. I
know that it is not used in your country, senor
—because I can read."

"I should think so," said Quentin, amused
by her simplicity; "is not every lady educated?"

"No—not in Spain."

"Why?"

"Lest, if handsome, they should write to
their lovers."

"And yet, senora, they had the rashness to
teach you."

"Do you mean that I am handsome, or that
I must have lovers?"

"I mean both—that being the first of necessity leads to your possessing the last."

"My poor father, the good old professor, who
was so barbarously slain by the French, was
careful to teach me many things, though our
female literary accomplishments are usually
confined to our prayers and rehearsing legends
of the saints, songs of the Cid Rodrigo, or
by Lope de la Vega. In England I believe
you have women who could lead the Junta or
shine in the Cortes itself; but what matters their
education, when it only serves to confirm their
heresies? And now, senor, place the bota in
the alforja, and sling that over your shoulder;
let us go, and I shall be your guide to Villa
de Maciera."

CHAPTER XXVII.

THE VILLA DE MACIERA.

" Innocence makes him careless now.
   *   *   *   *
Youth hath its whimsies, nor are we
To examine all their paths too strictly:
We went awry *ourselves* when we were young."
Old Tragedy.

Donna Isidora had now divested herself of the
large and loose woollen weed in which she had
travelled yesterday, and threw it gracefully over
her arm. In her short but amply flounced skirt
she tripped—as we are writing of a Spanish girl
we should have it glided—along by the side of
Quentin, who moderated his pace to suit hers.

The rain of last night had completely laid the
dust; the morning air was cool and delightful,
and save a Franciscan friar of Medellin, travelling
like themselves on foot, with a canvas wallet slung
on his back and a long knotted staff in his hand,
they met no one.

The heavy clouds were banking up from the
westward, but the sky was beautiful overhead,
and, refreshed by the torrents of last night, every
herb, flower, and leaf wore their brightest hues.
The Salor, a river which flows from the moun-

tains southward of Caceres, in Estremadura, and
joins the Tagus near Rosmaninhal, in the province
of Beira, and the bed of which frequently becomes
quite dry in summer, now came in sight, swollen
by the recent rains, and flowing red and muddy
between groves of olive trees, which were still in
full leaf, as in those regions the olive harvest
usually occurs about the month of December.

On the surface of the rushing river the large
flowers of the white and purple lotus floated, or
sunk to rise again, bobbing in the eddies; and
some brightly feathered birds, though summer was
long since past, twittered about, filling the air with
melody and song.

But the western clouds, we have said, came
gathering fast and heavily, and in sombre masses
that alternated between purple and inky grey,
while the wind rose in hot or cold puffs that
gradually grew to gusts; and these, with other
indications that rough weather was again at hand,
made the two pedestrians hasten on.

Ere they crossed the old Roman bridge that
spans the Salor, by arches that must whilom have
echoed to the marching legions of Quintus Sertorius, the sound of distant thunder was heard
among the mountains, and then the clouds
gathered so fast, that ere long every vestige of
blue was completely hidden in the sky.

"If rain comes, what a situation for you,
Donna Isidora!" said Quentin, turning to his

companion, to whose usually colourless cheek, the early morning air and the exercise of walking had imparted a lovely flush; in fact she seemed radiantly beautiful !

"Oh, fear not for me, senor, though to have one's only dress wetted, *is* rather unpleasant," she replied ; "besides, the villa of the Conde is close at hand."

At that moment one or two large drops of warm rain plashed on the road they traversed, causing them to quicken their steps.

Striking off from the main highway, Isidora led Quentin between two gate pillars, each of which was surmounted by a marble lion, seated on its haunches, with its fore paws resting on a shield. This gave access to an avenue, where two rows of giant beeches, now brown and yellow, mingled with ilex (whose leaves seem red as blood when viewed in the sunshine), cast their shadows on two lesser rows of dense and dark-leaved Portuguese laurels, myrtle and wild gentian; but in this silent and untrodden avenue, the rank grass and weeds were already sprouting.

"This is the villa," said Donna Isidora, as they came suddenly in sight of a château of very imposing aspect; "but Madre Maria ! what is this? It seems quite deserted !"

A double flight of white marble steps led from a green lawn to a noble terrace, the balustrades of which were elaborately carved, and had

at regular intervals square pedestals bearing each
an enormous porphyry vase filled with flowers
that diffused a delicious aroma. From the architecture of the villa, a large square mansion with
wings, which rose from the plateau of this stately
terrace, and by its Palladian style, many of the
pediments, cornices, capitals, and especially the
statues that adorned it, seemed to have been taken
from the various Roman ruins in the vicinity.

Around this terrace was a row of orange trees,
the fruit of which had never been gathered, as it
lay in heaps under each, just as it had fallen
from the branches when dead ripe.

The plashing water of a beautiful bronze fountain, where four Tritons shot each a jet of pure
crystal from a trumpet-shaped conch into a
yellow marble basin, alone broke the silence and
stillness of the place. Torn from its elaborate
hinges, the front door lay flat on the tesselated
marble floor of the vestibule, having evidently
been beaten in by the simple application of a
large stone which still lay above it ; and the
tendrils of the gorgeous acacias that covered the
front wall of the villa, had already begun to find
their way in at the open door, and to creep
through the shattered windows.

" The French have been here !" said Isidora,
with a dark expression in her eyes ; " De Ribeaupierre's dragoons have done this."

" The villa is quite deserted, senora," said Quentin, as they stood in irresolution and perplexity on the terrace. " How far are we from Salorino?"

" Six miles at least."

Quentin hallooed loudly two or three times, but the echoes of the tenantless abode alone responded, and the deathlike stillness there made Isidora shrink close to his side.

" I was not prepared for this," she said, while her eyes filled with tears; " yet what else can we expect while a Frenchman remains alive on this side of the Pyrenees?" she added, bitterly.

" There seems to be no living thing here, senora; not even a household dog."

" What shall we do, senor?" she asked, earnestly.

" Whatever we do ultimately, senora, we must take shelter now, for here comes the storm again, and with vengeance, too!"

So intent had they been in observing the indications of desertion and decay about this noble villa, that they had failed to see how fast the storm had gathered round them. A gust of wind tore past the edifice, strewing the terrace with withered acacia flowers and orange leaves, and then the rain descended in torrents, driving the travellers for shelter into the open vestibule.

In blinding sheets it rushed along the earth, from which it seemed to rise again like smoke or mist, then the thunder hurtled across the darkening sky, and the yellow lightning played like

wild-fire about the bare granite scalps of the
distant sierras, throwing forward every peak in
strong outline from the dusky masses of cloud,
amid which they " were an instant seen, and
instant lost."

" *Madre de Dios !* there seems a fatality in all
this !" exclaimed Isidora, as the overstrained and
half Moorish ideas of etiquette and female
propriety which prevail in Spain and Portugal
occurred to her ; then, looking at Quentin, while
a blush suffused her cheek, she added, " to be
wandering in this manner is a most awkward
situation, especially for me."

Quentin made some well-bred reply, he knew
not what ; but with all its awkwardness he felt
that " the situation had its charm," as he took her
hand and suggested that they should investigate
the premises and see whether the villa was really
so deserted as it appeared.

From the splendid vestibule, the lofty walls
and rich cornices of which were covered with
armorial bearings of the past Condes de Maciera,
many of their escutcheons being collared by the
orders of Santiago de Compostella, Santiago de
Montesa, the Dove of Castile, and the Golden
Fleece, with the crossed batons that showed how
many had of old commanded the Monteros de
Espinosa, or Ancient Archers of the Spanish
Royal Guard, Quentin and Donna Isidora as-
cended a marble stair to a large corridor, off

which several suites of apartments opened, and
through these they proceeded, every moment
fearful of coming suddenly upon some sight of
horror, as the French were seldom slow in using
their bayonets against any household that received them unwillingly, and the battered state
of the entrance door showed that the villa had
been entered forcibly.

The great corridor, like many of the rooms,
was hung with portraits of grisly saints and
meek-eyed Madonnas, and of many a lank-
visaged and long-bearded hidalgo, with breast-
plate, high ruff, and bowl-hilted toledo, looking
with calm pride, or it might be defiance, from the
flapping canvas, which had been slashed in mere
wantonness by the sabres of the French dragoons.

Save that a number of chairs were overthrown,
that several lockfast places had been broken
open, and that many empty bottles strewed the
floors, the furniture appeared to have been left
untouched. The gilt clocks on the marble man-
tel-pieces ticked no more, and the spiders had
spun their webs over the hour-hands and dials,
thus showing that the villa must have been
deserted by the family and servants of the count
for some weeks. The damask sofas and otto-
mans were covered with dust, and many books
lay strewn about on the dry and now musty
esparto grass that covered some of the floors,
which were nearly all of highly polished oak.

Quentin picked up a lady's white kid glove, and a black fan covered with silver spangles.

"These have belonged to the mother of the Conde, who resided here; where can the poor lady have fled—what may have become of her?" said Isidora as they wandered on, her voice and Quentin's sounding strange and hollow in the emptiness of the great villa.

All the bed-chambers were untouched, save in some instances where a mirror or cheval glass was starred or smashed by a pistol-shot; and so, ere long, the visitors in their search found themselves in the chapel, a little gothic oratory of very florid architecture, which had evidently formed a portion of a much older edifice than the present villa; for there, on a pedestal tomb, having a row of carved weepers round it, and little niches and sockets for twelve votive lamps, lay side by side the effigies of two knights in chain-armour, with their cross-hilted swords and military girdles on, and their hands folded in prayer. Quentin drew near them with interest, for he remembered the quaint effigy of Sir Ranulph Crawford, Keeper of the Palace of Carrick, in the old kirk of Rohallion, and while Isidora knelt for a moment before the little altar, he read on a brass plate this inscription:

"Aqui yazen el noble y valiente Conde, Don Fernando de Estremera, y su hijo, Don Antonio, Condes de Maciera y Estremera; fueron muertos en una batalla con los Infieles, en tiempo del Rey Don Alfonso de Castile, Leon, y Galicia. Requiescant in pace."

"More than seven hundred years ago," thought Quentin. "Sir Ranulph's tomb is a thing of yesterday compared with this."

He surveyed with emotions of pleasure and interest this little oratory, the sanctuary of which, with its half Moorish and arabesque-like carvings was a miracle of art and a mass of gilding. It must have been erected almost immediately after the expulsion of the Arabs from that part of Castile, and so those Counts of Maciera had lived and died before the days of the Cid himself,

> "The venging scourge of Moors and traitors,
> The mighty thunderbolt of war!
> Mirror bright of chivalry,
> Ruy, my Cid Campeador!"

for he had been born when Canute the Dane swayed his sceptre over England, and when Malcolm of Scotland—Rex Victoriosissimus—was nailing the hides of the Norsemen on the doors of his parish churches. It was a remote period to look back to, and yet, in some of her national features, particularly in a proneness to bloodshed, Spain was pretty much the same as when the Cid shook his lance before the walls of Zamora.

Light, many hued, crimson, blue, and green, streamed, with flakes of dusky yellow, through the chapel's deep-arched windows, shedding a warm glow on its carved pillars, ribbed arches, and lettered stones that marked the graves of the dead below, where the Condes de Maciera, "el noble—el magno," were mingling with the dust; but now their dwelling-place was desolate, and the heir of all their titles, a half-desperate outlaw and soldier, was serving as a guerilla in the band of Baltasar the Salamanquino.

Various stools and hassocks were still disposed near the oak rail of the sanctuary, as if to mark where several of the fugitive household had knelt but recently.

The chapel suddenly grew very dark, but was lightened as quickly by a terrific flash without. Against this glare of light the mullions and tracery of the windows were darkly but distinctly defined, and, as it passed away, a peal of thunder that seemed directly over their heads, shook the place.

Crossing herself, Donna Isidora sprang close to Quentin's side, and taking her by the hand, he led her back to a more cheerful part of the voiceless mansion.

The weather was completely broken now, and to Quentin it seemed that unless there was some change, of which there was no probability, as the year was closing, the army were likely to have a fine time of it, after breaking up from their snug cantonments in Portugal to open a campaign in Spain.

There was not the slightest appearance of the rain abating, so feeling the necessity for making themselves as comfortable as circumstances would permit, Quentin set about closing all the doors and windows, and selecting a room that had evidently been the boudoir of the Condesa, as its walls were covered by white silk starred with gold; there, too, were pale-blue damask hang-ings, starred with silver, a piano and guitar, with piles of music, illuminated books, sketches, statuettes, and ornaments, all indicative of a graceful taste and refined mind.

These were all untouched, so there Quentin installed his companion, whose eye was the first to detect a gilt cage, at the bottom of which a former friend and favourite, a little singing bird, lay dead and covered with dust.

She seated herself near the window to watch the black clouds whirling in masses around the peaks of the great mountain ranges that lay between her and her temporary home in Portugal, and on the rain plashing frothily on the marble terrace, gorging the gurgoyles of the parapet and the basin of the bronze fountain, which had long since overflowed.

Meanwhile Quentin bustled about; to have the run of such a house was not without interest. He soon procured a brasero, which he filled with charcoal, and lighted by flashing some powder in the pan of a pistol; and for warmth, he made Isidora place her dainty little feet upon it. Canisters of biscuits and of fruit of various

kinds, several flasks of Valdepenas and Champagne, a ham, and several other matters which
he found in overhauling the cook's department
and butler's pantry, with all the appurtenances
of the table, he appropriated with a campaigner's
readiness, and insisted upon his fair companion
partaking of a repast with him.

The storm—the rain, at least, as we shall have
to show—continued much longer than they
anticipated. But if it lasted for a fortnight,
there seemed to be still provisions enough in the
old villa to prevent them from being starved out
even in that time.

For a period both were now perplexed and
thoughtful.

Donna Isidora was considering how all this
unlooked-for deviation and delay were to be ex-
plained to her brother, who, as a Spaniard, was
naturally suspicious, and of whom she stood in
considerable awe. The latter emotion made her
conceive that the most peaceful and prudent
course would be, to say nothing whatever about
the casual discovery of her disguise, or her
wanderings on the way before reaching Portalegre ; but then, how was she to account for the
absence of the horse and mule, but for the loss of
which, after their flight from the French, she
and Quentin would have been last night safe and
separated at the place of their destination !

Then when remembering the haughty temper

of Cosmo, and the cold and hostile manner in which he was treated by him, Quentin felt some alarm lest his honour might be impugned by the protracted delay in rejoining the Borderers; while his own experience, and the hints he had received from Major Middleton, made him now resolve, however great his reluctance would be in leaving that fine old soldier and Askerne, Monkton, and other 25th men, to volunteer into some other regiment—perhaps in the 94th, if his friend Captain Warriston could scheme it for him.

The moidores which Ribeaupierre had so generously shared with him, made a transfer of this kind appear the more easy in a monetary point of view; and luckily the army had not yet begun to move, so his courage was still unimpeachable.

Reflection showed that Cosmo would render his life intolerable, and make promotion an impossibility.

"I shall seek out another colonel, if he can be found in the service. I can only fail in the attempt, and be no worse than I am," said Quentin, unintentionally aloud, so that the dark eyes of the Spanish girl rested inquiringly on him.

He now seated himself in the same window opposite Isidora, who having her own thoughts, was silent. Evening was drawing near—the short evening of a dark November day, and the ceaseless rain still plashed heavily down, while the wind howled drearily around the solitary villa.

CHAPTER XXVIII.

OUR LADY DEL PILAR.

" The foe retires—she heads the sallying host,
  Who can appease like her a lover's ghost ?
  Who can so well appease a lover's fall ?
  What maid retrieve when man's flushed hope is lost ?
  Who hang so fiercely on the flying Gaul,
  Foiled by a woman's hand before a battered wall."

BYRON.

" WHAT a singular adventure this is," thought Quentin; " and what a perplexing position for us both ! It is very· romantic, certainly. A deserted house, a lovely girl, and all that. 'Tis very like some incidents I have read of, and some I have imagined; but, by Jove ! I wish I could see my way handsomely out of it."

The last desire resulted from the unpleasant recollection of the Padre Trevino's face and intonation of voice, when he spoke so impressively of the *interest he* felt in the lady committed to his care, and the sternly expressed anxiety that she should reach Portalegre " without hindrance or *delay*."

Was the fellow only acting a part, or could it be that the ugly ogre actually had some tender fancy for Isidora? Whether he had or not, an unfrocked friar, especially of his peculiar character, had not much chance of success with the sister or support from the brother, so Quentin dismissed the idea.

"How charming she looks!" he thought, stealing a glance at the long lashes of the now pensive eyes, the soft features half shaded by the black lace veil, and the graceful contour of her bust and shoulders, in her low-cut scarlet velvet corset. "How delightful, if, instead of being lost in this barbarous place, she were at Rohallion or Ardgour; what a lovely friend and companion for Flora!"

Poor Quentin! Alas, this was but the sophistry of the heart, and was, perhaps, its first impulse towards the donna herself, and might end by her image supplanting Flora's there.

"Such desecration, that her hand should even be touched by such a wretch as Trevino!"

He had muttered his last thought aloud, so Donna Isidora looked up and said—

"You mentioned the Padre Trevino?"

"Did I?—surely not?" replied Quentin, as the colour rushed into his face.

"Yes—what of him, senor?" she asked, fixing her soft, dark eyes on him inquiringly.

"I must have been dreaming."

"Scarcely," said she, smiling, "while the thunder makes such a noise; you were thinking aloud."

" Perhaps."

" Of what? I insist on knowing."

" I cannot help reflecting, senora, that such actions as those in which Trevino seems to exult, must damage the Spanish cause in the eyes of Europe and of humanity, and thus—excuse me ——but I begin to lose faith in your countrymen, even before we test alliance with them fully."

" And what say you of the recent siege of Zaragossa ?"

" Ah, Don José Palafox is a brave man, certainly ; and brave too, is Augustina, the Maid of Zaragossa, who led the cannoneers in the defence of the Portillo against Lefebre."

" She had lost her lover in the siege, so apart from inspiration, her courage was no marvel."

" And you, senora—if you lost a lover ?"

" I have lost several ; but if I lost one whom I loved, you mean ?"

" Yes—and who loved you well and truly ?"

" I would face ten thousand cannon to avenge him !—Augustina did nothing that I would not dare and do !" replied Isidora, as her eyes sparkled, and she pressed her clenched hand into the soft cheek that rested on it.

" A beautiful little spitfire !" thought Quentin.

" But, senor, you must be aware that neither Palafox the Arragonese nor the girl Augustina could have achieved all they did, save for the aid of our Lady del Pilar ?"

"What lady is she?" asked Quentin.

"Madre divina, listen to him! It grieves me sadly, amigo mio, to think—to think——"

"What?" asked Quentin, as she paused.

"That you are a heretic, innocently, through no fault of your own, and yet born to perdition."

"You are not very complimentary, yet I pardon you, my dear senora," replied Quentin, laughing as he kissed her hand—which we fear he did rather frequently now.

"Shall I try to teach you, and lead your heart as I would wish it?" she asked, with a gentle smile.

"If you please, senora."

"I mean, to instil a proper spirit of adoration in it?"

"If it is adoration of yourself, senora, I fear my heart is learning that fast enough already," replied Quentin, with such a caballero air that the donna laughed and coloured, but accepted the answer as a mere compliment; "then tell me," he added, "about this Lady del Pilar, who aided Don José Palafox."

"She is the guardian saint of the city of Zaragossa, and save but for her assistance, he had never withstood the arms of France so long; for it was faith in her, and her only, that inspired Palafox to make a resistance so terrible!"

"But tell me about her, Donna Isidora."

"You must learn, senor, that after the resurrection of our blessed Lord, when the twelve apostles separated and went to preach the gospel in different parts of the world, St. George set out for England, St. Anthony for Italy, and the others went elsewhere; but Santiago the elder set out for Spain, a land which, say our annals, the Saviour commended to his peculiar care.

" Before departing from ·Judea, he went to the humble dwelling of the blessed Virgin—the same little hut that is now at Loretto—to kiss her hand, on his knees to obtain her permission to set forth, and her blessing on his labours. After bestowing it, she adjured him to build a church unto her honour in that city of Spain where he should make the most important, or the greatest number of converts.

" So the saint set sail in a Roman galley, but was driven through the Pillars of Hercules into the Atlantic ocean, and after enduring great perils along the shores of Lusitania, he landed in the kingdom of Galicia. Proceeding through the land, he went barefooted, preaching the gospel, teaching and baptizing, but with little success, until he came to a fair city of Arragon, on the banks of the Ebro and the Guerva, in the midst of a vast and lovely plain. Surrounded by fertile fields of corn, and by groves of orange and lime trees, its stately towers were visible from afar, glittering white as snow in the sunshine; but in its marble temples false gods and goddesses were worshipped by the people.

"Enchanted by the sight of a city so fair, the saint rested on his staff and asked of a wayfarer how it was named; and he was told that it was Cæsarea Augusta; so entering, he began to preach in the public thoroughfares, and ere long made eight disciples, who gave all they possessed to the poor, and followed him.

"Full of joy with his success he retired, one evening, to a little grove on the banks of the Ebro, with his eight new friends, and there, after long and holy converse, they fell asleep under the orange trees; but between the night and morning they were awakened by hearing a choir, possessed of a harmony that was divine, singing 'Ave Maria gratia plena, Dominus tecum;' yet they saw not from whence the sound proceeded.

"Louder swelled this mysterious harmony, and louder still, until they seemed to be in the midst of it.

"Listening in wonder and awe they fell on their knees, and lo, senor! a marvellous silver light, brighter than that of day, filled all the orange grove, and amid a choir of angels, whose golden hair floated over their shoulders, whose wings and robes were white as the new fallen snow, and whose faces bloomed with the purity and radiance of heaven, there, on the summit of a white marble pillar, stood the blessed Madonna, with her fair brow crowned by thirteen stars, and her robe all of a dazzling brightness. With a divine smile on her face, she listened to the choir, who went through the whole of her matin service.

"When it was ended, when the voices of the angels were hushed, their eyes cast down, and their hands meekly folded on their bosoms,

"'Santiago,' said she, 'here on this spot raise thou the church of which I told thee, and build it round this pillar, which I have brought hither by the hands of angels; here shall it abide until the end of the world, and all the powers of hell shall not prevail against it!'

"The saint and his eight disciples, who were all on their knees in reverence and awe, bowed low at this command; when they looked up, the Virgin had disappeared with all her shining choir, and nothing remained but the miraculous pillar of polished marble, standing cold, white, and solitary, amid the moonlight, by the bank of the Ebro.

"So around that column he built the famous church of Our Lady del Pilar, which has been the scene of a thousand miracles; about it, ere long, grew the vast Christian city now named Zaragossa, which, as my father the professor always assured me, is but a corruption of the original name, Cæsarea-Augusta.

"Santiago rests from his holy labours in Compostella, where he was martyred by the barbarous Galicians, and where his bones were discovered in after years by a miraculous *star* that burned over his grave. When danger threatens Spain, the clashing of arms and of armour is heard within his tomb, for he is her tutelary guardian, and so greatly do we venerate him, that of the canons of his cathedral seven, at least, must be cardinal priests : and there, at Compostella, he appeared in a vision to the king, Don Ramiro, before his famous battle with the Moors, and promised him victory for withholding the annual tribute of a hundred Christian girls.

" Time passed over Zaragossa, and even the infidel Moors respected the holy pillar, for it was found uninjured when the city was re-captured from them by Don Alphonso of Arragon.

" And so last year, when the French had pushed their batteries along the right bank of the Guerva, and had beaten down the rampart ; and when, at their head, General Ribeaupierre had cut a passage through the ranks of Palafox into the wide and stately Coso ; when Lefebre assailed the Portillo, and was repulsed with the loss of two thousand men, but returned with renewed fury, when a carnage ensued that must have ended in the fall of Zaragossa and the capture of Don José, *then* it was, senor, that the young girl Augustina, inspired by vengeance for her lover's fall, appeared among the soldiers, calling on Our Lady del Pilar to aid her chosen city.

" Then springing over dead and dying, she snatched a lighted match from her dead lover's hand and discharged a twenty-six pounder loaded with grapeshot full at the advancing foe, and animated the citizens to continue that awful struggle by which Zaragossa was saved, though the flower of Arragon perished. Foot to foot and breast to breast they fought, contesting every street and house, from floor to floor, till the French retired. Augustina received a noble pension, and now wears on her sleeve a shield of honour with the city's name."

By the time this story was ended, darkness had almost set in ; the rain was still rushing down in a ceaseless flood, and the vivid lightning, with its green and ghastly glare, lit up from time to time the gloomy chambers of the silent villa.

Remembering that he had seen a lamp in one of the rooms, Quentin was about to go in search of it, when the sound of a heavy door closing with a bang that echoed through all the mansion, made him pause, and as he was Scotsman enough to have certain undefined but superstitious notions, he turned to his companion, who on hearing this unexpected noise, had started from her seat with her eyes dilated and her lips parted.

"You heard that, senora?" said he.

"It is the private door of the chapel—the door through which we passed," she replied.

"What has caused it to open and shut?"

"The wind, probably."

"It can be nothing else, senora, though in

truth I was thinking of those two effigies that for seven hundred years have stood, with their stony eyes uplifted and their mailed hands clasped in prayer."

" What of them ?" she asked, with surprise.

" What if they got off their pedestals and took a promenade through the villa on this stormy night ?"

" Ah, senor, don't talk of such things !" said Donna Isidora, as she shrunk close to him and laid her hand on his arm.

END OF VOL. II.

www.ingramcontent.com/pod-product-compliance
Lightning Source LLC
Chambersburg PA
CBHW060522030726
47498CB00004B/1045